What if I told you, we were walking on a path that has already been set for us . . .

THE BRAND – BOOK 1

Publisher's Cataloging in Publication Data

The Brand

'Question Everything, Trust No One!'

Young Adult, Thriller, Suspense, Mystery

ISBN #: 978-0-9963209-0-0

Library of Congress Control Number: 2015906999

Published By: Nishan A. Kumaraperu

Authored and Edited By: Nishan A. Kumaraperu

Copyright © 2015 Nishan A. Kumaraperu

www.TheBrandNovel.com

"I do further promise and declare, that I will, when opportunity presents, make and wage relentless war, secretly or openly, against all heretics, Protestants and Masons, as I am directed to do, to extirpate and exterminate them from the face of the whole earth, and that I will spare neither age, sex, nor condition, and that I will burn, hang, waste, boil, flay, strangle, bury alive, these infamous heretics, open up the stomachs and wombs of their women and crush their infants' heads against the walls in order to annihilate their execrable race.

That when the same cannot be done openly, I will secretly use the poison cup, the strangulation cord, the steel of the poniard, or the leaden bullet, regardless of the honor, rank, dignity or authority of the persons whatever be their condition in life, either public or private, as I at any time may be directed to so do, by any agent of the Pope, or superior of the Brotherhood of the Holy Faith of the Society of Jesus."

– **Quoted from the Jesuit Oath** – entered into the Congressional Record, 62nd Congress, 3rd Session; House Bill 1523, Library of Congress, Catalog Card Number, 66-43354, Volume 49, part 4, pages 3215-16.

CONTENTS

CHAPTER 1: Ordinary Lives

2035:

The world as we knew it no longer exists.

The constant WHIRRING of the centrifuge broke the silence as the lights around the building auto-dimmed. Three of the four remaining scientists hurried towards the electronic doors to leave the laboratory for the night, pausing only to grab their coats. The short, balding man who was the last to leave, tossed his scrubs into the biohazard hamper as he walked past.

He removed and methodically arranged his safety glasses, gloves, and hair net on the anti-microbial table beside the exit; the risk of contamination to the experiments was high and something to pay the utmost attention to. Smoothing down the stray locks of his thinning hair, he appeared to change his mind about heading out, turning back to the lone female, impatiently waiting for him to leave.

She was clearly disappointed in his choice of action. *Whatever you forgot, I'll make sure to ship it back to the Idiot Farm,* she thought as he moved slowly towards her. Working with the man was one thing, but being forced into a conversation was a waste of precious oxygen. She waited for a moment for him to speak, but he just stood there staring at her. His creepy demeanor radiated discomfort all around him in a morbid sort of way, as if his aura was a warning for others to keep their distance.

"Did you forget something?"

"Are you sure you won't join us; we're heading over to Lansings Pub," he ventured as his much too long of a stare drifted up and over her breasts.

His enormous eyes, set in an angle on either side of his too-small nose, reminded her of the semblance of an alien. *Earth is full; go home creep!* "No- but thank you for the invite James," the beautiful woman replied quickly, already bored with his constant pecking. *Maybe I'm being too hard on the poor guy...Nah – I'm on a roll.*

She laughed inwardly to herself. Besides, James was *a dick*!

"You look like the walking dead you know, working so hard and all... You really could use a stiff one darling – drink or otherwise!" James tried to hold in his laughter, amused with himself for being so clever as he inched ever closer. The stink of sweat hung about him like a cloud, fouling the air.

Case in point, she thought, *every chance he gets – the little pervert! Worse yet, he knows I'm married!* At one time in her life she would have appreciated the humor in anything – even something as crass as that. Now however, she wanted nothing more than to kick this vile little man square in the balls, and throw him out onto his grubby little ass. *But-* she reminded herself, *he has his uses...*

James Massy was a phenom in his field of engineering and had vast knowledge of computer systems and electronics, with a proficiency that greatly surpassed her own; unfortunately his skills were vital to her research. She forced herself to smile even as the look he returned made her skin crawl, all the way down to her toes like tiny dancing spiders. He reminded her of a child molester - not that she knew many of those - *but still.*

"Listen James, I just can't. I, uhh...I have a lot more work to do," she replied, anxiously hoping that he would just leave without her having to waste any more of her breath on useless conversation. "Sooner or later, I'll have to take you up on that offer, just not today, okay?" *Much later than sooner.*

His thick tongue licked his lips. "I hope that's dedication talking and not denial darling...I'll see you tomorrow then," he replied back as he whipped on his worn corduroy jacket and ran to catch up with the other two. *And stay out - you pig!*

What was it with that guy?! To say that James Massy was harassing her was an exaggeration, but the man seemed to be everywhere at once, like an omnipresent shadow! Besides working alongside him for most of her shift, she'd oddly bumped into him on several other occasions: at least five times on her lunch breaks coming from various restaurants, a number of times in random places, twice as she was window shopping for new coats, and once on her way to the gym! It was unnerving to say the least.

Not that running into someone you knew was strange, only the times she'd seen him were much more frequent than the norm, almost routine! Sometimes, she felt like he was following her...and that was ridiculous. James was annoying, arrogant, and perverted; all the things she couldn't stomach in a man, but hardly a stalker...*maybe* a rapist. Thank God he was gone, any longer and she wouldn't have been able to hold back.

Dr. Jenna Methis sighed deeply, her porcelain face flickering with annoyance as she made her way around the jungle of disorderly placed equipment. The immediate area was scattered with Nano manipulators, Particle Growth Accelerators, and other highly technical machinery. Some of them were so new and advanced that they hadn't even been named yet. These were the tools of her trade and she was itching to get back to work.

The tiredness along her brow and her disheveled look did not belie the fact that if she had not chosen her current line of work, she could have had a far reaching and prosperous career as a high-fashion model. Her pale complexion contrasted perfectly with her honey-blonde hair and her elfin face topped a slim figure with ample curves to spare. Tall and graceful, she moved with determination to begin anew on her tedious tasks.

Busying herself from one table to another, Dr. Methis took her time, painstakingly taking notes on her HOL-COM of each stage her research was in. She checked the Nano parameters of the second batch, only to hear the beeping noise pronouncing the end of her current experiment. She walked over to the far end of the lab and seeing that the centrifuge had stopped spinning, she reached for the small vial containing the subtly glowing liquid. She brought it up to her spectrascope for a closer examination and let out the breath she'd been holding, quickly realizing the Swarm was still not accepting the control-protocol, *nor* the advanced directives.

Almost immediately, the nanobots destroyed themselves. Lately, her efforts had ended much the same: in boundless stress and frustration. Modern science could already create nano-enhanced materials and all types of other items. But the Nano-swarm was different; the hive-mind needed an autonomous leader, capable of directing the other nanobots! It was the next logical step in nanotechnology. With a 'queen' in place, it would be capable of amazing feats! Without it, or the long and tedious hours of manual programming for simple tasks, they literally ate themselves.

"Damn it," she quietly swore to herself. After countless months of research and multiple failed attempts, she was back where she started. Electro-magnetic stimulation; chemical directives; even DNA-based algorithms were of no effect. The problem was that none of those efforts produced the semblance of 'self-awareness' required to control the other Nanites! She carefully dumped the solvent into the disposal unit and began again with the Scanning Electron Microscope. Continuing her work, she spent the next few hours calculating the Nanostructures and determining the NMR parameters of the fullerenes.

The science of Nanotech was an especially complicated and delicate process. Heating the reaction medium to the appropriate temperature, the precursors were chemically transformed into monomers. Once these reached a high enough super saturation level, it would start the nucleation process. Finally, she gathered together the dispersed atoms and free electrons to form several Colloidal Quantum Dots and back in the centrifuge they went.

Colloidal Quantum Dots?! Oh my God; I've turned into a total Nerd! It seemed that over the years she'd forgotten what fun was all about. Work; work; work; that's all she ever did anymore. And it didn't help that life's ups and downs were distracting her from her progress. Constant stress was becoming a reality in her and Collin's marriage and with what had happened to Cole, it was only getting worse.

Lack of emotional comfort and understanding had taken its toll on their relationship, bringing about arguments over trivial matters and resentment from issues they never had the time to resolve. Most importantly though, their physical relationship had begun to suffer as intimate contact was lacking and far between. *I really need a social life...*she thought to herself...maybe even the prolonged use of a certain personal massager that she had aptly named 'Dick'. *Stop feeling sorry for yourself, Jenna; things can only get better!*

The rain-streaked window suddenly lit up with a blinding luminescence signaling that she had again lost track of time – it was daybreak already. Residing in Illinois, the snow-covered mornings were beautiful, flanking the outside paths in unbroken curves of frosty white powder. The snows enveloped the oak and maple trees scattered outside like sparkling crystals, reminding her of her most favorite time of the year – Christmas.

Soon those trees would unfold their leaves and the flowers would bloom, signaling the beginning of an early spring...After a while, the whiteness brilliantly reflecting off the environment hurt her eyes and she turned away from the delicate scene. *What a moment, if only Cole could have seen this*...Her son was the most important person in her life and Jenna missed his handsome smile and the brightness he could bring to a room when she was down. She wished things could be different, that- *Stop dwelling on things you can't control!*

Jenna Methis was a patient woman, but the latest demands from High Commissar Riordan were completely unreasonable. She did have another life besides catering to Psy-Gen Global and their endless pursuits of technological advancements. But the Special Projects Division was time-sensitive; they had to develop a specific product or application within a limited end-date.

So far, she'd produced no favorable results and the clock was ticking. This sector of Psy-Gen catered to all types of industries: agricultural, manufacturing, medical, military, and classified projects. The work she did now was related to the latter. Leisurely interludes for her had lost all meaning; due to the strict time constraints, the long, additional hours were sorely required.

The last time Riordan asked this of her - just six months prior- Jenna had reluctantly accepted the extra shift to help support Cole's hospitalization. She had thought it was a wise choice - after all, it was only a few more hours at work a day, right? But it also meant less time that she could spend with Cole at Princeton Memorial Hospital, and that broke her heart. Not that it mattered much - there was very little she could do for him regardless of her decision...

Now the pompous bastard -she would never say that to his face- was practically forcing her to forgo her own family's needs and put in more overtime than she had already agreed to. But the reality was that she needed as many Credits as possible to provide the constant care for Cole until he was better...or if a miracle happened and a cure was finally found.

For longer than she cared to remember, the only thing on her mind had been her research and her family. With her tenure in Special Projects, exhaustion and stress were now part of her regular routine. And if that wasn't bad enough, her position as head of research put all that responsibility squarely on her shoulders. Maybe she should have gone for a much-needed drink with that little worm, James Massy after all...but here she sat.

What a shame she hadn't become a medical doctor instead as the hospital would have included an amazing benefits plan and she would have had the knowledge and training to care for Cole herself. Instead she had pursued Nano-genetics, a technical and highly advanced field which only the most talented and brightest of scientists were accepted into.

Not that it was a bad thing, she received plenty of Credits in her line of work and she had a position that most people would envy. But the ever-increasing costs of extended medical care were usually more than what she brought in. In this New World, short-term care was fully covered, but long-term care was a bankruptcy waiting to happen.

Either way, Jenna hadn't expected that her daring career choice would eventually *become* her life. The constant physical and emotional stressors of her job made her feel as if the Hand of God was literally pushing through from the Heavens and placing all its pressure on her, always keeping her from picking herself back up.

And that was on top of everything else that had come crashing down over the past few years, affecting her time, her marriage, and the constant care for her son...*Oh my God, just shut up already!* As she contemplated all her internal struggles, she felt old...and tired.

Maybe not old, but *definitely* tired. She felt like she was much too young to have already birthed and raised a teenager - which she also knew was a ridiculous notion considering she was close to 40. Most people in her line of work could never juggle both the responsibility of a career in the sciences and a pre-adult at the same time; she should be proud of that! But somehow she felt as if she'd betrayed her family for a career...Jenna's life had begun and continued to go at full speed; there was no time to slow down now. *You're just making things worse; focus on the project.*

The three-dimensional data she received from scanning the Nanites with the atomic microscope showed that their hive modulation frequency was intact, but the control-protocols still refused to take and the bots would not assimilate them. For some reason the swarm would not self-replicate or choose their own directives. *Great, I've made it worse!* Was the only remaining solution to insert an autonomous master command module - a brain - into the hive? If so, Jenna had a feeling she would be working on this for many years to come!

A Nano-swarm was a night and day difference from simple Nanobots. It was...or would be a completely independent entity with the ability to govern itself. To create a Master-bot would be incredibly difficult and more akin to a human mind than a computer program. *Stop whining and get on with it!* There *had* to be another option; something they hadn't thought of yet. As she continued the painstaking experiments, her wayward thoughts drifted back to her unhappy childhood and with that - bitter memories that threatened to unhinge her.

Regrettably, there were many life experiences she had missed out on; simple things that she was never allowed to do! Her early years had been a whirlwind of chaos, consistently causing her internal pain and heartache. Jenna was actually pleasantly surprised that she had reached adulthood without having a complete mental breakdown or being admitted into some System-run loony-bin. But the reason she had not cracked had been due to one man. The person that had centered her and kept her grounded, both physically and emotionally; and did so even now. Despite their fractured relationship, she still loved him with all her heart.

His name was Collin Methis and she had first been introduced to him at Westmount Academy, an exceptional school for the Gifted. Jenna was quite young when she attended Westmount and she never did experience much of a real childhood. Friends were far and in-between growing up and most of the time, other children would not get along with her...or maybe it was *she* who could not get along with them. Either way, her peers always felt uneasy around her and consistently discluded her when their parents weren't watching. She kept to herself most of the time and even at a young age, people thought of her as a lonely recluse.

Her parents had noticed her boredom with everyday things at the tender age of three: playing with others; watching TV; things most toddlers were mesmerized with. Then again, that's about *all* they noticed. As far as parents go, there were two types: the ones who were invested in their children and the ones who were not. Unfortunately, she wound up with the latter. Not that she was an expert on parenting, but what she did know was that quality time and personal attention mattered!

Love and affection were something that every human being craved, but for a child - it was essential. You could give a son or daughter the most amazing, beautiful gift in the world, but there was a big difference in *watching* that child play with it or playing *with* them. From the vantage point of your comfortable leather couch, you would simply be a spectator. But actually *taking the time and making the effort* to get down to their level and play *with* him or her was something else thing entirely. She could not figure out for the life of her why some parents chose to have children in the first place. To some, it seemed more of a burden than a gift.

Throughout much of her young life, Jenna's parents seemed to be perpetually confused as what to do with a child. Her mother and father were even more baffled when her KP teacher, Ms. Meyers informed them through email that she had stumbled upon Jenna solving complicated math problems on the classroom chalkboard. Hearing this from a school teacher normally would not have been such a shock, except for the fact that Ms. Meyers was not just any old substitute teacher. She was only standing in as a favor for her daughter who was raising a newborn baby.

Alberta Meyers' primary job was as the AP Mathematics Professor at Piermont Institute and for her to see a five year old little girl performing equations well beyond her years was absolutely fascinating! Half of her previous advanced-year students could not have done what she witnessed Jenna Methis do that day so she knew at once this talented child was very special indeed.

Thinking she was doing them a favor, Ms. Meyers scheduled a conference with Jenna's parents and the education board. Once people began spreading the excitement around the small town they resided in, things spiraled out of control. The press had gotten word, turning the discovery into an all-out spectacle as Jenna became headline news: 'Wunderkind found in small-town America'!

At first her parents didn't know what to do or even whom to

contact; Jenna guessed not many people do when they find out their child has a genius-level intellect. Being that Jenna was so introverted and abnormally bright, her mother foolishly assumed she bordered on the Autistic spectrum. They had immediately taken her to a psychologist who had prodded and probed Jenna with stupid questions and useless conjecture.

Now that she was older and looking back on her past, she considered their actions a waste of time; psychologists were more trouble than they were worth. The problem with these types of therapists was that they based their long, drawn out hypothesis on a standard 'Discover, Analyze, and Solve the Problem' method that usually never truly helped anyone with their deep down personal issues.

The difficulty being that a psychologist did not live in the day-to-day situation so has to base these 'findings' on the present and from what he or she has learned from the patient. Unfortunately, being as all human beings have an Ego, that information is often misleading, one-sided, irrelevant, or simply untrue.

Therefore, the diagnosis or advice was based on assumption rather than the true facts or actual emotional strife of the patient. At least that was *her* opinion. Doctor 'What's-His-Face' had been such a pompous and arrogant ass, she had not even bothered to remember his name. Absolutely nothing had come out of that bout of 'therapy' other than the fact that she was *not* Autistic and a confirmation that she *was* intelligent well beyond her years.

Ultimately, they finally sent her to an IQ evaluation facility in the middle of nowhere. Trapped in a drab, grey cube with no windows, she was forced to go through multiple trials: verbal, numerical, spatial, and logical. Of course, she had blown through these assessments with relative ease and completed them much faster than was considered the average time span. After these experiences. Jenna did feel as if she now had a pretty good understanding how the test rats in her laboratory *viewed her*.

Sometime later, her parents had received the test results and extraordinary news that their spiritless child, Jenna Ann Methis had an IQ of 180! They had promptly placed her in a specialist charter school that advanced her quickly through all the general scholastic courses and provided her with access to progressive academics. It was more of a private boarding school than anything else, as she was given a small dormitory and practically lived in isolation with little contact with the outside world.

However, due to her exceptionally fast progress, she was allowed to spend one week a month with her parents. For Jenna, this was of no benefit; she couldn't get back to school fast enough! Being as she had never experienced much of the public school curriculum nor truly made any close childhood friends around the neighborhood, Jenna felt incredibly alone throughout those years.

She finally made the choice to focus solely on her education and turn things into a more positive outlook. Eventually, she was placed into Westmount Academy. Since entering the school, the most she saw of her parents was on major Holidays such as Thanksgiving and Christmas or the few uneventful occasions they deemed it necessary or just felt guilty enough to visit. Even then, she sensed an aire of nervousness and caution emanating from them when she was around; like she was carrying some type of contagious disease which may be spread through closeness and caring.

It hurt terribly to think that her own parents seemed to treat her as aloofly as some people would treat a stray cat. Then again, even she was kind-hearted enough to show an animal some sort of affection. As for the rest of the students at the school...well – to be honest she never did have enough time to spend with anyone to really get to know them and develop close relationships.

The robots...or teachers – as some students liked to call them – were like computer-programmed statues that had no semblance of personality or made any attempt at communication, other than teaching their lessons during their scheduled class time. She was bored, lonely, and most likely would have – if she had not met the man destined to be her husband – been depressed and perhaps even suicidal.

Collin Methis was a breath of fresh air! He was brilliant, kind, and partnered with Jenna for Advanced Labs, conducting molecular analysis experiments with certain types of cancers. When he first sat down on the lab stool beside her, the first thing she noticed were his piercing blue-grey eyes. She was lost in their swirling storm clouds as they shifted between the two colors, boring into her like two red-hot suns. His smile was a ray of warm sunshine, putting her instantly at ease and his tousled blonde hair framed his chiseled features and handsome face as if he were carved from stone. To this day, he was a perfect, physical specimen and she still couldn't figure out what he saw in *her*...

They had literally stared into one another's eyes until Professor Donovan finally nudged Collin on his shoulder and bade him to pay attention to the experiment at hand. Every few minutes, they stole glances at each other, chatting about everything other than their studies. From that moment on, the term 'love at first sight' had a much clearer meaning for her doubting disposition and she somehow knew that this man was *the one*. At that time in her life though, she probably would have fallen for anyone who gave her what she craved for most: love and acceptance. She was glad it had been Collin.

They began to spend time with each other immediately, starting with the occasional date between their studies and multiple courses. Any personal days were spent talking for countless hours on end, spending time together and doing mundane things. Soon their delicate relationship began to blossom into something more. It was Collin who'd introduced her to many of the new and exciting experiences she'd missed throughout her childhood: hiking, biking, camping, cooking, and all the other simple things that made the world go around. He was well-educated and worldly, with a great sense of humor. It was because of him that she'd finally come out of her shell and enjoyed life to the fullest.

One day on a beautiful spring afternoon, Collin took her for a stroll in Maymont Park. There was a barn filled with pot-bellied pigs, rabbits, chickens, and even a donkey you could feed. They hiked through the bamboo forest hand in hand, taking in the wildlife and watching the giant fish in the coy pond. Coming into a clearing surrounded by huge, ancient trees, she was pleasantly surprised to find a picnic lunch laid out on a patchwork blanket.

There, they'd spent the day getting to know each other more intimately and discussing their future plans; it was a beautiful moment. After eating, Collin had taken her to a hidden waterfall which they'd leapt across the large rocks to reach. Once there, he pointed out an immense tree towering over the water. Something was carved into the rough bark.

It read 'Jenna, You are my North, my South, my East, and my West. My working week, and my Sunday rest. Will You Marry Me?' She was in such shock that she almost feinted right there on the spot! It was one of the most romantic engagement proposals she had ever seen. Kissing and frolicking in the forest as the birds chirped around them and the clouds misted over, it was the most amazing time of her life; a day she would never forget. She didn't have to think twice before saying *'Yes'*. In a few more years at the foolish and inexperienced age of eighteen, she had agreed to marry him.

It had been a wild and exhilarating ride. Although Jenna had expected to finally have found a substitute family to enjoy and get close to, it turned out that Collin's parents had died when he was much younger. She had not known that he was a ward of the State. Throughout their whirlwind romance, he never said anything other than some random references to imply that he 'did not want to talk about it'. It was odd, but she was in love and nothing else mattered.

Since both of them were usually buried in their studies and working more often than not, she accepted and respected his privacy and focused her energy on loving him. She was starting something which was denied to her all her life: a family. The vitality of life with Collin was wonderful and most of all, sexually liberating. It was this part of her adolescence she had the least experience with.

Cole Alexander Methis was born two years later; a beautiful baby boy who had the similar impressive features of his father and the stubborn intellect of his mother. His cherubic cheeks and cheerful demeanor could melt even the hardest of hearts. Each time she held him, she always felt a warm, fuzzy sensation of joy accompanied with the fervent responsibilities of motherhood. She remembered that the preliminary tests shortly after Cole was conceived revealed no abnormalities, and a physical evaluation right after his birth showed that he was completely well both physically and mentally. Neither she nor Collin were prepared for the complications that would soon take a toll on their lives.

During this time, Jenna had continued her education at an accelerated pace. Finishing up her required studies, it was soon on to Advanced Placement Testing for Calculus BC, the more difficult of the two and then to Probability and Statistics and Mathematical Logic which again she aced, as she knew she would. She remembered Professor Fitzhugh having a sign attached to her desk that said 'AND THEN SATAN SAID, "PUT THE ALPHABET INTO MATH AND CALL IT CALCULUS".' – It was hilarious from an academic standpoint at least.

Early on, she dabbled in Quantum Mechanics, which she found to be an amazing and complicated field of science, but a little too much for her to handle at the time. From there she took studies in Biological Evolution, Organic Chemistry and Evolutionary Genetics, finally going onto the core programs for Nanotechnology. Some considered it an odd jump from one science to another, but at that point- Jenna desired to be a part of whomever was doing the most innovative and important research. She found that she had an insatiable appetite for knowledge that was never quite able to be fulfilled.

Raising Cole however, was proving to be a challenge in itself! He was an especially sensitive infant whose first few years of life were exhausting and emotionally wrenching for both her and Collin. Later on, his temperament evened out and he became much easier to handle. For most of his young life, things came easy to him and Jenna could tell that Cole was advanced well beyond his years; he had definitely inherited his parents' intellect. He learned new things quickly and he reached developmental milestones much faster than kids his own age.

He did extremely well both studiously and in athletics, excelling in ways that were much different than her own upbringing. She remembered being so happy for him; he had a great personality and lived life with no regrets. The strange symptoms he began to display years later were a profound shock to her, bringing Cole's aspirations and possible future achievements to a crashing halt. There had been no complications during the pregnancy and he seemed to be a picture of perfect health since he was born...or so they had thought.

The melodious tone of her Sat-Com brought her back to the present. The holographic screen projected Collin's three-dimensionally rendered face above the fluid display. He was frowning deeply; not in anger, but in what she could clearly see was concern.

"Hon, Is everything alright?"

Jenna was confused as to why he was asking her this question. She must look worse than she felt. "Yes, why?"

"Jen, your Com registered *seven attempts* before you answered it!"

Jenna took a moment to sort her thoughts. "No...Yes, everything is fine. I was just...nevermind." She could hear anxiousness in his voice and it had nothing to do with her not answering her Sat-Com. "What's the matter; you sound...Collin, what's wrong?!"

He faltered and that told her everything she needed to know before he had a chance to explain. "It's Cole..."

Before he even had time to finish his sentence, she had ended the call and was out the door and running towards the lone titanium-colored sedan waiting in the dimly lit parking lot.

CHAPTER 2: The Boy Who Would Be King

"We have a CODE BLUE people," Florence Henderson exclaimed to the other staff, "Room 702, Cole Methis again!"

The CPR / Ventilation machine was wheeled in by two desperate looking Nurses as Florence checked Cole for the sign of a pulse. Finding none, she strapped the Auto Pulse Cardiopulmonary Resuscitation Device onto his chest. The machine is composed of a constricting band and half backboard that self-measures chest size and resistance and delivers a unique combination of thoracic and cardiac chest compressions, she remembered from her training. She didn't know why, but that was all her mind kept repeating as she frantically tried to get Cole Methis to breathe.

"We're not getting anything," someone said, from afar.

"Keep trying," Florence yelled back over the chaos, "He's a survivor, this one! He'll come around."

After a few tense moments, a faint heartbeat appeared on the ECG monitor. The hospital staff gathered around, breathing sighs of relief. The last thing the hospital needed was for someone so young to die on their watch! After an uneventful forty-seven minutes, the ER Doctor on call finally gave the 'all-clear' and expressed to the nurses that Cole could be transferred back to the Intensive Care Unit.

He put in an order for all the standard tests: respiratory function, blood, sugar, oxygen levels, blood chemistry, and continued cardiac monitoring. As the staff hurried to follow his instructions, two large orderlies came in and moved Cole's exhausted body onto a gurney and wheeled him away.

Nurse Henderson wiped the accumulated perspiration off her forehead, letting loose a great sigh of frustration. She knew that any moment, Doctor Methis would be bursting through the doors with her husband threatening that they would sue the hospital should constant and intensive care not be provided. And who could blame them?

The poor kid was hooked up to all sorts of machines with the ever-present specter of death looming over him! If it were her son living his life like this, wouldn't she feel the same? Of course she would, but that was only part of the reason she had volunteered to be Cole's Intensive Care Nurse; partly it was because he reminded her of the trauma her own Mitchell had gone through early in life.

Mitchell was diagnosed with acute lymphoblastic leukemia at a very young age. Before his diagnosis, Florence and her family lived in a safe, small world; a consistent, predictable one where the worst thing that could happen was a bad case of the flu.

When you learn that your child, whom you've nurtured all these years could die from a life-threatening disease, the semblance of the life you once lived was shattered in an instant! The worst part of it all was trying hard to be upbeat for her child's sake, acting as if everything was going to be alright, but knowing it wasn't. Luckily, Mitchell had pulled through and after a long, uphill battle, was finally cancer free.

Florence had seen her share of death as well. Mostly from the ravages of SARCA-24, a viral contagion that had spread across the massive population of The Old World. It was highly contagious and killed indiscriminately; young, old, men, women, and children – no one was spared! Over the years, The System Authority on Disease Control had quarantined the sick and re-located them to The Slums. Other regions across the globe had followed suit and finally after what seemed like ages, a temporary solution was found.

A new antigen in the form of a prescribed tablet was created and freely distributed to the masses. It stopped the virus from reproducing but only inhibited the infection already ravaging the body. The main drawback was that if it was not taken on a daily schedule, a new outbreak could easily occur. For now, it could be held at bay. She had seen many people lose their loved ones to the disease, including her own mother. Yes, if anyone knew how Jenna and Collin felt - it was her.

Doctor Methis and her husband had dutifully had a home-monitoring network installed at their residence so that they could be notified immediately should anything out of the ordinary happen. It had been Jenna Methis's unconditional request that this system be put into place. This was the second time in the last year the boy had gone into cardiac arrest and as sudden as it was today, Florence was terrified it would be his last.

As expected, the emergency room doors soon flew open as Jenna and Collin Methis barged in, searching frantically for their boy. "Where is our son?!" Doctor Methis was flush with fear and in no mood for politeness, "Florence, please – where is Cole? Is he okay?" She was shaking uncontrollably, tears flowing freely from her sleep-deprived eyes.

They had searched high and low until they'd found this particular medical facility. It contained a special ward that catered specifically to Cole's sickness and had one of the best care ratings in the city. Something like this should *not* have happened! *What the hell were they doing; didn't they understand they needed to keep closer watch*!?

"Please...Doctor Methis...he's okay. He pulled through just fine." Nurse Henderson reached out and pulled Jenna in for a tight embrace, hoping that the action might provide some comfort. "Cole's a fighter, Hon; he's tough. But this happened....suddenly; there was no warning like last time. I believe we may have a bigger problem here than what was initially diagnosed."

"I want to see him; *Now!*"

"Jenna...please calm down," Collin pleaded.

He strode forward and took his wife aside. He knew from the fear lurking beneath Florence's eyes as the information was disclosed, that this was not a good sign. "Thank you Flo; I know you did your best. We chose this hospital for a reason...and we're still happy we did-"

Florence held her palm up to quiet him. "Please Collin; just hear me out - a cardiac arrest such as the one Cole had last time is usually triggered by a literal electrical malfunction in the heart," she explained carefully, "When it's pumping is disrupted like this, the heart cannot supply blood to the brain, lungs, and other organs. But that wasn't the cause this time. Something else is-"

Collin's head was crammed with so many stray thoughts that he barely comprehended what Florence had said. He was both drained and exhausted; more concerned with seeing his son for himself than listening to the same time-worn lecture about what was wrong with Cole. As soon as the monitoring system had gone off, he had immediately called the hospital and after receiving the terrible news, contacted his Wife. Everything had been a blur from that moment on. "No...no need, we understand, I appreciate your concern. We-"

"Collin, *listen* to me," Florence interrupted with an agitated look, "I'm so sorry to have to tell you this - but Cole's disease is *rarely* associated with these sudden cardiac arrests; this could very well be something else entirely...at this point we would need to run some tests. Even so, Doctor Ambrose is recommending that Cole also be examined by a heart specialist from Mercy Hospital in Ohio. I -"

Jenna quickly freed herself from her husband's grasp as she angrily cornered Florence. "What the hell does that mean, Flo?! Are you telling me that my son is dying a little more each day and the best medical facility in the Midwest can't figure out what the damned problem is?!"

Florence took a step back, visibly shaken by the sudden attack. Normally, Doctor Methis was the one with a high degree of self-control. "Jenna I'm sorry...I didn't mean to-"

Collin pulled his wife back and did his best to physically comfort her. "Just give her some time Flo, she's been under an awful lot of stress lately" Mr. Mathis's sad, tired eyes betrayed the look of hopelessness to Nurse Henderson. "I'm...so sorry about that...Could we please see Cole now?"

Florence paused in her retort and shook her head, but knowing how stubborn a parent could be when a child was concerned, she quietly stepped aside. "He's back in the same room; I doubt he will wake for some time, but if he does, you tell him to be strong for me, okay?"

As they started walking away, Jenna ran back to Florence and embraced her tightly. "I'm sorry...and thank you for caring for our son," she sobbed, "I just-"

"It's okay Jenna...I understand," Nurse Henderson replied sympathetically. *How odd*, she thought to herself, *these two were usually so distant around each other*. What a shame it takes the potential death of their child to bring them together...

Jenna and Collin hurried through the doors of the ICU and down the stretch of corridors to Room 702, only to find Cole sleeping peacefully. The latest ordeal must have been too much for him to handle; his body had succumbed to the stress, but he seemed to be okay. He was still breathing and that's all that mattered right now. The complicated array of monitors, tubes and beeping machines however, betrayed the seriousness of the situation.

Neither one of them wanted to disturb him so Collin gently pulled his sobbing wife towards him and held Jenna on the long leather sofa until she finally fell asleep; more from emotional exhaustion than anything else. He wished he could do more for both his son and his wife. Their entire family had been through so much already...

Life had been unfair to both he and Jenna and they each carried their own personal burdens of regret and sorrow. Before they were married, Jenna had laid bare her soul to her past and it had taken him some time to accept that. He was young and madly in love then; open to whatever challenges came his way.

Their time together had started with a blossoming romance and progressed from there at a steady pace into a loving marriage, filled with many new and wonderful experiences – mostly for Jenna anyway. He was happy for that time in their lives and had definitely not been prepared for what was to come.

Collin had every intention to be a good husband and a better father, but things had taken a turn for the worse once Cole became sick. All his hopes and dreams for his son were shattered in a matter of moments. At first, he was so angry; always asking himself why this happened to him and his family. They were good people and surely, they didn't deserve *this*! For almost an entire year, he was binge drinking and took up smoking more than a pack a day.

Highly irritated with boundless frustrations, he had started arguing about meaningless issues with his wife and became annoyed at the slightest provocations. Troubles began in their marriage soon after that, leading into feelings of mistrust and resentment between the two. Once he had finally accepted Cole's fate, he resolved to change for the better. Professional counseling helped, but as counselors usually go, they were mostly there to listen; not prescribe solutions. He tried support groups; self-help V-books; hypnotherapy; and even alternative new-age healing techniques. Nothing helped and the sadness remained, festering into a deep-seeded rage.

The one thing he could not get out of his mind was if Cole would be better off if he didn't have to suffer like this. He understood it was a terrible thought, but the poor kid had gone through enough hell for two lifetimes! His son's entire world had come crashing down around him; his once happy life fallen apart in mere moments!

The pain he must have gone through both physically and emotionally, Collin would never know, but he was certain Cole would not want to live like *this*. In the hospital, with his son lying beside them, he hoped that a higher power was listening.

"Please forgive me my thoughts, Son," he whispered, to no one in particular and laid down his weary head.

Cole Methis's eyes moved with furious intensity, twitching back and forth while he slept and dreamed of a different life than the one he currently lived. He had the vague sensation that his parents were close by and that made him feel at peace. All the same, he felt a constant and gnawing sense of guilt for the problems his rare medical condition had caused for them.

He was not born this way; in fact he'd lived a wonderful and most importantly - a normal childhood. He was raised a bright, happy, healthy child, with a normal life and normal friends going to a normal school in a normal town.

'Normal' was a time that he wished with all his heart he could revert his life back to. He, himself was far from normal as he was gifted with his parents' incredible intellect – which in itself was both a blessing and a curse. Thankfully Jenna and Collin Methis had provided him with a chance to simply 'be a kid', as most likely they had learned a lesson from their own bitter childhoods and did not wish the same for him.

Because of that understanding, he had been allowed to attend a public school and get to know and befriend his classmates, play sports, go to parties, and do just about everything an average kid his age would and could do. He even managed to date a few gorgeous girls during the years and although his many extracurricular activities took a lot of his time, that didn't bother him much.

In spite of the fact that he could have mastered his classes with very little effort, he had chosen to bide his time and learn...well – act like he learned at a regular pace - class by class, grade by grade. Cole did not want to be looked upon as a 'freak' who was above his fellow classmates, nor did he want to be perceived as one of those 'know-it-alls'. Those 'brainy' privileged kids who went around school acting as if they were born with these repositories of knowledge.

The only thing they were born with were silver spoons in their mouths! They were so arrogant and aloof, it made him sick! If only most of the others realized all they were doing was memorizing ideas, quotes, and lessons that were already discovered by somebody else. That was after all, the basis of education in this day and age. Some things never changed...Either way, his parents trusted in his judgment and allowed him to go on with his studies at a steady pace.

Cole's artistic side emerged as a young boy. He was active in most of the school plays throughout his formative years; his favorite style being Improvisation. He learned many skills during that time from singing on stage to doing impressions. The musical games which were designed to force creativity on the actors were his most treasured moments; they were just plain fun.

While they were good sports about it, many of the performers despised the musical interludes. For Cole however, the accompanying music helped to conceptualize his body's behavior and facial expressions that ultimately sold his performance to the audience.

As he delved deeper into the arts, he developed an interest in musical instruments, specifically the guitar. He joined the school band and learned everything they could teach him. Eventually, after mastering the basics, he began to teach himself more advanced chords and techniques that transgressed beyond the amateurish lessons being taught in school. Soon he was playing at social functions and even began teaching fellow students in order to save Credits for college. But he didn't do it for personal gain; instead, the soothing effect of simply playing calmed him and gave him a sense of emotional gratification.

Cole's unique intelligence even allowed him to excel at sports and soon by understanding and anticipating his opponent's plays, moves, and weaknesses – earned himself the title of Team Captain in both Football and Basketball –it was a big deal in high school anyway.

It was simply a matter of planning the right moves at the right time and to be honest very similar to chess, which happened to be his favorite game of strategy and guile. The entire focus of most sports was to outguess the opponents, find a weakness to exploit, and reach a pre-determined goal using both offensive and defensive movements to accomplish it.

In his favorite sport, Football, there were linemen which were like 'pawns', a quarterback who is like the 'queen', and other technical positions that were like 'rooks', 'knights', and 'bishops'. The team then devises a game plan for each different opponent, determines which plays are working well, and finds a flaw in their defense.

Even the head coach could be thought of in a similar manner as he is like the 'king' who determines the master plan to be used against the other team and helps design the plays to triumph over their rivals. For Cole, his solution was mostly a matter of geometry; keeping track of routine patterns in order to react faster and plan a few steps ahead. However it came to him, it worked. *Perhaps had the NFL still existed, they should replace all the muscle head jocks with the kids from the Math Club...*

His one obstacle however, was his weight; about 160 lbs soaking wet, and he was under constant pressure from his coach to pack on the pounds. Odd thing was that no matter how hard he tried to gain mass: lifting weights; drinking protein shakes; eating a I/2 jar of peanut butter a day; forcing down raw eggs– he just could not get any bigger! For some reason he always stayed average. Stranger still was that each year he played sports, it seemed to be taking a physical toll on his body. Not only that, but he had begun showing signs of losing actual muscle strength.

At first his friends noticed that his throwing arm kept drooping, usually right after a big game. Once his parents found out, they were worried sick. Subsequently, upon going to an orthopedist, he found that he was beginning to lose some of his reflexes and muscle tone. After a multitude of hospital visits, life started going into a downward spiral, right into the proverbial toilet bowl. Before he was even halfway through his senior year in high school, the doctor's concluded that Cole had an affliction known as Spinal Muscular Atrophy.

The medical professionals explained that SMA was a disease in which certain nerves in the brain and spinal cord die out, eventually impairing the person's ability to physically interact with the outside environment. These clusters of motor neurons controlled a person's capacity to sit up, crawl, walk, and stand. When these nerves die, the brain stops sending signals to the body's muscles. Being as the tissues do not get direction on how to move, they become inactive and get smaller, finally wasting away; a condition known as atrophy.

SMA was usually inherited, although neither of his parents had the mutation in their genes. His doctor had informed them that most people are not routinely tested for this disease, unless the parents know they are carriers of the gene or the baby demonstrates significant muscle weakness.

As far as anyone knew, it did not run on either side of his parents' families; it was a freak occurrence. Luckily, even though SMA directly affected the nerves in the brain, it did not have any detrimental effects on his intelligence. He still had the use of his most powerful asset...for much good that would do.

More rapidly than gradually, the disease would finally leave him paralyzed for much of his life – however long of that was left. With no cure or medical treatment for Spinal Muscular Atrophy, doctors could offer little more than palliative care. The only good thing – if you want to call it that – was that the type he had was rare indeed.

Most victims died in childhood, but for some reason his unique genetic make-up kept it in dormancy until well past puberty and allowed him at least a handful of great encounters out of life. 'Thank God for small favors', his mother always said; something his father found little consolation in. He never did make it all the way into college and a part of him always regretted not being able to have that experience. His only other regret – It would have been nice if he didn't pass from this life a *virgin*!

All he knew at this point was that he was dying....and fast. He was trying very hard to accept the inevitable and not be angry about the lot that was chosen for him. More often than not he found himself willing, even longing to give up fighting and just lose himself in the darkness that eagerly awaited him.

Sometimes, laying in the darkness, he would try to convince himself that his parents would be better off not having to struggle to use medical Credits for someone who had a limited span on life anyway. Somehow, he knew deep down that it would hurt them more to know that he had given up; but that would not be fair to him either. He was still alive and here for a reason and hopefully soon, he would know what that reason was.

CHAPTER 3: The System

High Commander Lucien Bovier moved with purpose, he had an inspection to conduct. Walking into the barracks, he encountered the normal hustle and bustle of the new recruits as they settled into their unfamiliar quarters. The barracks were generously spacious and ready for habitation, providing not only the rows of twin sized cots, but also two full sized double refrigerators, two microwaves and a stove, a complete entertainment center, and its own laundry room.

For the 'grunts', Old World technology was substituted in place of the new to toughen them up to the reality of the battlefield. The soldiers' belongings were all in place; surprisingly neat and orderly. He knew Tom had given them a break between drills and allowed the troops some time to get situated and tidy up.

You're much too good of a guy, Tom...Personally, I would have worked them to the bone during the first week. They would have welcomed me that same morning and hated me by noon!

Noticing who had just walked in, the soldiers immediately dropped what they were doing, lined up in neatly filed rows and saluted him with the respect due his rank. *Another round of young men willing to give their lives for The System,* he thought, *they have no idea what they're getting themselves into.*

"For those of you who did not take high school history or *too stupid* to get an education in the first place, I am going to give you a lesson on times long gone that better be seared into your memories from this moment on – or until a rebel finally puts a bullet through your head!"

"Understood High Commander," the soldiers replied as one. One good thing about these Newbies was that they were taught respect right from the get-go!

Lucien paced back and forth among the rows of men as he spoke, finally stopping in front of the entire platoon. Commander Lucien Bovier was six foot two and had some impressively muscled bulk to him, but his physique was not as imposing as the various medals and badges on his uniform. The meanings behind two of these demanded the utmost respect by everyone who knew what they stood for.

The Medal of Honor and the Silver Star were two of the highest military decorations of the Old World. They were only awarded to those that had distinguished themselves through conspicuous valor and heroism at the risk of life above and beyond the call of duty. The soldiers who looked on in awe as he recited his speech from memory, understood exactly that.

"The System was created soon after the third World War and from there, it prospered for the benefit of the people. Before it was initiated, violence and corruption had permeated the world's governments and politics for centuries. The people had lost trust and faith in our leaders and representatives.

The System has turned things around and brought unity in all things: Government; Religion; Economics; and Resources. You are here to serve and protect the New Order! We must protect The Amalgam against tyranny. We must fight for the good of all and to establish order within the New World. We must obey the System."

The gathered group of soldiers before him responded in unison as they struck fist to palm in salute.

"We are as The System commands!"

"Those who are gathered here will become part of my unit and as a Cateton of The System, you will follow and obey my direct executive orders or those of my Second, Justice Master Quinn! None of you are ordinary and have been chosen from a select genetic stock and for having a unique skill-set that can be utilized when the need arises," He paused to take a breath, taking into account the gathered soldiers in the crowd.

The faces staring back at him were serene with not a trace of doubt. They all knew they belonged here. In fact, most of the soldiers before him were a direct scion of the 13 Bloodlines; as was he. 'The 13 Families', as they were called had descended from some of the most notable and aristocratic figures in human history: from the Egyptian Queen Cleopatra to the Emperor of the West Charlemagne, to King Edward the Third. Since the beginning of early civilization, they had always been involved with politics, banking, and all things where power was concerned.

The 13 Families had amassed incredible wealth, unquestionable influence, and global connections throughout history and were instrumental in the creation of The System. The members of these Families were born into prominent status, much like nobility. Lucien however, happened to be at the tail end of his bloodline as he was the last surviving member of a Family that had bred soldier after soldier, finally ending in an unforeseen problem on *his* end – he was sterile and would never have children.

His family's legacy ended with him. Although he accepted it, others looked at him in shame or disgust. But that wasn't the only problem. Lucien's father had long ago, steered his own family away from the politics and drama that fueled the 13 Family's far-reaching goals.

Adam Bovier never did explain his reasons for doing so, but Lucien had the feeling that these reasons were better left unsaid. His father had purposely kept Lucien in the dark about his family's past and as a result, Lucien knew very little about their history. The small amount of information he did gather were whispers he caught here and there from other notable members. The backlash from the other Families was transparent in their antagonistic behavior towards the Boviers; it was almost as if they were considered outcasts.

If it wasn't for Lucien's almost legendary reputation as a war hero, he would have been demoted to Citizen Status. His military prowess and leadership skills kept them at bay; he was far too valuable to be cut loose. There was also a public image to protect so they needed him. As he scanned the new recruits, for a fraction of a moment he wondered what they thought of him. *Screw 'em!*

"Some of your fathers may have been progenitors of The System and because of that, you may feel you are above your fellow soldiers in that regard," he continued, carefully taking a measure of each man before him, "However, I will brook no egotistical tendencies or superiority complexes from anyone, am I making myself clear?!"

Whatever the consequences may be for disobedience, none of them took the time to consider as they roared back to him. "By your mandate, High Commander!"

"From this moment on, you will give yourself over to The System!"

"We shall *do* as The System commands," the soldiers shouted back.

A Sat-Com signaled an incoming transmission as Justice Master Quinn swiftly turned to Commander Bovier and saluted, striking a fist to his chest, then flipped about reflexively and did the same to the men. "You are dismissed!"

"For now," Lucien added.

As the gathering of soldiers split up to go their separate ways, High Commander Lucien Bovier stepped away and took the call in private. Minutes later, he and Justice Master Tom Quinn walked side by side in silence towards the MPT line. It was a sophisticated marvel of modern technology, which was the main method of transportation throughout the city.

But it didn't end at OZ; millions of miles of underground tunnel systems were constructed that reached to every corner of the four Sub-terrestrials. Built on specially charged ion-magnetic tracks, these extreme high-velocity trains could reach speeds of 500 miles per hour or over should the need arise. The new trains were called Hypertrans and down here, more than two miles deep within the earth - they were the fastest way to get from one place to another.

"You're too easy on them," Lucien stated, breaking the silence.

"I can say the exact opposite about you."

"They need discipline!"

"Yeah well, I never finished my 'asshole training'", Tom replied with a grin.

"No Tom, I'm pretty sure you've got that down perfectly," Lucien said in irritation, "You know how these guys are: cocky; arrogant; most likely to get themselves killed without someone holding their hands."

"I'm on it, Commander. You're killing my mojo by getting involved,

029 | P a g e – T h e B r a n d

you know. They're very receptive to the way I'm handling things."

"The only 'mojo' you got is what's hiding beneath those pants. Just make sure they are ready, alright?"

"Sounds like you've been speaking with Fiona again."

"As I recall, Fiona left you high and dry."

Tom flashed him a hurt look. "You really have to work on your 'people skills'; both with your friends as well as your recruits."

"My 'people skills' are just fine. It's my tolerance for *idiots* that needs work...and *you're* getting on my nerves."

"Careful Commander, you're actually starting to show some emotion; we wouldn't want people to get the wrong idea."

Lucien shook his head. He couldn't decide if he wanted to laugh or clock his friend in the head. "That's enough, Tom; you're testing my patience! I'll expect a full report by the end of next week."

"Yes Sir. One last thing Sir."

"Yeah, what is it?"

"About that 'asshole training', Commander. When will you be teaching your next class?"

This time, he clocked Tom in the back of the head. "Have I ever told you that the hardest part of my job is being nice to *stupid people?* What the hell has gotten into you?!"

"Well, let me-"

"Tom!"

"Okay, okay."

Tom's always the joker but he's a bit too much lately, Lucien thought to himself. No matter what he said, you just couldn't stay mad at the guy. Then again, he was the only one with the audacity to speak to Lucien this way...and get away with it. It was refreshing actually; to be able to get some honesty for a change. It was a rare occurrence in public as they both had high stations to uphold; one where the requirement was to act angry, demanding, and uptight. Cocky bastard or not, Tom *was* his best friend and a man he trusted implicitly.

But he was also easily manipulated by the troops; Tom felt a kind of fatherly love for them and they usually used that to their advantage. Regardless, Lucien *was* worried about this new batch of recruits. They were younger than the last and that brought about its own set of problems: lack of discipline and respect, with a know-it-all attitude. He didn't want their deaths on his hands; he was already carrying enough guilt all on his own. Lucien made up his mind to re-confirm their training exercises when next they met. *Better safe than sorry.*

Entering the station, the next shift was starting and the crowds had swelled. Half of them were trying to come to work; the other half rushing to leave for home. At this time of day, it was a huge pain in the ass to get anywhere. They swiped their wrists across the biometric scanner which read their G-ID chips, confirming their Global ID and walked through the automatic doors, where they boarded the magnetically powered bullet train.

Standing amongst the other black-ops soldiers...or Catetons – as they had come to be known as after The System had been put into place - and the few civilians aboard, Lucien peered out the sturdy glass window at the expanse of the city. He didn't think that he would ever get over his awe at the sophisticated engineering feats that must have gone into building an entire city underground!

From the enterprising vision to the complicated construction, the secrecy involved at creating something like this went beyond his meager comprehension, but he had discerned some of the stories of how these things were accomplished. The erection of these super-structures had begun about 25 years ago under the guise of tract development. The construction crews had actually built an immense square of hollow buildings surrounding the immediate area so that the real work could begin underground.

Eventually, once they had the first level complete, they had banned the entire site, stating some type of radioactive ground contamination. All the collective public knew was that there was some small town in development which was later abandoned for whatever reason.

As far as the rumors went, it was a restricted and unsafe area, which no one wanted to go anywhere near in the first place. Regardless of this fact, construction smack dab in the middle of the Ozarks granted enough privacy as the area was very remote and the mountain-living population was scarce and were a clannish lot, who asked very little questions.

These underground tunnels were made using nuclear powered laser drilling machines whose patents were never released to the general public. These newer, updated machines quite literally melted their way through the rock and soil, actually transforming the waste into a solid and incredibly strong glass-like substance.

There were news stories during that time about strange noises being heard and unexplained shaking of the ground, but they were quickly explained away as a swarm of many small earthquakes which took place in a short amount of time. Who knew that the true cause of the mysterious happenings were the result of giant tunnelers burrowing massive holes beneath the earth!

It wasn't until a few years later that the effects of mass tunneling through the earth made itself known. All over the world, birds upon the thousands fell dead from the sky, hatching dark rumors about apocalyptic plagues, UFO's, or insidious experiments being responsible. The real truth was that the drilling had somehow breached the magnetosphere, causing disruptions in the magnetic field. The alternating strength and polarity of the field was the reason why it was affecting the birds.

It was shown that specialized cells in a bird's brain record detailed information on the Earth's magnetic field, a kind of biological compass. Birds used these fluctuations to navigate based on the direction and strength of the field itself. The disruptions caused a kind of vertigo to the hippocampus of their brains, causing them to stop flying mid-flight and come tumbling down. At least that's what the scientists say...

Yet, there were many other occurrences besides the birds. Fish, who imprint on the magnetic field for navigation and also used it to find their prey were dying off all over the world by the millions. Course charts and maps needed to be fine-tuned to account for the subtle changes to shifts in the poles. Skin cancer rates had increased. Large sinkholes began appearing in various countries, opening up the ground and causing untold chaos.

Storms around the world became much more violent and unpredictable, unleashing torrential rains and sudden tornados. Strange cloud formations and eruptions of long extinct volcanoes were a sign that something unnatural was going on. Drastic weather changes were taking place on a regular occurrence with no end in sight. The detrimental effects to the rest of the Ecosystem were yet to be seen, strange things were indeed happening. Global warming definitely had its part to play in this, but the more drastic effects began with the rupture to Earth's magnetic field.

Either way, the construction of these underground tunnels were a most impressive feat! Even with millions of tons of earth pressing against them, the beautifully inlaid tunnels that allowed train, vehicle and pedestrian transport, were mostly impenetrable. Above ground, a person could see a number of mini-cooling towers that were designed to provide ventilation and clean oxygen to the subterranean city below.

These were intermingled amongst the partially built structures, parks, and trails that ran across the false development. Small outposts equipped with security cameras and motion sensors were scattered about in several defensive positions and hidden weapon systems manned the grounds. Rarely were there trespassers, but for those that did – most were never heard from again.

Below ground, OZI City was one of the four major Sub-terrestrials built and placed in strategic locations around the world. They were immense communities, with state-of-the-art facilities stretching almost 60 miles in either direction! The ever-encompassing Solar Simulation Grid blanketed the entire city, creating and providing artificial sunlight that sustained both health and productivity.

It consisted of everything needed to survive and prosper, with enough excess to spare: innovative battery-powered vehicles, fitness centers, medical and testing facilities, various types of grocery and retail outlets, a multitude of clean-air factories that manufactured everything from staples to high-tech ammunition, and of course an extremely secure base of operations for The System.

The site also included a water and air purification plant as well as a small lake fed by fresh water from underground springs. All said and done, it was a marvel of both science and engineering.

There were many smaller underground bases of operations, but only four large ones: OZI City in the United States; CABALA City in Kazakhstan; DAGON City in China; and ASURA City in India were the main administrative and regulatory bodies. OZI City; known as the OZ Initiative to its inhabitants however, was special- it was the autocracy for The Amalgam, also referred to as The Council. This political regiment was formed of its own internal board of directors and the few influential people who controlled most of the world's bureaucratic regulations.

There were whispers that while The Amalgam was certainly a very powerful entity, they were not the ones making the decisions regarding the masses; rather it was the 13 Families, acting behind the veil and being the guiding influence. Whether that was true or not, Lucien was not privy to anything that did not concern his immediate position as High Commander of the OZI City Catetons.

Everything had changed in this New World and even he was aware that rights and freedoms as we knew it, did not exist anymore. Interestingly enough, in order to provide a false semblance of democracy, each individual country and state was allowed to keep its original name, but was ultimately governed...or *dictated* by The System.

"We have arrived, Commander," Quinn said redundantly, as the train went from high speed to an immediate stop in a little under four seconds.

"Yeah, thanks for that. Maybe you should see if there are any openings in the Conductor's Guild; with your skills at intuition, they might be able to use you."

Tom smiled back at him and moved forward, parting the row of passengers to allow himself and High Commander Bovier room to step out onto the walkway. They continued their descent towards the city's main structure by taking a shortcut through the adjacent alley.

"Commander-"

"Oh, *enough already,* Tom," Lucien laughed and patted him on the shoulder. "We are in private as *we can be*...enough of that '*Commander*' bullshit; you sound like some damned robot!"

He frowned. "Sorry, my mind is not where it should be."

"Is it ever?"

Tom didn't answer. His face was a pale shade of red and his brows were furrowed with uncertainty. He stopped in the middle of the alley, prompting the High Commander to turn and walk back towards him.

Lucien stared at him for a moment, expecting him to speak. "Are you alright? You don't look well."

"Listen," he began hesitantly, "I've had something on my mind for some time now...I'm thinking of getting out."

"Out of what?"

"Everything! All of...*this*."

He paused and gave Tom a sideways glance. "Very funny, you almost had me there."

Tom didn't say anything, only put his head down. Whether it was in shame or indecision, Lucien couldn't tell. He looked distressed, hesitant...this was *not a joke*.

"You're serious."

"I don't know if this is for me anymore."

"What?!"

"It's different for me, Lucien. Someday I want to start a family of my own and stop placing myself in the line of fire. We've been fighting a long time-"

"We're fighting for a cause," Lucien interrupted, with a bit of anger. "What are you saying? You're just going to *quit*?!"

"Retire, maybe. You think this isn't difficult for me?! I know you need me. Maybe I can head up the training unit-"

"Tom..."

Either his commanding officer didn't believe him or they were about to get into an argument right here in the alleyway. "Look, this is obviously not the right time for this. I shouldn't have brought it up. Let's keep moving."

Tom started walking again. After a moment, Lucien picked up the pace and caught up. This was definitely something unexpected! A half hour ago, Tom had been joking around and acting normal as can be; actually more of a jackass than anything else. All that silly banter must have been his nerves talking. Tom was always flippant when he was nervous. *I should have seen this coming!* He'd never mentioned anything about having doubts about any of it; especially to Lucien. Perhaps *that* hurt more than his sudden declaration...*Let it be for now.*

"You're right – this is a discussion for another time," Lucien stated, breaking the awkward silence, "I assume they are ready for us?"

"We'll be meeting with just Doctor Lockwood as far as I am aware."

Lucien pursed his lips in irritation. That evidently meant that Rand would not be there - again. Did the man feel he was too good to be seen with 'the help' or was he simply being careful? It was about high time they met face to face! Quentin Rand was the leader of The Hand of Light, the global resistance faction which fought against the extreme indoctrinations and dictatorship of The System. In The Old World, he was once a top executive of a mega-corporation called Grains Unlimited based in what used to be Europe.

Lucien knew very little as to what caused his defection, but common knowledge was that Quentin had discovered that the company he worked for had developed a genetically-modified grain that was slowly poisoning millions of people. According to the rumors, this was done with the full knowledge of the company's Board of Directors.

Whether the contaminated grain was deliberately created for some dark purpose or if it was an accidental engineering blunder, Quentin Rand was convinced of a shadowy conspiracy within the corporation. It may have had something to do with his father, Balthazar Rand who was a radio host and documentary filmmaker who focused specifically on scandals and controversies in the Old World.

Many of these had been proven true and Quentin had been raised to question, investigate, and doubt circumstances that were strange or unexplained. Whatever the case may be, Rand had purposely leaked this information to the public. Outcry was immediate and the company's stocks plummeted. Investors were outraged and pushed for action. For months, no one knew who had been behind revealing the scandal.

Quentin Rand began collecting data on all ties the company had with other similar businesses and the foundation for the Resistance was forged. Once the Board found out that he was moving un-authorized funds to a private location and forming militant views; even building contacts with 'undesirables', they put two and two together and quickly moved against him. He was framed and accused of corporate espionage and libel.

With two separate law enforcement agencies hunting him, Rand had gone into hiding for eight years and when he resurfaced, The Hand of Light was already a global force to be reckoned with. That a one-time executive of a mega-corporation had now become the leader of an inter-continental militia was strangely ironic. It was said that during all those years as a fugitive, Rand was taught combat tactics and warfare by the Black Republic, a large sect of anti-System revolutionaries operating out of Colombia. Once he returned, Grains Unlimited was their first target and after that, global corporations had every right to be afraid.

Still, although he had never met the man in person, he and Rand had a begrudging respect for one another. If he chose not to be there, he had a damned good reason. "Looking forward to getting some good news for a change," he muttered under his breath, more to himself than Tom.

Tom nodded silently, in agreement. He had known Lucien Bovier a very long time and considered him more like a brother than as a friend. He wanted some good news as well. All this secrecy and the constant danger of being exposed had been getting to him for some time now. His nerves were frayed from always having to be on edge and tension headaches had become a part of his daily routine.

As a soldier, he was used to taking risks; even to the point of recklessness. His team had been involved in many battles and countless incursions and he had survived each and every one of them. But *this*; this was something else. The significant danger of being exposed as a 'traitor' was a constant; this was *his life*. All these years and only now, the realization was hitting home! Why was it happening now? Maybe he was finally burnt out. *Pull yourself together!*

Three weeks earlier, Tom had been sanctioned to Atlanta for a complicated mission that was contained weeks sooner than originally estimated. Lacking anything better to do afterwards, he'd decided to stick around for a while. This redneck capital of the world was where he was born and raised for much of his pre-adult life. Gun and ammo shops, cowboy retail outlets, and local taxidermists fit right in here, amongst people who thought that going to the big city strip club was the next best thing to taking a vacation in Disneyland.

It was strange coming back home after so many years. Most of his family were either deceased or living abroad so there was no one to really visit. Instead he had some drinks with a few old friends and hooked up with an ex-girlfriend for the night. It was the day after when the fear set in; a premonition of bad things to come. Caution had led to doubt, which had turned into worry and finally become dread. *But for what?* He was a religious man, but he was far from superstitious. Still, he was smart enough not to ignore a gut feeling either.

It had slowly gnawed at him for two days until he had dared to set foot back into the abandoned remains of Blessed Saints Catholic Church. Tom never thought he'd see this place again; especially after his falling out with the faith. He had gone in, thinking he could get some guidance through meaningful prayer. Instead, it had brought back a tirade of spiteful memories, he should have known were better left alone.

He was raised Catholic and attended Blessed Saints Private School, which was attached to the Church. It was one of the best educational institutions in the nation at that time. Mass was every Wednesday, with Confession on Fridays, and a weekly Religion class held on Thursdays. His mother and father were strict and disciplined Catholics, determined to bring Tom up in line with their faith.

His experiences with the school brought back feelings of resentment. After all the years of annoyance with how he had been treated here, he'd come to the conclusion that he had done nothing wrong. It was the self-righteous and arrogant teachers who were truly at fault.

Tom's troubles at Blessed Saints had all begun with a simple question he'd asked during a Thursday Religion class. Father Waran, the firm and oftentimes iron-fisted priest loved to impress upon the mindless students, his amazing knowledge of the Catholic religion.

He could preach all day about why things were the way they were and how everyone should be devoted to the faith's indoctrinations. But what Tom noticed was that Father Waran would never explain the reasoning behind these actions. Throughout the weekly classes, curiosity had built itself a home within his mind. He had questions as all young students did, however, his were the kind that bordered on blasphemy.

"I want you all to go home and read through the first few chapters of the New Testament. After dinner tonight, I want you to say three Hail Mary's before you retire for the night, and ask God for forgiveness for your sins," Father Waran had said one day, "Next week, we will review-"

"*But why*...why talk to *Mary*," he had asked.

"What was that?"

"Why the Hail Mary's?"

"*Please, Mr. Quinn*, why don't you enlighten the rest of the class on your *dispute*?! I'm sure we'd all like to hear where this is going..."

Tom didn't realize at the time how condescending Father Waran was being towards him.

"Sure, Father, I don't mean any disrespect...I understand she is the Mother of Jesus, but shouldn't I be speaking to God Himself? Wouldn't it be sacrilegious to pray to anyone *other than God*?" It was an innocent enough query...or so he had thought.

"Blasphemy," the priest screamed, his face contorted in rage, "Who do you think you are to question a servant of God?! You little sh-"

Obviously, the Church judged differently. The tirade that came down on him by the disciplined priest was akin to the Wrath of God Himself. Tom was reprimanded in front of the entire class and made to look like an impetuous fool. His giggling classmates thought it was some kind of joke and that had only made matters worse.

Perhaps questions about faith that needed answers were considered sacrilege when it came down to religion! *Nod your head and follow the sheep...that was the way things seemed to go.* Throughout the next few weeks, he had even more 'heretical' inquiries, spurred on by deep down feelings of curiosity and frustration.

"Why do we have to genuflect each time we come into church?"

"Why is the Mass *always* the same, to the point of being cultish?"

"Why do we have to confess our sins to a priest, who in turn tells them to God? Why go through a 'middle man' instead of speaking to God directly?"

"Are you telling me that I can commit all variety of sins throughout my life and all I have to do is ask for forgiveness to get into Heaven when my time comes? That's it?!"

"How is it possible to be forgiven for my sins simply by saying five 'Our Father's' and seven 'Hail Mary's'?"

At the moment, they all seemed like common sense questions. The answers that came were vague and without substance; it was as if they did not know either. But of course, the chastising and punishments appeared with no hesitation. Hadn't they taught him to think for himself? It seemed that the Church was resolute in their ways, without really teaching the how's and why's of the religion they were preaching; an interesting contradiction to faith itself.

There was a joke he'd heard his father tell at family gatherings when he was young. It went something like "When I was a kid, I would pray every night for a new bike. Then I realized that God doesn't work that way. So, I stole my neighbor's bike and prayed for forgiveness." It was hilarious at the time, but now it forced him to think things through in a whole new light.

After a meeting with Sister MaryAnn, the principal, his parents and Father Waran, he was expelled from the school. It was unfair and he knew it, but Tom never looked back and considered himself simply 'Christian' from that moment on. Tom was a reverent and God-fearing man but he felt betrayed by the Church itself. He remembered his mother being so angry with him. Their entire family had attended Blessed Saints and now, that legacy had come to a crashing halt.

For Tom however, he could not blindly follow any doctrine without first having the answers he sought. He still respected every person's right to believe what they wanted to, but for him blind allegiance to *any faith* simply would not do. He had applied the same principles to his outlook on life. He never took anything for granted after that and he would find the answers he needed before committing to any cause.

That night in the skeletal remains of the Church, Tom prayed to God for the wisdom, strength, and guidance to get him and his comrades through the dangers that were to come. Ultimately after hours of soul-searching, he had come to the conclusion that *he wanted out*. All the madness, death, and mayhem that seemed to be a constant in his life did little for his sense of self. He wanted something more, something pure. He didn't want to be a soldier anymore. After he left Blessed Saints, he felt as if an immense burden had been lifted from his heart.

He felt...relieved. Sometimes, a little faith did wonders for the tortured soul...Since then, he had been searching for the 'right time' to tell Lucien but never seemed to find it. His revelations were never meant to have spilled out in the middle of an alleyway. But what could he do about that now... Hopefully once they had more time, they could have this conversation the right way. For now, they had other obligations to attend to.

The two men followed the alley onto the West walkway which

curved around the station and boarded one of the deep red lifts that went up towards a moon-shaped building above. Bovier scanned his G-ID chip across the panel and his 5th level security clearance activated.

There were many such high-speed elevators all around the city that not only serviced the multiple levels of the super-structure, but also took passengers horizontally across vast distances throughout the city. A few of these, such as the one they were on and differentiated by a very tiny symbol placed between the doors, led to buildings and places of extreme importance that had a high security clearance. Only a 5th level Chip could mobilize it.

CHAPTER 4: Rebels

The Citadel was not exactly the given name of the moon-shaped building that they entered, but that was what it was referred to by most of Oz's inhabitants. It was a whirring, buzzing nest of sophisticated tech which ran and controlled a number of the weaponized security hardware used around the city in place of additional manpower. Laser grid systems; ion canons; security cameras; and even the surface to air missiles located in the unseen silos above could be both manually and automatically controlled right from here. There were offices and large meeting rooms on both sides of a hallway that travelled in multiple directions, ultimately leading to the Tech-Ops Laboratory.

Here, researchers and scientists worked together in secrecy to invent and manufacture new and highly advanced weaponry and other useful gadgets. Each time Lucien had been here, there was something cutting-edge and unique that was being developed and ready for beta testing. They were to be used for operations that sometimes not even he was privileged to know about yet. He had a pretty good suspicion that although these technophiles *built* the weaponry, they had no idea what they were meant for either. This time unfortunately, he would not have the time to have a little fun with the 'new toys'.

But Lucien wasn't here to play around with exotic weapons; he was here for a meeting. One that had taken careful and considerate planning to accomplish, while at the same time choosing a specific date and time where The Citadel was least occupied. Something that had been incredibly tough to do as this was one of the main nerve centers of OZ. This place was usually crawling with Cateton security and research scientists.

Today, however, was a special day. The annual New Year's celebration had emptied most of the workers from the building, leaving a skeleton-crew of guards. Each of the Citadel's Directors took a turn manning the installation so only one was mandated to stay behind during these special events; the one they would be meeting with. Since all the lead science officers would be required to attend the festivities, most of the division was empty, providing them with the necessary privacy they needed. Thankfully for Tom and himself, attendance for the Cateton Guard was optional.

They finally entered the laboratory and walked towards the wall in the far corner. Lucien reached down towards the lower right portion of the partition, and pressed on a subtle protrusion that appeared to be a mere defect in the structure. Immediately a hidden door opened and they walked into a large glass-like room. The entire surrounding structure was made of a thermal-glass hybrid material. The insulation -developed by another satellite location of The System- made the extended area completely sound-proof.

The room was equipped with a long metallic conference table and comfortable leather-backed chairs, a bathroom and a kitchen. No other openings were anywhere in the room, with just the hidden door they came in leading in or out. A number of surveillance Holo-monitors were hooked into the corners of the ceiling and showed a clear view of the outside and other areas around the facility. The far-left wall was lined with holographic display terminals that could control the security defenses in the building, directly from the inside.

Very few knew about or were even aware of this place. It was specifically designed for the upper echelons and the heads of the engineering division to discuss the new weaponry and tech at their disposal. There was one other use for it, but wasn't public knowledge – it was also a Panic Room to be utilized in case of a security breach. He looked the area over from one end to the other. What this room lacked in style, it more than made up for in functionality.

A mousy looking woman in a long white lab coat greeted them as they approached, fumbling with a number of documents on a clipboard. She was of average height, her eyes set a bit too far apart with a bigger nose and full, wide lips. Her stance portrayed a confidence in her work, but also betrayed a nervousness around members of the opposite sex. A few white-blonde tresses tumbled about her blue-green eyes while the rest of her hair was neatly woven into a braided ponytail. Dr. Ayla Lockwood was in great shape for a lab rat and if she would do something to tidy up her appearance, she would be considered very pretty indeed.

She acknowledged them with a polite nod. "Good Afternoon Gentleman, glad to see you made it; please take a seat."

"Ayla, how are you?" Lucien nodded and sat down.

"It could be better Commander," she replied respectfully, and reached out her hand to Tom

Instead of taking it, Tom pulled her into an endearing bear hug. He was always the 'Lady's Man' or trying to be anyway. "Come now Ayla; as Lucien keeps telling me – we are *not* in the public eye anymore...you can do better than that!"

"I suppose I could," Ayla smiled as she pecked him on the cheek and motioned him towards the table. She handed each person a portable holographic personal computer, commonly referred to as a HOL-COM, so everyone could keep in pace with what she was about to discuss with them.

"Right down to business, eh?"

"You know what they say about me: All work and *more work*," she answered, and then switched to a serious tone, "You both know the layout of this place well so I won't have to go over that; there are pastries and tea on the table if you're hungry or thirsty and the Comms are live in case you are recalled for duty. So if there are no more tiring and simply boring questions, shall we get started?"

"The floor is all yours Ma'am," conceded Tom, between large mouthfuls of a frosted strawberry pastry. She had an edge on her, that one – especially when she was nervous about something...

Dr. Lockwood eyed him with an exasperated look, using three perfectly manicured fingers to brush the hair from her pretty face. "Alright gentleman, let's get to it. Rand has requested that I get you both up to date, but there's one last thing..."

The annoyance at her statement built up in him yet again. *Why doesn't Rand come and give us the orders himself,* Lucien thought. He was the first one to admit that he was highly irritated with the fact that Quentin Rand seemed to always be hiding in the shadows while the rest of them were out in the open, taking the risks, getting things done! Regardless, it was clear that he trusted Ayla enough to confer this knowledge to them through her. Lucien did too, so he calmed himself before he said something stupid.

Ayla reached into her pocket and used her thumbprint to unlock a black carbon-fiber case and handed Lucien a small Terra-drive. *"This* is for you, Lucien, he instructed me to get this to you. I've keyed it to your G-ID chip so it's ready to be accessed. DO NOT allow this out of your sight; it has vital information and rest assured – you really *don't* want to be caught with it!"

The Commander accepted it, quickly slipping it into a hidden compartment on his person. "I am aware of what this means to you Ayla; I will keep it safe...and thank you." The information written on this drive was something he had been very curious about. When he had more time, he would look through it more carefully. Right now, there were more important matters at hand.

She nodded in acknowledgement. "I'm going to make this quick so please follow along...last thing I need is for that arrogant bastard, Wychert to come in here and-"

"Temper, temper, Ayla," Tom said, with a big grin, "You know, oftentimes you remind me of Fiona; she has that same irritability about her. Ha - when she'd get angry, sometimes she'd tie me up and tickle my-"

She stopped him mid-sentence with an irritated stare. Seeing as they were listening, she continued. "As you both know, the targets have been chosen according to intelligence smuggled in by Dagon City agents. System operations have stalled in five sectors and have affected multiple programs set forth by The Amalgam, especially the new chip upgrades. Even that Tech will soon be halted completely.

The Hand continues to recruit members from higher echelons at an increasing rate, including Core Minister Allastor Kallen, right here in OZ. He will be invaluable in accessing the city's unmonitored safe routes and procuring internal data. He will also be the inside contact for your team. I have encoded all relevant information into your G-ID Chips."

"*Kallen*? I know that name..." Tom said. "There was a Benton Kallen who was killed in the Cypher Labs explosion six years ago! Any relation?"

"A much deeper significance, actually," Lucien explained, "Benton

Kallen was the Core Minister's son. Makes sense why he switched sides then. He will be a great asset to The Hand."

That was as long as the Core Minister could keep his personal vendetta in check...Before the tragedy, Cypher Labs Industries used to be located 60 miles past the northeast sector of St. Francis National Forest, far above OZI City. They had been conducting experiments with Dark Matter, using a highly advanced particle accelerator to create and form it.

It was to be their 'penance' in a way from what humans had already done to the planet...Pollution and decay from generations of using the three major fossil fuels: coal, oil, and natural gas had finally taken its toll on the planet. Environmental problems such as global warming, air quality deterioration, oils spills, and acid rain had caused more than its share of damage and deaths around the globe.

However, Dark Matter was not the first alternative energy to be introduced. The powers-that-be had already failed them many years ago when they introduced Uranium-powered nuclear power to the masses instead of the revolutionary natural compound they could have utilized. Thorium was a white, silvery chemical that was a basic element of nature, found in soil, rocks, and water. Unlike Uranium, small amounts posed little danger to human health and was in much more abundant of a supply.

What was amazing about the chemical was that a very small amount: 1 ton, could produce as much energy as 200 tons of Uranium! In the 1950's, it was a safer, stable alternative to the more hazardous isotope, but was discarded by the simple fact that Uranium could be weaponized and Thorium could not! All the progress of Thorium research was stopped because an entire industry had already developed around the use of Uranium! Money played a huge motivating factor in the decision; they were making millions with nuclear power! By that time, it was too late.

As was then, so was now. Again, they had reverted back to the pre-built industry of oil and other high-priced fuels, suppressing the research into smarter, safer alternatives. All these years later and fossil fuels still accounted for 80% of the world's primary energy sources used in the New World. After seeing first-hand, the damage that was caused to the Earth itself, public outcry finally deafened the ears of the global corporations. To that end, The Amalgam was forced to appear as if the people actually had a voice in all of it. As such, a new source of energy was promised to the masses to be discovered and harnessed.

Dark Matter was an innovative new study at the time. It was unique due to its characteristic of being its own antiparticle. In that sense, it did not need to fuse with its opposite or be split into separate atoms like nuclear material did. Cypher Labs had built an Antimatter Relay to collect and collide dark matter particles to produce a 100% efficient source of energy that would be free and virtually unlimited!

It was to be one of the greatest breakthroughs in scientific history and Doctor Benton Kallen was the lead physicist who was heading up the project. Accurately predicting that they would lose power, control, and untold wealth, The Amalgam had other plans. On the day of the reveal they somehow detained Benton at his home and proceeded with the testing. Without him present, a leak in the containment field had released the Dark Matter. Once unleashed, it had started a gravitational chain reaction that had destroyed not just the laboratory, but everything in its path for five square miles!

There were hushed whispers that The Amalgam had intentionally extinguished any chance that the world would receive clean, free energy. What's more, the blame had been pinned on one man: Doctor Benton Kallen. He was not only an innocent victim, but a patsy as well. The site had been immediately restricted and all the evidence pointing to Kallen was based off a single investigation by a Cateton Search and Retrieval Unit, loyal to The System.

Core Minister Allastor Kallen had fought tooth and nail for the case to be re-opened and a new inquiry to be authorized. Neither of those things happened and the world quietly went back to coal, oil, and natural gas as their leading sources of energy. Benton Kallen was imprisoned and subsequently murdered in a riot. Although he continued to perform his many political duties, Allastor Kallen was never quite the same after that. And now, it seemed that the notable and powerful man had become not only a friend to, but a trusted informant of The Hand of Light.

"I don't believe Kallen's views were in line with The System's to begin with, Lucien. Anyway, he's with us now," Ayla stated. "Kallen was a Robotics Engineer before he became the Core Minister for

OZI City. He was working on a neural interface for A.I. - Artificial Intelligence."

A.I.? "*Interesting*...I'm listening," Bovier prompted.

"It's ours, Lucien," she said excitedly, "Kallen gave us full access to his research. Our Techs have been studying it non-stop for months now and we've made significant progress!"

"I guess that certainly cements our relationship then," Tom commented, and turned to Doctor Lockwood. "But what does that mean *for us*? I mean that's great and all, but how are we going to utilize something like that...and *for what purpose?*"

"Come on, Tom, use your head," Lucien butted in, "Think of the military applications it could be procured for! We could-"

Such a one-track mind with him..."*My interest*," Ayla interrupted, obviously irritated, "is primarily for scientific uses and war is hardly the function I had in mind! Don't you two think about anything else...Imagine the lives it could *save*, not the ones it could take. The applications are endless: scientific discovery for one; enhanced security; concept processing; medical advances – hell, it may even be able to find a cure for diseases such as SARCA-24!"

SARCA-24? Could it really be possible to eradicate that terrible plague?! "Okay, okay – sorry I spoke," Lucien relented.

"How far have you come," Tom asked.

Giving him a flashing grin, she continued. "Okay then...As you know, sometime after The System was established, we set out to do the impossible: *replicating a human brain*! Twenty-five years ago, it was deemed by the majority of the scientific community to be undoable...even taboo-"

"I thought we'd already developed the brain scan," Lucien put in.

"We've barely scratched the surface; what we currently have is rudimentary at best. It is nothing more than a precursor to the final product, which will be significantly more advanced. Let's see how I can explain this...we'll start with the basics. The human brain has a power consumption of only 20 watts, but that outclasses even the world's fastest supercomputer when it comes to performing common tasks based on sensory input!"

Seeing the look on their faces, she paused. "Did I lose you already; I must be melting brain cells as I speak!"

"*You lost me* when we sat down," Lucien laughed, "but go on, please continue."

"Okay – so the human brain...Because its neural networks continuously adapt and self-organize, it can process information in parallel and on a massive scale. The initial goal was to create a computer brain every bit the equal to its human counterpart. It was thought of as...*the basis* to creating Artificial Intelligence. Take a look at the data charts on your HOL-COM's of the DNA model."

Both men ran their fingers along the spines of the Tablets and activated the holographic projections. A double helix of a DNA strand appeared in line with brain wave algorithms above each of their screens.

"The first obstacle we had to overcome was seriously understanding what it meant to be human."

"*To be human*," Lucien questioned, "You mean walk, talk, and think like a man?"

"She means in the literal sense," Quinn cut in, "There are many things humans can do that a machine cannot...For example, we take many of the inherent feats we can accomplish for granted; things we don't even think twice about that come naturally to us."

She peered down at Tom from above her spectacles as if a petulant child. "Well, I think you are being very vague when you say that; the principle is sound, but you have to apply specifics to the-"

"I understand you are the technical genius here, Ayla, but I wasn't born yesterday," Tom snapped and then turned his face down, noticeably embarrassed about his sudden outburst. He really liked Ayla Lockwood. She was a genius in her field and over the years, had become a very good friend, but she could be so damned-right condescending!

And I have a temper? "My apologies, Tom. I didn't mean to-"

"No, *I'm* sorry. Sometimes I take your input a bit personally...Regardless, what Ayla means is that there are many things we as humans know, that we don't even know we know and we take those things for granted." Tom shook his head in frustration. "Okay, well that didn't come out quite right. What I meant was-"

Lucien felt both sufficiently cowed and baffled at the same time. "Huh? What are you going on about; it's like I'm speaking to a reincarnation of Sigmund Freud!" He shook his head in exasperation, "You want me to comprehend what the hell you're saying, then explain this to me as if I'm a child! Bad enough we already have *one* resident genius in the room..."

Quinn chuckled out loud, jerking a thumb in the Commander's direction, "Did he just insult himself?!"

Tom could be such a pain in the ass, with his intellectual ramblings... "Shut up and get on with it Tom!"

"You two are like a married couple," Ayla chuckled, "My mother always said guys are sometimes just boys in men's clothing and I'm starting to agree with her."

A frown of confusion was evident on Lucien's face. Ayla stifled a laugh. "From where I stand, I'd have to say he's on the right track," she said. "It appears I've underestimated you, Tom; you just *look* like a dumb jock...let's allow him to continue, shall we?"

She stepped into the adjacent kitchen and took a tarnished black kettle off the small stove and filled it up with water. She'd had this appliance from The Old World installed six months ago; for some reason the water came out tasting better from a kettle than a thermal-inducer. This conversation was getting deep, which meant *tea* was in order.

"Thank you...*I think*," Quinn stated, accepting the obscure compliment graciously, "Uhmm – let's see if I can explain this in simple terms...For instance, all of us know that the walls in this room are substantial, right? We know that we cannot go through them, unless we have an opening; they are for all practical purposes

- solid."

"So," prompted Lucien.

"So, we learn things like this before we can even walk, and we only have to learn it *once*. Therefore, this is information our brain's process that *we* take for granted, but we also comprehend and understand this as basic 'common sense'. We know that when someone dies, they stay dead; we know water has no color; we know we smile when we are happy and so on. I'm-"

"Oh God, help me," muttered Lucien. He was impatiently rapping his fingers on the table. The High Commander had a habit of getting upset when he could not comprehend matters he was unfamiliar with. That didn't mean he was stupid or scared; being a leader of the Catetons, he just worked smarter and more efficiently when he had all the details.

"Let him finish Commander," Ayla urged as she poured three cups of steaming black tea and added a dash of cinnamon and a wedge of lemon; she distributed them amongst the small group.

"I'm no expert on the subject," Tom answered hesitantly, "but if I had to formulate a hypothesis..." He got up from his chair and began pacing around the table. "In order for you to create a *true* Artificial Intelligence, the program must be able to think, comprehend, and reason for itself. It needs a way to be able to absorb information like a person can." He stopped pacing and stared at the wall. "But it's even bigger than that, isn't it?" he said to himself, "It not only needs to be self-aware, but it also has to have a conscience of some sort; maybe even the capacity for wisdom or subjective thought..."

"It has to be *human*," Doctor Lockwood finished, "at least as close as it can be. But you're right – deduction, reasoning, and problem-solving are the first steps towards a working neural net."

The room was silent for a moment. "Maybe Tom here should have been under *your* command instead of mine, Ayla," teased Lucien, with a smirk on his face, "I didn't realize I had such a brainiac on my hands...and you became a *soldier*?"

Tom stared at him sharply for a moment and then laughed. "To put it simply, Lucien, I'm smarter than *you are*." He nodded in Ayla's direction, "From what you're implying, I assume you and your team have succeeded?"

Her eyes glittered with excitement. "Well gentleman, what I'd like to say is a resounding yes. However it is a bit more complicated than that. Are you two understanding the theories behind this so far?"

Both men nodded their heads, eagerly waiting for her to continue. "Okay then...We've accomplished a great deal and although we do not have a self-aware robot we can send back in time yet," she joked, "we *do* have a prototype artificial intelligence!"

"You're kidding," Lucien murmured quietly.

"*However,*" she clarified, "it is only semi-sentient and has a half-life."

"How did I know there'd be one of those?"

Side-stepping Lucien's disappointment, she turned to face his second in command, "You did extremely well Tom, but left out a few relevant details."

"I'm sure that's the understatement of the year," he replied sarcastically.

"You have the gist of it, but the A.I. must also be able to plan, learn, and communicate in order to be effective. Another issue we've run into is abstract logic: nothing is completely true or false in the way it defines. For instance, if I were to bring about a bird in conversation, most people would typically envision a small animal that sings and flies. However, these things are not true about *all birds*. An ostrich, for example is a *large* bird that *cannot* fly. Default reasoning brings about a whole other set of problems! But most importantly in this case, there has to be a *compatibility quotient!* Here, let me put this up on the Holo-view so we can all take a closer look."

Dr. Lockwood reached forward and waved her hand across a tiny sensor embedded into the table and a holographic image of what looked like a human brain took shape. She reached into the three-dimensional representation and performed a few intricate gestures and it separated into the different areas of the human brain.

"As I've said, The System developed a rudimentary version of the brain scan to identify and map large portions of the human brain, but with Kallen's research, we've taken it to a level beyond anything we could have imagined! What you are looking at is called a B.I.O.N.E.X.- a Bio-Synthetic Neural Emulation Xenogen, created by scanning and mapping a biological human brain in minute detail: from the processing data through electrical pulses, to the complete structural and functional neural connections of the mind! Its entire state is copied into a computer system and the simulation model is then uploaded into a chip. As of now it is only a prototype, but by far the greatest scientific breakthrough of the last century."

"Whose brain is it," Tom blurted out. What he was looking at was unnerving to say the least.

Ayla paused, nodding in his direction, "Now that is actually an interesting question, Tom. It brings us both to our solution...*and our problem*. When we first thought to achieve this, whomever this brain belonged to simply did not matter. At least that was what we had all assumed. Unfortunately the natural order of things had a different idea altogether.

We soon discovered that although this unknown person is long dead and gone, the adaptive neurons and behavior elements craved the original user in order to function correctly. At this point, even though it is technically a predecessor to A.I. - we still need to program its functions and give it direction. The emulation overlay will provide it with a human-like consciousness which will encompass all of these variables I mentioned and it will eventually become self-aware. However, it is not autonomous yet, nor will it be, unless we have the original user to take control of it."

"So what you are telling us is that it is completely *useless*," Commander Bovier pointed out irritatingly, his right knee shaking excitedly. His calculating mind had played out various scenes of the multiple military uses a working model could be used for, but this was an obvious deterrent. "Or that we need to somehow locate, exhume, and turn a dead man into a Frankenstein monster!?"

Ayla frowned and completed another series of gestures and a set of calculations and four faces with relevant details below each one appeared before the brain model. "I wish it were that simple...Not only do we need a consciousness for the A.I. to bond with, but also a mind that is at least 67.5% compatible to the neural network of the brain we've already mapped."

"And these are the four people who share that same similarity," Tom stated, pointing at the holographic images.

Ayla took a sip from her cup of tea, and then cleared her throat. "Yes, and as I am sure you both are aware, when the Global ID chip was introduced years ago, The System mandated a brain scan of all high-level employees for security clearances. We clearly could not test person by person as this would have taken far too long, so having this data readily available was *most helpful*. Using the B.I.O.N.E.X. Algorithm and the Neuroimaging Topographer Kallen obtained for us, we were able to map a significant portion of each individual candidate's neural network."

She gestured at the life-like projections of the four individual images floating above the conference table. "The four you see before you are our best candidates. High Commissar Kyle Radner was killed three years ago by rebel forces; there is no clear report on what exactly happened, but we only found out this morning. Zhou Dongshan is by far the best match, but he is approaching nearly 80 years of age. This leaves Professor Akun Bantu in ASURA and Doctor Jenna Methis topside who are the most readily available subjects we can approach. As you can see, we have very limited options."

Lucien fidgeted with his sweat-stained palms as he nervously listened to the conversation. It was so disturbing how scientists and doctors casually referred to human beings as 'subjects'. It was both degrading and demeaning; out of sorts with his moral center. Regardless, she was saying that out of the remaining five billion people in the current occupation of the world, they had *four* suitable candidates...scratch that – *two* people they could approach!? And then what? *What* exactly did they have here?

"So why not map a different brain altogether," Lucien interjected.

Ayla flashed him a condescending look. "Would you like to donate *yours*, Commander? A single B.I.O.N.E.X. mapping took us months to complete! It is both a complicated and experimental procedure. We have a 40 percent chance of success; another scan would give us much the same odds of finding a relevant candidate. Besides, to locate a suitable match would be like looking for a specific grain of sand at the beach...we're lucky we found these four!"

Woah, settle down. "Okay, you're the expert," he stated with hesitation, "But I still don't understand what the problem with the A.I. is?"

"As I said, the furthest we could get so far is a simulation of an artificial intelligence that is only semi-sentient."

"Yes, Ayla – I get that part. But what does that mean?"

"Let me finish, Lucien. The advances we've made using Kallen's research are leaps and bounds over what we initially had! To be realistic, in the scientific community, the term 'semi-sentient' does not exist. Either it *is* sentient or *it is not*. We can create a semblance of A.I. but, it will burn itself out in 12 hours. It's unstable at best. A true artificial intelligence needs time to learn, adapt, and process information. This is how it becomes self-aware. Half a day is barely sufficient enough time for a game of chess."

"And the Neural Emulation will resolve this problem?"

"Theoretically speaking, yes. It would imprint a persona and simulate a central nervous system. The-"
"Okay, okay. I get it."

In all honesty, he didn't. He was just tired of wrapping his head around the concept of a machine being sentient. But, if they could succeed with it, the Resistance would have a fighting chance...and a weapon that could 'even the odds', maybe even surpass them! Lucien wasn't quite certain about the various capabilities of a true artificial intelligence, but he was sure it would prove a powerful ally. Hell, if it didn't work, they could always use what they had to make a better robotic vacuum; at least *that* was doable.

He pondered if it would be possible for the A.I. to enable them to hack into The System and its cells all at once? If that could be accomplished, it could bring them down for good! Now that was more fantasy than reality, but it *was* the most obvious way to do it as The System was like a Hydra. You cut off one of its heads and it was just replaced with another. They needed to hit the 'nerve center'! The things he could do with that kind of power in his control...It would have been nice to have something like this back in the day; who knew what advantages it could have given them...If they did, perhaps the A.I. would have never allowed The System to come to power in the first place!

Before that tyranny was initiated, life had been very different. The Old World had its faults, but peoples' freedoms were still intact and self-expression was evident everywhere you looked! Back then, he was a platoon leader of Navy Seal Team 4; a very capable and accomplished Special-Ops unit. Lucien had led his men through countless incursions with minimum loss of life; it was quite an achievement for someone who was not yet past 27 years of age at the time.

Of course, he'd been trained for this since he was a boy. His French-Canadian father had not only been a high-ranking Officer in the Navy, but also a Survivalist who had taught the High Commander everything he believed his son would need to know someday, from hunting in the wild to surviving in the most desolate of environments.

Lucien had taken to his training whole-heartedly and even though this cost him close relationships with friends and classmates, he did not mind as much as he probably should have. Even at a young age, he'd considered himself a Patriot and accepted the necessary sacrifices needed to become the perfect soldier for his country. Little did he know then, how bad things would eventually get; how corrupted the world really was...But that was the time and government of The Old World; the only thing that existed now was The System...and it had become much worse.

His thoughts shifted to Tom, who was having one of his intellectual conversations with the good Doctor. Justice Master Quinn was a man who had seen his own share of hard times before and during the last world war. His rough demeanor and massive six foot five frame were an odd combination with his handsome face and large doe-eyes that usually displayed a serene portrait of comfort and caring. He was unusually intelligent for a soldier and his military prowess in planning, strategy, and leadership were a direct reflection of that.

Tom Quinn had been his first trusted Lieutenant and quite possibly, one of the best damned Snipers he had ever seen. He was a proficient and excellent marksman with a modified AS50 semi-automatic sniper rifle and once took out three Taliban insurgents from a range of 2300 meters, which now that he thought about it – could very well have been a world record!

Tom was a brave man with a good heart and an even better friend; a man that you could divulge your closest secrets to and sleep soundly, knowing that he would protect them with his life. It was for these reasons that he promoted Tom to the position of Justice Master. Tom had never been one to shirk his duties, so his decision of leaving it all behind was most confusing. Then again, the stressors of war could certainly take its toll on anyone. He was fairly certain even he would have to cross that bridge eventually...

Both men had fought side by side during the third World War and each had lost both friends and comrades in the horrible conflict that arose. What The Old World referred to as World War III had begun with the chemical bombing of the American Embassy in Syria and then shockingly, the Pentagon in Washington D.C. Hundreds of innocents were killed instantly and the ones who were unlucky enough to escape the blast had slowly succumbed to severe toxic poisoning.

The investigating U.S. government had discovered that classified security information had been leaked to the terrorists by a high ranking 'spook' in the CIA by the name of Robert Beem. Beem was later found to have been a member of a terrorist cell called 'The Illuminated Ones', a globally powerful cult that based their teachings and beliefs on the clandestine Illuminati. It had all been very 'hush-hush' from that point on; no one knew quite what the true goal had been. What they *did know* was that the terrorists were smuggled in and funded by the ruling Arab Libertarian Party. This was the starting point of the War.

Everything had gone to hell in a domino-effect from there: Oil and interest rates skyrocketed; Housing markets, currency value, and economic prosperity came tumbling down around the world; China recalled all foreign debts; financial markets crashed, bringing the Dow to the verge of collapse; Riots and chaos ensued! The people lost their homes and their livelihoods, forcing them into despair and shrouding them in hate for the ones who did this to them. They demanded retribution!

The United States of America had gone to war with swift retaliation, recruiting its Allies into battle. With their close and supportive relationship with the United States, the Nation of Israel had joined immediately, seemingly more than happy to destroy their ancient Arab enemies. Both sides slowly gained other world players, all of whom allied with specific countries dependent upon what they had to gain and it eventually became the namesake of a true World War.

The 100 kiloton Trident missiles were first launched at Iran and Syria, and then retribution came from around the globe in the form of space-based weapons and high energy lasers. Back and forth the attacks went until the casualties numbered in the billions! Finally a cease-fire was negotiated by powerful representatives on all sides and an agreement reached in order to keep the human race from literally annihilating themselves.

Global corporations came into power, promising to the masses - gifts such as global healthcare, an umbrella of protection from crime, a guarantee of safe communities for all, and an end to the war! All they wanted in return, was an allegiance to a way of life meant to bring about these beneficial changes; an instrument that would establish order out of the constant state of chaos the world was in. Increasing exponentially in power and with the support of the people, they disbanded world governments, labelling them as the true villains and eventually creating The System as it was known today. It was a virtual...

"Lucien...Lucien," He could faintly hear Tom in the background. He felt like he'd been woken up from a slumber while under water, "...Commander!"

High Commander Bovier shook his head, rubbing his hands across his eyes and replied absently. "Yeah, yeah – I'm fine Tom...sorry about that. What were you saying?"

Tom pushed himself up and walked around to place his hand on the Commander's left shoulder. "You *don't look well* Lucien; we need to be open about all thoughts and ideas here, okay?" He wasn't quite sure if any of them were doing any better than his friend was. In this war with The System, every step had to be taken very carefully;

every move planned in advance; and every detail accounted for.

If they mis-calculated in any way, he had no doubt they would all be executed or imprisoned. Most importantly, it was vital that their leader keep himself focused and Tom needed to support him every step of the way...and call him out if necessary.

Tom was correct in his assumption - Lucien knew that. He needed to keep his senses sharp and his emotions reigned in. "No, you're right. It's just that...we can use all the help we can get. This shit we're in...It's deep and there aren't many hands reaching in to pull us out."

"And here I thought I was the only one having cold feet about what we're doing," Tom commented. Ayla gave him a confused look, but he didn't clarify his comment.

"Don't get me wrong, Tom," Lucien cautioned, as he cleared his thoughts, "I believe in what we are fighting for; I have no doubts about that! But we're up against an entire way of life here; once people are used to something, it's hard to change that - this isn't going be easy...The Amalgam will do anything to keep themselves in power, which means before this is all over, a lot of people are going to die and the blame will likely fall on us! Things are moving much faster than anticipated and we need to be prepared to act."

It was no surprise that Lucien cared; what was though, was that he was finally voicing it. "I see your point, but Tom's right, Commander. We have to be clear-headed if we are to have a chance at succeeding," pressured Dr. Lockwood, "You two brought me into this and although I share your ideals and goals, we need a sturdy leader who can keep it together...and that Sir, happens to be *you.*"

And he *was* trying. Maybe it was Tom's words earlier that that brought these stray thoughts into his head...or maybe it was his own self-doubts. "Regardless, I apologize for my brief foray into...absent-mindedness." He nodded in Ayla's direction, "You were saying something about Dr. Jenna Methis?"

"Yes, do you know her," Ayla asked.

"I know *of her* because I hear she is on a project for High Commissar Riordan; I don't know her personally. However, the only other candidate we have is some guy in India whom even if we could get to, we would have a very slim chance of smuggling out without a damned good reason. Methis is closer and any information on her is more readily available."

"Makes sense," Tom conferred.

They sat in silence for a moment and finished their cups of cinnamon-lemon tea.

CHAPTER 5: Conspiracy

Ayla gathered the empty mugs and took them into the kitchen as Tom and Lucien continued their own separate conversation. She was fretful as well, but for other, more personal reasons than Lucien. And she had every right to be.

She filled the kettle with more water, put it onto boil once again and started clearing the dishes. Her father had a penchant for tea, as it seemed, did she. Green, black, white, oolong, herbal; whatever she could get her hands on. Each type of tea had its own characteristics including different tastes and health benefits. But most of all, some of her favorite teas had a certain calming effect that helped Ayla soothe her regular symptoms of anxiety.

Unlike the men at the table, she had close family topside; a sister and even a six year old niece. What if they were discovered; what would *they* do to her loved ones?! She had a very important position as a Senior Technocrat within The System; she made more than enough Credits to grant herself a wealthy and extravagant lifestyle; and received all the perks she could have ever wanted to live a long and happy existence!

But she *wasn't* happy...she hadn't been for some time now. She'd found out the truth about things she truly wished she'd stayed ignorant and blind to. No matter how many excuses she kept giving herself to simply turn tail and run away from all of this, she knew she wouldn't. Her impeccable allegiance to her father's morals and commitment to The Hand kept her grounded and true to their mutual goal – to bring down The System.

This had all begun with such a ridiculous notion that even now, she laughed out loud when she thought back on it. It was many years ago when she had gone to visit her father, Professor Daniel Lockwood, called to his home in the middle of the night. It was a Tuesday in the cold, snowy month of December. She remembered it as if it had occurred just last week and...it hurt just as much.

Daniel had been a Professor of Historical Studies at Berkeley back in The Old World and also had a Masters in Chemistry. His first career option had strangely been in the field of genetics, but he had dropped out before he completed the program; although he still kept in touch with several of his friends and colleagues. Daniel blamed his constant hopping from one thing to another on his self-diagnosed ADD.

The Professor was smart and well-educated, if not exceedingly eccentric. He had retired at the early age of sixty and spent most of his available time researching what he claimed was a mass cover-up of true American historical facts; he believed the universal public had been deceived and we were all living our lives within a pre-determined master plan. He insisted that it had been put together by a group of extremely wealthy and powerful individuals whom he referred to only as 'The Elite'.

Her father was convinced that we, as a people have been manipulated from the moment we were born as the things that are most common and important to 90% of the world's population begin as purely emotional concepts. The human being has an ever-encompassing desire to be loved, wanted, and accepted. They need to belong to a community holding similar ideals and perceptions; a system of belief to provide morals; and of course – support when they are down, or to accomplish any given goal.

Without these things, he said, most humans would be isolated, depressed, and eventually suicidal, perhaps even driven mad by loneliness and despair. Emotion and ego drives *everything* from success in life and business to a person's basic relationships with others. It has a profound effect on their needs, wants, and goals for all things material, and even religious fervor and patriotism. This was mainly a proponent that had been thoroughly enforced by the United States of America much more than other countries around the world.

Professor Lockwood preached that to be continuously striving for more is second nature to many of us. We are mistakenly led to believe that 'more' is better: the five bedroom home with a white picket fence; the top of the line automobile; the far-reaching career and position; the higher income; or the status, power, and control that come with a combination of these things.

We subconsciously surround ourselves with people and information that match our beliefs and pay more attention to stereotypes than we think we do. Clever advertising and marketing of products and wants; bits and pieces of information by the media, had driven us into as much towards complacency as animals are steered into a pen to be slaughtered. In his perspective, the people were merely 'sheep', to be herded in one way or another to accomplish a specific goal set forth by someone else.

The point he was trying to make was that for most of us - individuality had ceased to exist. There were, of course the few and in-between who have had the veil lifted from their eyes, but more-so are the ones that have been taught, through indoctrination and years of subtle manipulation – not to question the status quo. He was referring to the general populace, who strongly believed they could not make a difference and 'went with the flow' rather than upset the delicate way of life they were 'taught' to follow.

The ones who were happy with their 'nine-to-five' jobs and lived paycheck to paycheck, with no thought towards anything other than the next big item they needed to have on their wish lists. These were the masses, kept too busy trying to survive and feed their families; further oppressed under the weight of life itself. Controlled, managed, and directed; they had no foresight to see through the 'global smokescreen' simply because they were never afforded the necessity of 'true' information or the luxury of time. Time enough to sort through the deceit and lies being sold to them on a daily basis...

But *why* did the people, who've had their blinders pulled from their eyes, *continue* to ignore the truth?! The deeper he delved, Professor Lockwood was convinced that in retrospect and on a very base level, it all came down to survival! In fact, scientifically and physiologically speaking, the human brain's ultimate goal was to make sure that we survive and reproduce; everything else is secondary! However, the brain must create and use emotions to achieve this goal. Hate; love; fear; desire; passion; they are all extremely strong emotive responses to specific stimuli. Interestingly enough, hate seemed to be the strongest of these sentiments.

This unique emotion created its own distinct circuit which generated aggression and prompted action, while allowing a person's responses to be both cold and calculating. Hence, it was this emotion that most of us were ruled by; what could vaguely be considered to humans as hard 'logic' and 'reason'. At the same time, it was also our most animal-like instinct. All these theoretic principles her father drilled into her, and as crazy as it seemed - caused her to re-think her doubts on his state of mind.

He fervently believed that countless governments and countries throughout history have controlled large populations by constructing a 'hated other'; whether it be an individual or a group of people to fear. These political entities have used catalysts such as differences in religion; the threat of limited resources; fear of change to the norm; or even such petty excuses as skin color and strange cultures to fuel anger and hate to the point where people do things they would normally never conceive of. This, her father believed, was practically the driving force for every war we have ever fought - from the Crusades to the Civil War, finally culminating with the three World Wars.

Being an individual of rational thought, Ayla had been not only embarrassed by her father's ideas, but also tried to avoid much contact with him in public or otherwise. At that naïve time in her life, she was afraid it would have a detrimental effect on her career and her personal life, so she gave Daniel Lockwood as wide a berth as possible. What a fool she had been! If only she had trusted him, things may have turned out differently.

Every two weeks though, she would make the long trip to visit with him and make sure he was doing well; after all he was still her father and she loved and cared for him. Thinking back on everything she'd done or could have done, she felt ashamed and laden with guilt. *You should have been there for him. If you were, he might still be here with you...* These were the thoughts that plagued her dreams and sometimes, even her waking moments.

But that night had been different for her; that night she was forced to come to terms with something she never could have thought possible - he may have been right all along! Her father had sounded so anxious and frightened that she had dragged herself out of bed and drove there as fast as she could, barely taking the time to put on a robe and slippers.

After knocking on the door and ringing the doorbell for at least five solid minutes, her father had slowly opened the door, looking pale and flustered. His normally kept hair was disheveled; he had noticeably lost weight, and he had grown almost half a beard in the three weeks she had seen him last! He hurried her in immediately, looking past her with sleep deprived eyes to make certain that she was alone; a look of fear clearly etched across his face.

She remembered her first instinct being to call an ambulance or maybe even 'the men with strait jackets' to come and take him away, but eventually he had persuaded her that he was alright and what she saw before her was simply the image of a lack of sleep and utter exhaustion. Finally convincing her to sit and stay, he had told her that during his research, he'd found something so abhorrent that if the general public got wind of these occurrences, there would be worldwide panic! If things weren't strange enough by that point, what he had told her was to the point of being laughable.

"Dad, you're scaring me. What has gotten into you?!"

"*I'm* fine. It's the rest of the world there's a problem with!"

"What does that even mean? You're talking nonsense..."

He scratched at his overgrown beard. "How I wish that were so. Please, take a seat."

"I *am* sitting, Dad."

"Yes, yes, so you are...Has anyone followed you," he asked as if it was the most normal conversation piece between a father and daughter.

"What?!"

"I'm just...never mind."

"Fine. Now, what is the matter with you?"

He was visibly shaken and upset, that much was apparent. "You must understand Ayla that these people are trying to hide the truth! They know about my findings! The common public is ignorant to what is truly happening. I sincerely wish now that I had never delved this deep into what I am about to tell you!"

"Slow down Dad, you're losing me; *what people*?"

He ignored the question, remaining silent. The Professor had this insatiable habit of smoking cherry flavored tobacco from a custom-made English pipe when he was upset or nervous. He took a moment to pack a large wad of the foul-smelling leaves into the chamber and light it, sending smothering wafts of smoke directly into Ayla's face.

"You've known about my investigation and research into human psychology for years, yes?"

"Yes Dad, the 'brainwashing' of countless millions and how-" she started, sarcastically.

Apparently, her father was offended by her remark. "This is *hardly* a joke my Dear and I would appreciate you showing me a little respect," he vehemently spat, "I did *not* say brainwashing; this is far from some damned fairy tale; this is really happening and *still is!*"

Ayla blushed in embarrassment...or fear, she did not know which, but this was one of the few times in her life her father had lashed out at her like that. He was usually a calm and gentle man. Whatever had him so riled up must be important. She gave him a hurt look, but stayed silent.

She could tell that he immediately regretted his angry outburst. "I'm sorry Honey...I didn't mean to get so-"

"It's okay Dad, I shouldn't have – please go on..."

He appeared to be lost in thought for a moment and then he must have remembered where he was going with this. 'Absent-minded Professor' was a good description of her father. He was a master at losing track of everything.

"I just want...to be clear. You know my research and my beliefs and yes, some of them are quite far-fetched, I understand that. I know that often times you think me a fool, but I must tell someone what I've uncovered. It's important to *me*."

"Oh Dad," she sighed, "I don't think that."

He gave her a small smile and continued. "This is not psychological warfare or social influence I am talking about this time...It's much more of a deception than that! You should know that the manipulation of human emotions has been linked to many of the problems we had within The Old World...but what I have found goes far beyond simple misdirection. I am speaking of *forced pacifism*!"

Oh boy, here we go again, she thought. The last time the 'crazy old coot' had gone to these lengths was when he had led the charge on the incident in New York. She struggled to recall it: something about two planes that had crashed into a building called the World Trade Center. She had been quite young when it happened, but such a shocking act of terrorism was fresh in the minds of the people who lived through it.

Daniel Lockwood had organized a large number of protestors to call for an impeachment of the President of that time. He was convinced that the government had allowed the acts of terrorism to purposely take place in order to start a war and facilitate a monopoly on oil. More importantly, to move the West into a permanent military occupation of the Middle East, establishing a hold of various resources, while destroying the sovereignty of individual Western nations.

She had to admit that he had definitely put up a number of rational arguments that made sense. Strange occurrences *had* taken place before, after, and during the attacks. Things he claimed were more than mere coincidence. He had given several examples that allayed her doubt: an extraordinary amount of put options were placed on United and American airlines stock; there was a lack of presence with Air Defense; the tower collapse appeared similar to a controlled demolition; and the plane that crashed into the Pentagon hit a vacant portion of the building with no substantial wreckage ever being found. There was a lack of jet interception over the Pentagon and New York City with 'training exercises' and 'war games' planned for and in process that very same day. This clouded military radar with false images of airplanes whizzing to and fro, causing mass confusion.

And *box-cutters*?! Flimsy blades that only came out ¼ to a ½ inch? Come on! All those people suspected they were going to die a horrible death and they did nothing? It was hardly realistic. That was like some jackass using a can of silly string to hijack a cruise ship! Then again, no one really knew what happened up there; it was all just speculation. At least that was *her* opinion.

Odd as it may seem, the passports of the terrorists somehow survived the fiery explosion and cell phone calls were made at altitudes that could not have possibly received reception. Further still, 4,000 World Trade Center employees took off work the same day of the attacks; only three of the four black boxes were found with only a single one being in good enough condition to listen to; and there were many other details that raised suspicion. Worst of all, relevant intelligence reports were largely ignored or suppressed, bringing about even more questions! Add to that, just six weeks before the Towers collapsed, the owner had an insurance policy drafted for 3.5 billion dollars and you had the makings of a conspiracy!

The most shocking result of all this was The Patriot Act. It gave the government the broad sweeping powers to conduct surveillance of American Citizens and others within its own country's jurisdiction. In other words, the Act 'legally' took away our civil liberties and basic rights as a people, without any blowback! It was a 342 page Bill which was strangely passed through Congress in little over a month! The Professor believed it was written long before the attacks and 911 was a pretense to usher in the Patriot Act. Either way, there was solid evidence of circumstances that did not add up which only seemed to swell as new details were revealed. No – to her father, 911 was another Pearl Harbor.

Ayla was no fool. Obviously some of the proof he presented was sound. She knew that the media played an important role in what people believed and that most times, no one was getting the real story. There were cover-ups and scandals abound in governmental rule and as shameful as that was, every single individual had their own personal problems to deal with. Unless they had some modicum of power and status, there was very little they could do.

A part of her felt terribly guilty that one of the reasons she had trouble accepting her father's accusations was that these issues did not affect her *personally*. This seemed to be the constant that made the world go around; if a problem was not perceived as a personal threat, it was better left ignored or largely forgotten! The other half of her simply thought it was too terrible to conceive. Regardless of what happened in the past, what in the world was going on in her father's head now?

"Can you stop being so vague and give me something substantial?"

"I am telling you that things are not as they seem."

"Things rarely are...so what does that mean for us?"

"For *us*, it means complete submission; for *them*, it means total control."

"Who are *they*, Dad? Why are you always so cryptic?"

He laughed at her annoyance. "Yes, I suppose I am. Sorry...I'm referring to the people behind our political leaders; not the ones who are the public puppets of our government, but the ones who pull their strings."

"Okay, so if they have all this power, what are they afraid of?"

"Open your eyes, Ayla...There are many strong willed people in the world's population who have unlimited potential. Historical figures such as Martin Luther King and JFK fit that bill. If given the opportunity, they may become leaders of revolutions or fight against injustice and oppression. These people are a threat to them. You, yourself are so damned stubborn and pig-headed-"

"Very funny," she scoffed.

"My point is – that even with the constant manipulation of events, it still isn't enough. There still has to be a way to '*pacify*' or control the majority. Once in place, even should these leaders rise up, the people will be hesitant to follow. There are many things I've uncovered which point to mass corruption, but this one is most interesting. Are you familiar with Sodium Monofluorophosphate?"

She laughed inwardly. "I'm a Tech, not a Chemist."

"Oh you *know* what it is, alright...you just don't recognize it by its scientific name. This goes all the way back to our 'Industrial Age'. Sodium Monofluorophosphate was a known toxic byproduct of large industrial companies in the early 1900's such as the Aluminum Company of America, US Steel, and a then plastics producing company by the name of Monsanto..."

"Mega corporations have always been cheaply disposing of toxic byproducts into the environment for years, that's not a surprise."

"That is *not* my point. But yes, you are correct. It wasn't until toxic waste became the target of negative press that people actually took notice."

"Then *what is your point*?!"

"Perhaps it will help speaking of it in more common terms: Sodium Monofluorophosphate is better known as Fluorine...or *Fluoride*. I know it sounds-"

"What?! Are you crazy?!*" Maybe she was wrong; maybe he *had* gone out of his mind. Fluoride was everywhere you looked: toothpaste; water; even processed foods...This was way beyond rational!

He flashed her a condescending look. "No, you heard right! If that sounds laughable to *you*, imagine how I felt when I stumbled upon it!"

Ayla brought her hands over her face, trying to process what she'd been told. She was not prepared for this..."Alright Dad, I'll humor you. If this is true, wouldn't they have figured this out long ago?"

"They've been poisoning our water supply for years, Ayla! Let me explain...In those days it was very expensive to dispose of: between $1.50 to over $2 a gallon. Being as the standard minimum wage at that time was somewhere under or slightly above $1 an hour, you can see the comparative costs involved for these companies should they do things safely...or legally. The easier and cheaper alternative was to simply dump it and other toxic chemicals at any readily available site: lakes, streams, rivers, or even the public water system. Not too long after it permeated the water supply, they began to notice some of the more malicious effects that fluoride had on human beings."

Strange as it was, Professor Daniel Lockwood preached to her with a straight face. At that point, Ayla was seriously considering getting up and walking right out the door. This was...*weird*; what did all this have to do with anything?! She felt as if she was in some alternative studies class back in college. This may very well have been looked upon as the sad ramblings of a mad man...still it was her father so she forced herself to stay put and humor him. But she didn't have to stay silent either.

Ayla took his hands into hers and patted them reassuringly. "Dad, listen to me. I know you think all this...subversiveness in the world is at the heart of one of your 'conspiracies', but...you look like you haven't slept in days...what has this got to do with...I mean, how am I supposed to take all of this?"

At just over sixty-five, her father was not what she would have considered old, but on that day he seemed to have aged another twenty years; he looked ancient and bone weary. His calm face wrinkled up in an expression of hurt and sadness. *Shut up before you say something else to hurt his feelings.*

"I'm sorry Dad...I just-"

Professor Lockwood loudly cleared his throat, interrupting her apology. He loaded another ample supply of cherry tobacco into his pipe. Patiently lighting it with an engraved stainless steel Zippo, he inhaled and replied at the same time between puffs of smoke. Her mother had given it to him on his 42nd birthday. It was the most cherished item he owned. If she was still alive, what would she have thought of her husband now?

"Honey...I know I'm just an old coot and sometimes the things I say don't make much sense to you. Please let me finish, okay," he had pleaded, "I'm getting to the point, but...let me step back for a minute. It may help if you understand some of the facts about this first. You can make your own decisions from there and I won't hold you to anything after that, fair enough?"

Ayla nodded back in acceptance and allowed her father to continue. "The larger question you should probably have for me is: What are the detrimental effects of Fluorine on humans? The answer may scare you, it certainly did me...Fluorine is a *toxic poison*. I made some relevant notes; listen to this." He picked up a small notepad from his desk and began to read. "Fluorine disrupts enzyme activity and attacks DNA and protein. It has been implicated as a cause of memory lapses, dementia, autism, kidney disease, and even cancer. Now this is interesting - declassification of government documents stated that the manufacturing of atom bombs required millions of tons of Fluoride. In fact, many lawsuits and injuries that were conceived by involvement in the Atomic Program, were for Fluoride exposure and *not* due to radiation!"

"That's insane," she muttered under her breath.

"And that is only the half of it. The most interesting *side effect* of Fluoride is *not* that it helps fight tooth decay, but that it affects a section of the brain that regulates our reactions to stressful situations. The chemical reaction weakens resolve, thereby making human beings easier to control and be placated! Do you see now what I'm trying to-"

"And this has been going on for how long exactly," she interrupted. Strangely, some of this had started making sense. There had been a great many scandals; both political and otherwise that had gone on in the latter part of the last century that even though people were aware of the corruption and atrocities that were involved, very little had been done to oppose them. People were wary of getting involved with anything that didn't have a direct impact on them. Even she sometimes felt that the only reason she couldn't accept things for what they were was because they didn't affect her own life.

Her father had almost looked relieved to hear her say those words as he continued, knowing that the questions she asked betrayed her interest. "This was before your time, but a tyrant you may be familiar with by the name of Adolph Hitler was one of the first to start using Fluoride in German water systems. It was seen as a means of controlling the Jews and other prisoners in ghettos and concentration camps. The Nazis strongly believed that it promoted passivity among the captives, amounting to easier domination of the human mind with minimum outbreaks of resistance. So the knowledge of what Fluorine can do has been around for almost a century!"

Ayla knew her history..."I'm well aware of the damned Nazis," she spat. It was disgusting that something like had even taken place!

"Watch your mouth, young lady; you know how I feel about that type of language."

Oh my God; I'm not a kid anymore..."Yes, Dad...So why hasn't anyone done anything about this?! We just accept this and are okay with it?"

A wave of anguish flowed across his features. "The government of the last century knew of the effects it had on its people, but it was largely ignored or buried under bureaucratic red tape to contain widespread panic! But I believe that even then, people would not accept it. The majority would deny, no – *rationalize* – reasons for these occurrences because to know the truth is often times, a terrible burden...

You must understand that this and other pertinent information has been quietly removed from public knowledge over the years; even from the schools in The Old World. What hasn't been taught from childhood is strange and unknown. It is easy to doubt something that no one else believes. In this world, we are conditioned to follow the many; not lead the few."

He was right. Human beings found security in habit. Change requires adjustment and adjustment required adaptation. It forced people to make mental and physical re-arrangements for things that were difficult to accept, and not too many wanted to take the time to think that hard. "This entire thing...is so unbelievable," she mumbled, in reference to both the Professor's comments and her own thoughts.

"*It is* and I don't blame you for thinking that," he agreed, "But unfortunately, it is not fantasy...What you will notice are the rising statistics in fluoridation: twenty years ago, 66% of the public drinking water in the United States was purposely fluoridated for health stated reasons and more so after The System was initiated; it is now at 92% world-wide. Why do you think that is, Ayla?"

She didn't even know how to reply. If she agreed with him, she would be inadvertently reinforcing his delusions. That was probably the last thing he needed right now. If she disagreed, she would face the wrath of a slightly overweight madman. She decided it was better to keep quiet. But something in the back of her mind told her that these were *real statistics*, not the ravings of a disturbed man. If that was the case, shouldn't she at least keep an open mind? Maybe he *was* onto something...

He sighed deeply. "If you don't think I realize how preposterous this sounds, I do. But that is *exactly* why it works!" Professor Lockwood tiredly walked over to the open, spacious kitchen and poured himself another steaming cup of tea. "Would you like some tea?"

A lot of what he was saying seemed to have proof, but it was so difficult to take in all of it in one night.

"Of course, after what you've told me, a nice hot cup of tea will make everything better," Ayla scoffed sarcastically, "And later, we can organize a picketing at the Amalgam Annex and accuse the Executive Bureau of a world-wide conspiracy! That would go rather well, don't you think?"

Chortling humorously, he had walked back, sitting heavily at his magnificent desk. He was silent for a minute before he finally spoke. "Ayla...I understand the position I have put you in. I cannot force you to believe me and I understand how I must sound...an old man slowly losing his mind, living alone, locked up in his house, withering away..." He had stared directly into her eyes as he finished, "You are my daughter and I love you. Do you at least trust me?"

"You shouldn't even have to ask me that, Dad."

"Then let me put it another way. More than sixty-five years ago, we placed a man in a mechanical contraption made from aluminum and sent him to the moon! Only a few years before that, if someone had told you what NASA was planning to do, would you have believed them? "

"That's a separate example in itself, but I see your point."

"Okay then – all these over-the-counter medications that have been recalled and are now off the market, why does this happen?"

"Easy enough – it takes time and testing to determine the side effects. If there is a danger to a person's health, they pull it."

"Yes, that's correct. Now then tell me – I've just told you about the risks of fluorine, why haven't they pulled *that*...why haven't they informed the public?"

"I...I don't know."

"What would you call something that is purposely withheld even though all statistical data points to the endangerment of human health?"

A conspiracy. Okay, you got me. "Dad...I-"

"You don't have to answer that. I firmly believe that *anything* is possible...In fact, I have something for you that may open your eyes on things a bit more."

Professor Lockwood knelt down under his large solid-oak office desk and lifted off a number of the dark stained floorboards. He reached in and pulled forth a large lockbox that had both a G-ID scanner and a complicated electronic lock. Un-clasping his locket from around his neck, he used the magnetic key inside along with a wave of his wrist to open the box.

"Take this," he said, as he handed her a slightly scarred Terra-drive, "It's everything I have been researching and compiling for years. I can't tell you every little detail now...or show you *here*, but I know you have 5th level clearance to secure servers. You don't have to accept everything I've said Ayla, but I beg of you to at least take a look."

"You're hiding this under your floorboards," she asked, incredulously. He didn't respond.

Ayla hesitantly reached out and took the drive. *Do I really want to know what's on here?* The look in her father's eyes betrayed no sense of madness; he truly believed everything he was saying and had now handed her something that was perhaps, important proof of that. She was doubtful, but she wasn't stupid. Her rational mind kept telling her that this type of thing only happened in the movies...but she'd also seen enough films to know that when someone doubted what they'd been told, it was usually true. Knowing she was hardly in a fictional situation and this could really be happening, she resolutely committed herself to have an unprejudiced outlook on this and really taking some time to think things through.

"How do you come up with these things," she asked rhetorically.

"The truth is out there if you only know where to look," he said in a serious tone, "You asked me earlier why people have not taken a stand to what's happening around them. Think about it Ayla, the greater population has simply been too overloaded with *life*. People are too overwhelmed, over-committed, and over-stressed. It's not that they don't know what is going on out there; it's that most times, *they don't want to know*!

Credit, debt, personal and economic strife – these are the relevant problems that exist for them and run their lives. They've come to expect all their news and truth to come directly from the media; it's more expedient and convenient for someone else to collect, analyze, and present the facts. I suppose you can call that *'brainwashing'* in a way. I just pray that somehow I can expose my findings to the people..."

Ayla's Sat-com pager had gone off then and she grabbed her robe and quickly put it on. "I...don't know what to say Dad, but you *have* managed to scare the hell out of me. I think I'm going to need some time...or some very expensive therapy after we are done here. Listen, I have to go. I'll be back in a few weeks, okay?"

He smiled and pulled her into a tight embrace. "Just promise me you'll think about what we discussed here. I've been compiling this data for years now...but even I still have certain doubts. As I said, there's much more on the drive than I care to speak of today. I can't expect you to accept everything I've just told you in one night," he had acknowledged, "After all, who could have thought of the American Dental Association as 'the enemy', putting mind-altering substances in our toothpaste, right?"

"That's not funny."

Professor Lockwood had put up his hands in mock surrender and laughed softly as he made that joke. Years later, she understood that it wasn't meant to be one. Ayla didn't know whether to laugh or cry as she turned to leave. Conflicting emotions were hitting her like a ton of bricks. Opening the door, her father had left her with one last comment. "Do you remember what Von Goethe said - *'None are more hopelessly enslaved than those who falsely believe they are free'*?" There is more truth to his words than you think."

That was his favorite quote; he used it every time he wanted to express his views of 'global subjugation' on someone else. "I have no doubt in my mind that you will one day, make sense of all of this...I love you, Ayla, always remember that." Sending her off with a warm, fatherly smile, he quietly closed the door behind her.

That was the last vivid memory she had of Professor Daniel

Lockwood. To Ayla, life from that moment on was filled with doubt and suspicion and not as enjoyable as it once had been. Two weeks later, after not so much as a phone call from her father, she had gone looking for him. All she found was an empty house. Strangely, not much had been disturbed since the night she was there.

Ayla and her sister had contacted friends, staff at Berkley, and put up posters of his likeness all around the city. Finally, after waiting weeks with the hope that he would make contact, they filed a missing persons report with the new Cateton Field Agency. The investigation concluded that there was no foul play or malfeasance involved with her father's disappearance. There were no signs of a struggle or a break-in. He was simply...gone.

As for the Terra-drive her father had given her, she did not dare look into it for many months after, fearing that he had indeed found something conspiratorial and the false semblance of the world as she knew it would crumble down before her. She was not ready for that. Every few weeks, she would take out the drive and stare at it, thinking about her father. She wondered if the information contained on this device could be the cause for his disappearance. But each time, she'd place it back without opening it; afraid of what she was going to find. It took the better part of half a year before she built up enough resolve to finally do so and the things she discovered - should have indeed stayed buried.

Darkly disturbing and secret plots beginning with The Old World and reaching into The System itself. Information that she wished she had never been so unlucky to have been handed in the first place. Things that lent credence to all of her father's mad rumblings. During those long cold months, she barely skimmed through a third of it before she realized how dangerous what she had in her possession truly was.

After that, Paranoia and fear were her constant, faithful companions. Understanding that this propaganda may put herself and her extended family in terrible danger, Ayla had decided not to delve into the information contained on the drive any further! Instead, she buried it and tried unsuccessfully to move on with her life.

The discoveries on the Terra-drive and her father's sudden disappearance had scared the hell out of her! With the ever-increasing suspicion that someone would soon be coming for her as well, it had spurred her into action. She put all her effort into seeking out others who may know more about these events than she did.

Slowly learning of, locating, and making contact with the resistance faction - The Hand of Light, Ayla hoped they could help her find out what had happened to her father. The Hand was a global organization, with ties and connections to many high valued assets and individuals hidden in not only the four major Sub-terrestrials, but also above-ground.

When she'd first met Rand at an undisclosed location, Ayla felt lucky not to have been executed on the spot! But Quentin had been impressed with her tenacity in searching out The Hand; not too many people had been able to seek them out, much less meet their leader face to face. What a shock it was to learn that Quentin Rand had known her father many years ago, in passing! It was probably the same reason she was not killed! Nevertheless, he promised to do what he could to help locate Professor Lockwood.

He was more curious about why she had tracked them down and to protect the rebels, Ayla was put through intense bouts of interrogation. Once she had informed Quentin the reasons for her defection, he asked her to keep what she had learned to herself. This information was extremely valuable and would be used once the time was right, he told her. Until then, it needed to be kept hidden away and from falling into the 'wrong hands'. The Hand would need time to set things in place before it was revealed to the masses.

During the years, Ayla and Quentin had become comrades and later, good friends. He trusted her implicitly and she soon became his agent in OZI City. Her position afforded her the means to valuable information, which she forwarded on to the rebels as needed. She'd been with Rand for years and was one of the most trusted members of the Resistance.

It wasn't long before she met Tom and Lucien, who shared similar ideals. Having discussed their individual experiences and discoveries with each other, they had immediately begun with a common goal. All three became fast friends and worked together to foster a better future for the people. Ayla, Justice Master Tom Quinn, and High Commander Lucien Bovier were the leaders of the

OZI faction and they were all very dedicated to the Cause.

All these years, she had obeyed Rand's orders and kept her father's secrets to herself. Four days ago, she'd been given express authorization to hand over a copy of the drive to the High Commander. She wondered what he would think about all this...She glanced over to the two men conversing lightly as they waited for her to return, wondering how much personal pain and strife they had gone through in their own lives. Ayla desperately wanted to go over to them and give them some good news for a change, but she still had to explain the dangers of the B.I.O.N.E.X. process.

What the hell was that woman doing in there?! He and Tom had been forced to converse amongst themselves for some time now and his patience was running thin. They would have to get back to the troops soon and focus on their training! Leading this double life was utterly exhausting; he could see where Tom was coming from... Lucien was committed to The Hand and their ideals, but the dangers of discovery were ever-present. *I sure could use a drink!*

Ayla must have read his mind as she walked back in with a bottle of whiskey and 3 small glasses. And it wasn't just any old whiskey; what she had in her hand was a rare bottle of Macallan 1939! Lucien anxiously snatched the glasses from her hand before she even had a chance to sit back down. He opened the bottle and poured himself and the others a generous helping of liquid bliss.

He hadn't smiled this big in weeks. "This is a Macallan; where did you-"

"My father," she replied, anticipating his question, "I found some well-aged bottles in his cellar after he – It doesn't matter. Enjoy it; as expensive as this is, it will only come around once in *your* lifetime."

I won't argue with that! In The Old World, bottles such as this went for over $12,000 a pop! Lucien had no idea how someone could pay these extravagant amounts for alcohol...or for anything which was ultra-expensive. The rich needlessly spent loads of money for no reason other than status; it was beyond him. Money was a funny thing; it truly changed people...and not for the better. Regardless, The System had changed all that.

Currency as they knew it: the Dollar; the Yen; the Franc; the Euro; the Pound; and just about every other type of legal tender that was commonly used had been eradicated years ago. Old World currency was replaced by one universally recognized virtual instrument called the Global Reserve Bancor Credit. In order to utilize this new system, what was left of the human population was required to have a Global ID Chip implanted on their person. A painless inoculation, similar to a flu shot, was used to inject the Chip under the thin skin of the wrist. This was the only way 'monetary' trade, distribution and transactions could take place.

In addition to Credits, the Chip was a practical library card catalog of information about each individual from their name and address, to their criminal background, to their medical data logs. Personal, financial, and at times - collected information unknown even to the Wearer were immediately available with a simple scan of the wrist!

According to The Amalgam, the Chip's security protocols were state of the art, completely firewalled and coded to each individual's unique genetic structure; they were thought to be un-hackable. Lucien knew that was not the case. Once a person received the G-ID chip however, they literally belonged to The System.

For those who *did not* accept the Chip, they were forced to fend for themselves. They had no choice but to grow their own food and forage for supplies and shelter, even barter for items like they once did ages ago. No form of medical care, employment, or even wages were allowed to be accessed by these people; they were *completely* on their own.

If that wasn't hard enough, they were considered 'Outcasts' or 'Undesirables', frequently isolated from the rest of society and abused by the Citizens. They were banned from entering System boundaries; if they dared, they would be shot on sight! It was a damned shame, really – but this was the way of The New World...

Lucien gulped down the rest of his drink. "What do think Tom?"

"I do believe this is the smoothest damned whiskey I've ever tasted," he answered grinning from ear to ear as he poured himself another shot.

"Something tells me this was not offered to us so Tom could feel better about his looks, is it Doc?"

"Huh, when did you get a sense of humor," his second retorted.

"No," Ayla answered in preparation, "No it was not."

CHAPTER 6: Coffee Break

Jenna slammed down her delicate fist into the glistening epoxy-coated laboratory table and just as quickly pulled it away in a rush of pain, nursing her hand as if she had been burned by a hot flame.

"Damn it!"

Four weeks! Four long, uninspiring weeks had gone by with only limited success! She was close, but she still had to find a solution to the deterioration of the Nanites; everything she had recently tried did not tip those scales in her favor. Over the past month, she had had very little sleep and was in constant pain from long hours of sitting, standing and bending over microscopes and other equipment.

The throbbing headaches and muscle cramps were new; they had begun only a few short weeks ago. She was increasingly frustrated with this project, wanting nothing more than to take something that was more than foreign to her – a lengthy and deserving vacation.

An explosion of some magnitude sounded in the background, causing her to drop the slide she had been holding with her good hand. Angrily, she directed her gaze towards the screen to catch a news report showing the re-play of an explosion at the Executive Bureau building.

"Oh my God," she muttered under her breath.

The attack itself was horrifying, but the flaming bodies that spewed forth from each of the separate levels of the burning forty seven story building were a worse sight to behold. The structure was in ruins. Engulfed in smoke and flame, some victims were jumping to the balconies far below, hoping to somehow survive the fall rather than be consumed by the fiery red death that awaited them. Pleas for help and screams of pain were heard coming from all around the tattered remains of the Executive Bureau Building.

People appeared to be suffocating on the noxious fumes of tar and smoke as they tried desperately to shout for help. Rescue workers, including the Fire and Emergency Brigade had their tank-like trucks raising escape ladders skyward even as large sections of the building itself rained down destruction from above. Some were throwing H.A.G's – heat absorbing grenades into the fire, hoping to smother the flames.

She could almost imagine the smell of the acrid ash as it swirled around the full-blown inferno. Amidst the carnage, a reporter at the scene was spouting off something about the Hand of Light being responsible for the attack, but Jenna was so dazed by the on-screen violence that she barely registered much more than that.

The members of The Hand of Light, the rebel faction that spanned across the globe was just as secretive as that of The Amalgam, the main political arm of The System. They went about their affairs in utmost secrecy; members from each side going to a lot of trouble to make certain that their actions and identities remained unknown.

Even before The Hand of Light became notorious to the general public, they had been at war with The Amalgam and all their dominions. The Hand was responsible for three previous carefully orchestrated skirmishes that had primarily hit effective and high security targets, amazingly with minimum loss of human life. Not that it mattered; even one life was far too many.

The Amalgam, as they were called, were the centralized power within The System; they made the decisions that would eventually effect everyone else in the civilized world. Similar to The Hand, the general public had no idea who they were, what they looked like, where they lived; for all anyone knew one of them could be serving tea right next to them and none would have been the wiser!

The Hand's latest conquest, the Executive Bureau Building was the *source* from where these new rules and laws were devised and formulated. Now the most secure and heavily guarded location in the world was no more than another burned out husk.

The hawk-nosed, sharply dressed young woman who was reporting the tragedy gazed off into the smoke-filled distance as the deafening sirens wailed around her. "...This will put a significant delay on the NAS Chip...What is most mystifying is how the perpetrators managed to get Red Thermite into the vault itself!" She paused a moment to listen to something on her earpiece. "We have just gotten word that *all nine* Justice Administrators died of asphyxiation just hours ago on the eleventh floor Law Archives as-"

A KNOCK at the door broke her concentration.

"Excuse me Ma'am, I apologize for the intrusion."

Jenna spun quickly around to face...*GI JOE*? She smiled inwardly as the ludicrous thought came to mind. *You've gotta be kidding me!* To the 'T', this well-built, medal-emblazoned soldier was the literal cutout representation of 'The Marines' advertising posters she used to see around the city in The Old World. Albeit with a sureness about him that bordered on the verge of cocky...but also athletic and beautiful in a personable sort of way.

He was tall and broad-shouldered; having a firm jaw with a small curve to his lips which accentuated his strong cheekbones. His eyes were set with a fierce determination; at the same time conveying a distant sadness that haunted his being. In other words, this man was very good looking! *Your married* she scolded herself; *down girl.*

"Uhh...the recruitment offices are *that way*," she said humorously, pointing with her thumb to the far off buildings outside the window.

"You are Doctor Jenna Methis." It was more of a statement than a question.

"*I am*...and you are?"

"My name is Lucien Bovier, High Commander of the Catetons in OZI City. I'm with a special unit called Blackburn, I'm here to-"

"Blackburn is *Special-Ops,*" she snapped back accusingly, "To what do I owe the *pleasure* of your visit?"

"Obviously we don't seem to have a very good reputation," he said, taken aback by her outburst.

"*No*, you don't. Now what can I do for you?"
"Ma'am, I'd rather not speak about this here," he replied bluntly.

She was growing anxious by the minute now. What is a Blackburn System mercenary doing topside and what the hell did he want with her? "I've heard of you people! Catetons show up and people disappear, isn't that how it goes?! Why don't you tell me what you want from me and we can skip the pleasantries!"

The intruding soldier seemed strangely patient and took her sharp comments in stride. He appeared to be taking in the layout of the room and his surroundings. "You have nothing to worry about, I'm only here to talk," he stated calmly, "Is there a place we can speak in private Ma'am, may I buy you a cup of coffee perhaps?"

What does he want, a date? "I think you have the wrong woman here. Am I in trouble or something? Look...I'm just a scientist."

"I'm sorry Ma'am...I don't mean to intrude like this, but it's urgent that I speak with you. I understand that this is most unusual, but I didn't have time for formal introductions. Can we-"

"Stop calling me Ma'am; you're making me feel like a Grandmother! Just tell me what it is that-"

"Doctor Methis, I can explain *everything* to you... but it appears you have associates about," he gestured through the large pane glass window to her co-workers in the cluttered main lab, "you may not wish for them to hear what I have to say. I would prefer some privacy myself...and I assure you I am not here to hurt you in any way. And no, you're *not* in any type of trouble."

Well, at least I'm not getting arrested. "Jesus, this reminds me of every cheesy scene in all The Old World thrillers I used to watch. I can't believe I'm just...*I don't even know you*, I'm simply supposed to take you at your word?"

"Yes."

His flat response immediately brought into mind a movie she had seen long ago. "Oh...okay. I was expecting you to say something a *little more flamboyant* like 'Come with me if you want to live'...but I guess *'Yes'* works too."

"I'm not without a sense of humor Ma'am," he replied, smiling back at her.

She slowly shook her head lightheartedly and removed her lab coat, unceremoniously throwing it onto the time-worn coat rack. "There's a coffee shop across the street and my *name* is Jenna. Come on then." *What are you doing Jenna; this guy could be a rapist or something!* Then why did she seem so at ease with him?

They walked in silence across Central Boulevard and past the bustling foot traffic. The gigantic white cutout of a coffee cup which adorned the backdrop of The Java Mill loomed in the distance. Noticing how packed the streets were, Jenna quickly realized it was lunch hour. She was always losing track of time as always...She followed Lucien like a lost puppy into the coffee shop, wary, but intrigued at the same time.

As they entered The Java Mill, the buzz of multiple conversations filled the air. This coffee shop in particular was world famous, offering webline and freeband accessibility that networked privately to the customer's G-ID Chip. The super-comfortable lounge-like seating was spread sporadically around the spacious area and provided the added benefit of air-flow temperature regulation for each separate booth.

In the dead center of the building, the steel railings and copper pipes added a steampunk-like feel to the array of various coffee bean grinding tanks that dropped down from the ceiling. These were designed to provide customers with a faster self-service option, which most people took advantage of. Instead, Lucien led them towards an unoccupied booth in the far corner.

As they sat down on the fashionable leather seats, it occurred to Lucien that he didn't even know how to begin; he had not planned on coming to see her this soon - but time was of the essence. He had done enough research on Doctor Jenna Methis to know the basics, but not anything substantial. *Let's see if I can get to the point quickly without scaring the hell out of her any more than I already have*, he thought as he slid his wrist across the biometric table scanner. He moved two images of 16-ounce cups of Black Mountain Caramel Lattes into his credit bay and then noticed Doctor Methis irritatingly staring at him.

"Hrumph...It must have slipped my mind that you are not only a Cateton, but a psychic as well."

"Excuse me?"

"Well, it seems that you already know exactly what type of coffee I wanted and what size, right? Is it okay for me to have cream and sugar too, or would you prefer I drink it without? Are you always this presumptuous?"

Oh my God! Please tell me this woman wasn't some Amazonian Feminist or worse – part of some underground Women's Lib Movement that equates the type of coffee a man buys her to male dominance! All he had done was order two coffees and she's already going off on him like he's a male chauvinist. *Remember, you're a soldier. You've tackled things worse than this before.* He laughed inwardly at the preposterous thought. "Doctor Methis, I apologize if that was how I came off. I did not mean to presume-"

"I'm only joking, you big oaf," she said, with a laugh, "I'm sorry, but you should have seen the look on your face, hahaha!" Jenna had decided to break the ice more for her own sake than anything else. The High Commander of the OZI Catetons showing up out of the blue and requesting a private meeting was highly unusual! When her nerves were shot like this, she usually resorted to bad humor.

Thank the Lord! "Ohh...I uhh..."

"I'm not without a sense of humor either. I may be a Scientist, but I'm hardly a prude."

He chuckled in amusement. *Okay, maybe not as ice cold as I'd thought!*

She sobered quickly and began. "Okay Lucien, let's-"

"One moment please." He interrupted, pulling forth a small device, placing it on the table and pushing a switch to turn it on. It made a soft humming noise and all the ambient noise in the room quieted to a dull din. "This is a Noise Dampener; it will keep our conversation private and lessen the background noise. I hope you don't mind."

Jenna eyes lit up, perplexed. *That is some cool tech!* There was more to this meeting that she thought if he went to these lengths to keep their discussion private. That made it all the more unnerving and she struggled to stay calm. "So Major-"

"High Commander Ma'am, 'Major' was a rank in The Old World,

but *please* call me Lucien."

She silently crossed her shapely legs and sat back in her seat. Their hot coffees were delivered to their table and she snatched the nearest one, bringing it up to her moist, pouty lips. *She sure was a sexy woman!*

"Okay Lucien; mind telling me what you want from me?" *God, if she only knew.* "Let's skip the small talk and get on with it, shall we?"

She seemed anxious for some reason. It was barely noticeable, but it was definitely there. "Sure, why not...but I'd like to ask *you* a question first. Over the past three weeks, I've been doing my research on you, Doctor Methis and we both appear to know someone in common – High Commissar Michael Riordan."

"You've been *doing research on me?*"

Great, now she thinks you're a pervert! What is it with this woman? "It's only procedure, Jenna. We're *not* spies, if that's what you think." He shook his head. "Well...*we are,* but-"

"*But* you seem to know more than you ought to, is that it?"

"No, that's not-"

She didn't let him finish. "That may be alright in your book, but it's highly irregular in mine. Snooping into another Citizen's private affairs is *illegal*...but I'm sure you already knew that."

Is she always this paranoid? He ignored her reply. "Michael Riordan," he repeated, "What do you know of him?"

"As much as you claim otherwise, this is starting to sound like an interrogation instead of a coffee break! I *work* for him...but you obviously know that too. What's it to you?"

Alright, maybe a bit stubborn as well..."He happened to be my Senior Instructor many years ago; last I heard he was recruited into an agency called the Global System Defense Front. I haven't heard good things about their organization, they are Black Operations. How did you get involved with *him?*"

"Small world, right," she replied monotonously, as she ran her thumb across her nails.

"Not so small- and I rarely believe in *coincidence*. I have a 5th-level security clearance, which is the highest I know of, but your work remains inaccessible and that is...*highly unusual*. Is that Riordan's doing? What does he want with this project? I know most of what goes on within The System so-"

"Whoa, slow down. If you're here to find out about my work, I'm sure you already know that I can't discuss it – it's *classified*," she lashed out at him, annoyance reflecting in her bright green eyes, "And if you are going to *threaten me* with whatever you soldier-types use as a form of intimidation, I'll be the first to-"

He shook his head, putting his hand, palm up towards her. "No, no you misunderstand my intentions– I am *not* your enemy Ms. Methis. Anything that you wish to share with me will remain confidential. I am simply not used to being locked out of high-level material. This is a first for me..."

The Doctor calmed herself down in a professional manner, but her eyes were still slit with suspicion. "The only thing I can tell you is that I am working on a Classified Project for the High Commissar. If I didn't know any better, I'd think that you already-"

"We are aware that you are in the development of a Nano-swarm," he stated, knowingly.

For once she was silent with nothing in retort. Good – now they wouldn't have to play this back and forth game of useless intrigue, he didn't have time for that.

Lucien continued, "As I'm sure you already know The System has deemed that technology to be a 'Code 6' classification due to the dangers it presents. The OZI Cateton Agency should have been made aware of this. You understand the-"

"The project was approved by the High Commissar! It's not up to me to get the proper clearances; that's *not* my job. I was hired to head up the- It doesn't matter; who gave you the information about the Nano-swarm?!"

"James Massy. We brought him in a week ago," he explained, "And no – we didn't threaten or hurt him, but offer a person an incentive and he'll be much more forthcoming. And I believe that man has an *obsession* with you. You may want to think about the people you associate with, Doctor."

She was beginning to feel as if she had somehow been violated. He seemed to know everything about her, yet she knew *nothing* about him. Her eyes flickered back and forth in anger, finally finding her voice. "I don't believe that pervert's wants or needs are any of your concern! If you already have the information you're searching for, what the hell do you need me for?! Why am I even here?"

"Whether we need you or not, we don't know yet," he lied, "I must say however, that this was a great surprise to us at the Citadel. You see, we normally stay well-informed of the latest Tech; in fact, most of it is *ours*. Your file shows that this undertaking has gone on for a number of years now, how far have you come?"

There it was again; a small shadow of doubt...or was it fear that he observed? If she's not hiding anything; what does she have to be afraid of? He was confident in his skills at both interrogation and intuition, but this woman sure was hard to read. She paused for almost a full minute before she replied; patience was not one of his virtues.

"Maybe you should be asking *Riordan* that. I'm sure if he wanted you to know, he would have told you...or are you just a *lackey*?"
He had to keep himself from reaching out and throttling the smug look off her face. *Keep your cool.* She had an unusually high amount of hostility. *I guess I can't blame her...I haven't give her any reason to trust me.*

"I thought I would ask *you*, but if you don't want to share, let me give you a peace offering first...I assume you are stuck in the same place we were. The Nanites have many bodies but *no brain*, isn't that right?"

Doctor Methis appeared to be confused for a minute, contemplating in silence. When she finally spoke, she didn't sound as surprised as she should have been. "So the Catetons are also working on a Nano-swarm..."

"Of course we are...*or were*; *Blackburn* remember? Almost a year ago, the project was disbanded due to the same problem you've run into. We could not direct the Nanites; they went haywire: building, dismantling, absorbing each other – every nanobot was fighting for control of the other; they needed a control protocol- but it had to be separate from the Swarm." *Give her something to gain her trust.* "In fact, I believe we can help each other out."

Jenna pulled in closer, her eyes bright with undisguised interest. "What are you saying Commander; that a bunch of slime ball Mercs have figured out a solution to the *control protocol* in less than twenty-four months? A problem that the best scientists in the world have been working on for all these years with no luck?! Come on now. You expect me to believe that-"

"You can *believe* what you want Ms. Methis. In fact, you can stand up and walk away from this right now if you'd like...I won't stop you. But please remember – I will not make this offer a second time. The choice is yours," he replied confidentially. He waited patiently, letting everything sink in.

"Shit - you're serious," Jenna stated after some thought, "I am all out of ideas at this point! I've worked out the other details, but the *control protocol* is the most puzzling piece. We need a 'leader' designated within the Swarm, otherwise we would still have to direct their behavior with manual programming. It would literally take millions of bits of code for even simple command phrases and then there's a processing issue! *How* did you get past that?!"

Take a breather lady. Lucien knew he had her, but he didn't want to lay all his cards on the table just yet. And there was another offer he could propose - one of *mutual benefit* that would keep Doctor Jenna Mathis's loyalty and allegiance to him...and the Resistance, should they be exposed. *Now's a good time as any.*

"Slow down, Ms. Methis. I didn't say we have a *solution* to the control protocol, however I can give you the next best thing. But let's come back to that, I want to ask you about something very important."

"And *this isn't important?*"

He smiled. "I promise you that I will fill you in and get you copies of our research data as soon as the time is right...*if* we can come to an arrangement."

"Of course there's a catch, right?"

Oh, how frustrating this man was! This was the first real breakthrough she'd had in months! If Lucien Bovier could help her to successfully create a Master Directive, she could bring about a New Age of technology! She could-

"What's in it for you," she inquired, suddenly.

"We'll get to that in a minute."

Tread mindfully with your choice of words, you don't want to upset her any further. Lucien cleared his throat and took a sip of his coffee. "I understand that you have a son – his name is Cole, I believe. I realize that he is under medical supervision at-"

Jenna's hands shook in anger as her face reddened. The presumptuous prick would use her son as a bargaining chip?! "You son of a bitch," she cried out in retaliation, "How dare you bring *my son* into this?! He has absolutely *nothing* to do with *my* work! If you're going to use him as some kind of bargaining chip, then you can shove your offer right up your-"

But his eyes did not reveal that he was threatening her, instead he appeared compassionate about her situation. As if he wanted to help. Maybe she overreacted...

"I'm sorry," she blurted, "You come in all 'James Bond like' and start talking about my son and things you shouldn't know..."

"It's okay. I should have been more...careful about approaching the subject. I don't normally rush into things like this, but we are running out of time. We'd like to make a proposal of sorts."

"We? You keep saying 'we'?"

Who is this guy with? What the hell does he want? Jenna had a hundred different questions, but perhaps it would be to her advantage to get as much information from this man as possible. *Calm down Jenna, he couldn't possibly know...*He had to be speaking of something else. She should not jump to conclusions; hear him out and let him finish.

"You're *observant*, I'll tell you that. My people are unimportant right now; you'll meet them in due time. Right now, let me see if I can *help your son*. Why don't we start by having you tell me what you know of The System and its Healthcare Initiative?" Leading in with this was the logical option considering Doctor Methis' son was a 'prisoner' of the Initiative and so Lucien went with it.

The Healthcare Initiative? What did that have to do with anything? Jenna felt she could breathe a bit easier now that her previous fears were proved untrue. So this man wanted a trade...*But in return for what?* Although he had shown no signs of aggression towards her, she wanted to be fully aware of her surroundings – in case she needed to run. *That would be foolish, he's offering you a chance at advancing your work...but why?? And what was with all these odd questions?*

"I know what everyone else knows. I can tell you that The System helps to keep my son alive. With the Healthcare Initiative in place, all short term help is provided to the public at no cost. Employers must match a certain percentage towards healthcare and they are angry about that. The only other catch is that any consecutive medical care after the 30-day limit must be paid for out-of-pocket. These services are available only to those who have accepted the G-ID Chip implant. Everyone else has to fend for themselves..."

"That is all true, but there's more to the Initiative than you know," Lucien offered cryptically.

As she turned her face inquisitively towards his, Lucien decided to explain what he could, hoping she was open enough to accept the reality they all lived in. The earlier plans had begun with what was first called the Medical Directive right before the third World War. The ruling powers at that time knew they had to give something first before anything was taken away...

They had gained public praise and support through its gift of global Healthcare and everyday households were able to afford the medical health plans and most importantly – keep themselves and their families healthy. Something so common, yet so precious to countless communities around the world and even this, The System would soon subvert to their malicious goals of global servitude.

What the general populace *did not know* was that the advantages and benefits of having the Healthcare Directive in place had a steep price – and not in the way most people might think. All the talk at that time – at least what the public had been manipulated to believe were along the lines of conjecture rather than fact: Medium to large size businesses would cut hours to force full-time employees into a part-time position to avoid additional expenses; small businesses would not hire more than a certain number of new employees in order to come below the mandatory starting coverage numbers.

Students planning on becoming doctors and others interested in the medical field would no longer be putting in the long years needed for their specific degrees, thereby causing a shortage of numbers in their fields. It would bring about additional taxes and costs and so on. To the common folk, these were legitimate concerns and no one could blame them for making these items a priority. These things were of no benefit, but this was not the true goal. That came later.

The endgame was to put the people under a 'leash', as medical care is one of the most important essentials of the recent century. It was a managed system with the ability to improve, restore, and maintain public health and a sense of well-being! It held off and prevented disease; annihilated deadly viruses; initiated cures and new technology to combat health issues; and most importantly – saved countless lives in the process.

The people were pleased with the benefits they received, until the mandates soon began to change. Once The System was in place, they introduced the Healthcare Initiative, which were a subset of rules and regulations that twisted the fabric of global healthcare to their own ends. The System reserved not only the right to grant these 'free and available' services, but to deny or withhold them based upon each person's Citizen Designations.

Members of The Amalgam were given full health services and the ability to grant special waivers or selectively enforce medical care options. Initiates who had G-ID Chip implants were given conditional benefits, based on their allegiance and blind obedience. Commoners or 'Undesirables' who had not accepted the Chip were on their own, but could sometimes purchase care through favors and bribes. Revolutionaries and rebellious groups such as The Hand were completely denied any such System medical care; at least the members they knew of.

What The System was not aware of was that the last two groups had several trained surgeons and physicians who used a combination of herbal and medical knowledge to ensure the survival of their people. It was an underground system that operated on the antiquated network of barter and trade.

The Global Healthcare Initiative was a fraudulent program that ultimately gave way to disaster through corruption and subjugation of the people. More so, it kept people in line. A choice was given between allegiance to a dictator-controlled institution which provided medical care and facilities and the 'freedom' to seek your own aid. The Amalgam realized that the majority would be too afraid to abandon the medical services provided to their families in return for their loyalty.

Whether that be for the care of a diabetic child or a father suffering from lung cancer, the global outreach provided to them by The System was essential! It left most with very little choice, but to accept things as they were. But most of all, the people would do anything to keep their loved ones safe and healthy in their times of need. And herein lay the truth to their reality. There was always a price to pay when dealing with the devil!

Jenna listened with a sense of curiosity and suspicion. Wasn't this guy a commanding officer for The System? *Why would he be sharing this information with me?* Shouldn't he be *defending* it? "So you're telling me that we are being held *hostages* to the Initiative, is that it?!"

"Oh more than that, Ms. Lockwood. I'm telling you that we are a *prisoners* of *The System* itself!"

"You realize that what you are saying borders dangerously close to dissension?"

"*I'm aware*...Unfortunately, I don't have the patience to sugar-coat this. You see, time is of the essence and mine is limited. Although, I would *appreciate* you keeping this conversation to yourself."

She looked amused. "Don't worry; you know what they say – 'What happens in the Java Mill stays in the Java Mill'...

"You mean Vegas," he blurted out, before realizing it was a bad joke. "*Oh...funny.*"

Jenna laughed. "Since you've already let the proverbial cat out of the bag, why don't you tell me what you mean by *prisoners?*"

Lucien sighed. *Why not...*Doctor Jenna Methis was an innocent victim who knew nothing about the stranglehold The System had placed upon its people; she was only a mother who wanted to keep her son alive. But he needed her help and didn't have the luxury of 'wining and dining' her into acquiescence. And so – grudgingly, over the course of the next four hours, he told her all that he knew of the oppressive nature of the lives they lived; the 'short version' anyway.

Jenna Methis walked back into the laboratory, mentally and emotionally exhausted. Everything the High Commander divulged to her at first seemed like total fantasy, but the factual, scientific side of her could put two and two together and what had come out of that was...mind-blowing! Without any urging whatsoever, she had already decided to keep everything she had been told to herself; especially lest anyone think she had completely lost her mind!

Everything that she had been taught to believe since she was a little girl seemed to now be made of half-truths and illusions of the reality she truly lived in. Lucien had deemed her trustworthy even as he had informed her of the pulse monitor he had coded to her Global ID Chip. If she were lying or subversive in any way, God only knew what would have happened!

Still, Lucien Bovier was an admirable man in his own right, she doubted he would have harmed her. As to his reasons for approaching *her*, he had kept that to himself and she hadn't asked. It was an odd situation altogether, but Jenna had a feeling he was being honest and up-front about his actions, so far anyway...Quite good-looking too. Where did that come from? *Shut it, Jenna!*

Commander Bovier seemed to be working towards her best

interests; he had even offered a solution to further her work with the Nanites. Artificial Intelligence - a partial aspect at least; she had never even considered this, as it wasn't her field. It would not provide the true control faction she needed, but in a limited way, it would certainly keep them from destroying each other.

The Nanites themselves would be independent of each other and would still need to be programmed, but with one immense benefit – all code could be inserted just once, instead of written for each separate instance. From there, the master directives could be sent to each individual nanite at the same time!

The prospect of finally having a partially functioning Swarm would not only grant her a more than considerate raise in GRB Credits which would help support Cole, but also the gratifying fealty of High Commissar Riordan himself. Once she'd shown some results, she could get on with her real work.

Bovier's group had also promised an additional amount of Credits large enough to help pull her out of the current medical debt she was in. But Lucien had asked of her something so very odd. He had requested her to freeband over a current brain scan to a specific cyber-address and at some point later – to participate in something called a B.I.O.N.E.X procedure. It was deemed 'classified' at this time, but was supposed to be similar to a brain-scan – easy enough.

Blackburn assholes....why did everything *always* have to be so secretive?! The only thing that truly bothered her was that she had been strictly directed to keep all of this from her husband. She was not to speak of this to anyone, especially Collin – otherwise the deal was off. Bovier would be in contact with her soon.

But the thing that raised suspicion was why he would offer her these things and ask for something so simple in return. Jenna knew that if something sounded too good to be true, then it usually was. She'd have to find out everything she could about Lucien Bovier and this B.I.O.N.E.X procedure. There were important things that he was not divulging and she hated being kept in the dark.

CHAPTER 7: Introspection

"I had no choice-"

"Lucien, you offered her the A.I. Matrix before it's even complete! And that's if she survives the B.I.O.N.E.X procedure! We cannot give her something that is not fully functional yet; this is *my* project, you should have come to me first! And this High Commissar Riordan...what does he have to do with this- he was Blackburn like you. If he's involved, he'll see through all this fluff immediately."

"We had to give her *something*, Ayla. She doesn't know who we are and she sure as hell doesn't trust us! The A.I. could fix part of the problem with the Nano-swarm. It's a fair trade for what she has to undertake."

"It would only function for 12 hours, *you know that*! You're deceiving her, it's not right."

"I told her I had a solution for her problem and I do. I didn't make any guarantees on how long it would last."

Ayla turned away from him, seething with anger.

Boy, was she pissed! She did have a point though. "Listen, we already have a semi-sentient data cluster of the A.I. Matrix. Load it up into an Adaptive Interface Module and I can pass that off as-"

"It won't work," Ayla insisted, "Riordan will run the biometrics and figure out its all bulls-"

"By the time Jenna Methis or Riordan even figure it out, we'll have the emulation in place."

"What does that matter anyway?! An innocent woman may die and she doesn't even know why! She's a *Mother* for Christ's sake. You don't think she deserves to make her own choices," Doctor Lockwood yelled back in a flush of emotion.

So that's where her anger was coming from. Ayla was more concerned with Jenna's welfare than Lucien offering her the A.I. Matrix. Strangely, so was he.

A lump in his throat suddenly formed and he felt as if he couldn't breathe. Peering down to the streets from the balcony 325 feet above, he could see a small group of children playing 'Simulation Wars'. It was a game which each person constructs a 3D-rendered holographic structure as the others take a limited number of turns trying to knock it down. The challenge was to use only four types of virtual ammunition: a large rock, a steel ball, a titanium ball, or a cannonball.

Each one had a specific weight and trajectory. Thrown only by a Trebuchet which was a type of siege engine used in the Middle Ages, more or less a catapult, it was a challenge. The person who built the strongest foundation usually had the largest portion of his building intact and would eventually be declared the winner. The two small boys and three taller girls laughed, and played, and jeered, and teased, completely oblivious to anything other than their game.

His heartbeat sped up as a sense of sadness flooded his being. They were so unaware of their strife. These children...*they* were the innocents...*they* were the future. None of them realized the misery of the world they lived in. They too, would eventually lose their rights; their freedoms; and most likely, their hopes and aspirations. *We have to do something!* Even if sacrifices have to be made...

"She volunteered Ayla," he suddenly snapped, "This is utterly ridiculous, I can't be responsible for everyone!"

Ayla eyed him cautiously. *Why was he getting so worked up?* Guilt, perhaps? That didn't sound good...what would he be guilty of? Unless he didn't...*oh no!*

"You did tell her *everything*, didn't you Lucien," Doctor Lockwood interrogated. She wasn't a fool. The only way someone would agree to participate in a dangerous experiment was if the poor woman was not fully aware of the process or the risks involved! It was not the emulation that was the problem; that part was easy and had been successfully done before with the brain scan. No, it was the electrical feedback of the bonding process that was the danger. It could literally fry the brain or at best, leave the subject with permanent brain damage!

"I told her everything she needed to know," was his flippant reply,

"What she does, she does for her son...Ayla, this is too important to take a chance on and we don't exactly have an excess of volunteers rushing for the doors, now do we?!"

High Commander Lucien Bovier prayed with all his heart that it didn't have to happen like this. He hadn't wanted to lie to Doctor Methis and he sure as hell didn't want anything terrible to happen to her either. The odds of a successful B.I.O.N.E.X emulation with her compatibility ratio - the scans had given her an 89% match- was nine in ten, but the probability of survival during the process was much lower than could be accepted. But they did not have a choice; the Hand of Light needed an advantage and this could very well be the trump card they needed to win the war.

Ayla was bitter, but she knew what was at stake. She could not argue against hard logic: one possible life for the freedom of billions. Either way, she didn't want to talk about it anymore. "Have you received any communication from Tom?"

Tom was topside, meeting with an Agent named Katya Prulova, a deep cover operative of The Hand of Light. She was a global arms dealer who owned a private military company which also manufactured Ion-pulse Rifles, various other weapons, and new age Tech for The System militia.

The regal woman was extremely wealthy, being very well connected in both the public and private sectors and luckily for them – was also Tom's 'on-again off-again' lover. National Republic Armaments was a global player in the manufacturing, deployment, and distribution of firearms and munitions as well as the primary off-the-books supplier for the Hand of Light's militant forces.

Years ago, they had figured out a way to get these weapons into the hands of the Resistance without alerting System agencies by coding them to individual Chips of soldiers who were missing in action. In addition, Katya's operation also provided training to the militia in the use of firearms, tactics, and survivalist instruction.

Under the guise of a System-integrated company, Katya and her people had the necessary clearance authorizations and freedom to sell or trade anytime and anywhere they liked. She was the 'go-to person' who knew the ins and outs of most of The System nerve centers and secret bunkers scattered across the globe; more importantly – how to hit them and where it would hurt! Tom, it seemed - was already organizing the next strike.

"You know the risks involved, I can't rush them anymore than you can; Tom should be in contact soon," he answered bluntly, still unwilling to meet her gaze.

"Fine, but I need the updated blueprints as soon as possible."

"I'll have him get them to you."

Ayla punched in some new data into her HOL-COM as Lucien quietly looked out into the distance. The Midland Gardens provided a much needed distraction. The tension between the two was thick right now. The seven towers of the Gardens loomed less than a mile from where they stood. A cross between plant-life and concrete, these 'trees' provided a peaceful and relaxing atmosphere for Oz's inhabitants to take a stroll or simply admire its beauty. Standing at close to 40 feet tall, wide paths wove around each dome, merging with the Sky Road which went spiraling down to the ground level.

Like many structures or buildings in OZ, the Midland Gardens had a dual purpose. They provided an emergency supply of clean oxygen in case the regulators were damaged or went off-line. The process used a type of biomimetic approach to simulate photosynthesis in the enclosed area where the Gardens lay. Carbon dioxide was pumped out to be harvested as energy for the city while the newly created oxygen was stored in underground vats. From there, the gathered oxygen could be forced through the ventilation ducts in case the need arose. It was a creation of unparalleled genius!

As he quietly watched the people walking the structure, his mind amplified the culpability he was feeling. *Perhaps you should have chosen a different career path, life would have been much simpler then...*After a moment of silence, Lucien finally voiced what was on his mind. "Maybe it would have been better if Tom had met with Doctor Methis. He-"

Ayla stopped him right there. His self-guilt trip was really starting to grate on her; it was exasperating and an unfair play at justification! The dichotomy about this man was aggravating; he always took everything upon himself, regardless of the situation.

But, she thought, *he had done the best he could...*"Okay, I get it Lucien. We need her and it's *not your* fault. Can we get past that now?"

Then why did it feel like it was? "I'm sorry Ayla; I'm just tired is all - gonna get some shut-eye; we'll talk later." Without waiting for a reply or nod of acknowledgement, he turned and rushed out the door.

"You need to tell her the truth," she yelled after him as he disappeared, hoping against everything that he'd heard and would do the right thing.

Lucien *did* hear her last comment, he just chose to ignore her. Ayla had a soft heart, but *he* knew what needed to be done. If that meant convincing a Citizen to make a sacrifice for the greater good, then so be it, it would be *his* cross to bear. He took the elevator back down and made his way towards the Cateton Complex. He was surprised to find the paved paths so crowded. There were vendors everywhere selling fresh goods to passerby's

Then he remembered today was 'Market Day', which was indeed a special occasion! It was increasingly difficult to grow crops above-ground in the polluted soil so a few times a year, farmers would sell fresh fruits and vegetables to the OZI Citizens. Man-made pollution, radioactive chemicals, and human waste had dissolved away most of the important nutrients and changed the composition of the Earth's soil. Industrial activity and acid rain made it that much worse.

Therefore, it was hazardous to grow plants and grains in a natural environment. Long term exposure and ingestion of contaminated crops could literally affect the genetic make-up of the human body. Fear of congenital illnesses and chronic health problems forced most of the Citizen population to avoid consuming anything that was not manufactured by alternative means.

Greenhouses were erected in the underground cities which allowed those with agricultural knowledge to grow what little they could. But the absence of natural sunlight below made it a slow and complicated process. Four times a year, 'Market Day' provided an opportunity for the people to purchase these sought after items; natural foods which were considered more or less organic.

As he took a short-cut through a deserted alleyway, he came upon a large group huddled around a robed man, standing on a raised dais. He wore a simple grey garb; an older fellow, his face etched in wrinkles and long hair falling about his shoulders in a tangle of silver locks. Lucien pushed his way through the crowd to hear what the preacher was saying.

"...And I beheld when he had opened the sixth seal, and, lo, there was a great earthquake; and the sun became black as sackcloth of hair, and the moon became as blood' – and so it is written in the Book of Revelation, Chapter 6, verse 12. Mark my words, Citizens - this was the prophecy for the beginning of the End times!

The fourth blood moon occurred just before the last World War, bringing with it darkness and despair; death and destruction from above. It was a warning for us all and *we did not listen*! I tell you now that we yet have a choice to save ourselves and walk hand-in-hand with our Lord, Jesus Christ. You *must* repent; you must-"

The preacher was abruptly silenced as three System Catetons surrounded the man and escorted him away. The crowd slowly dispersed and Lucien felt a sickening in his stomach as he watched the struggling preacher being dragged towards the Council Chambers. He grappled with his internal urge to help him, but he knew there was nothing he could do without exposing himself. The poor man would be tried and executed, as religion was outlawed and he was spreading dissension against The System!

Forcing himself to turn away, he sighed and continued towards the Cateton Domiciles. Every so often a brave soul like the old preacher would try to sway the majority with a public declaration, but each time they ended in failure. The New World was insistent upon order and most Citizens were too frightened to oppose The System in any way, lest they be made an example of. It was a reality that all too often kept individual thoughts silent and constrained. *This* was the world they lived in...*But one day - it will be different*!

Thirsting for a strong drink, Lucien stumbled into his modest residence, the anger of what he had witnessed still bothering him. With a wave of his Chip, the doors opened to allow him in. It was a simple, yet comfortable place of living with all the amenities that a soldier needed, including a small bathroom, kitchen, and even a wall-mounted Holo-tube. He primarily used the place for sleeping or eating as he was always on some type of mission or likely in the middle of planning one.

As such, a comfy memory foam mattress laid perfectly in a slightly bent metal bedframe, a plush white couch, and a small oak table were the only other comforts he needed. A pile of faded and tattered magazines, remnants from the Old World, were scattered about the table. Sometimes, the actual physical sensation of thumbing through pages were more comforting than scrolling through a V-book.

He sat down and paged through a small gardening book, finding the article he needed. Reviewing the directions for the second time, he tossed it back on the ever-growing pile of old publications. Stepping out to the balcony, he watered the small Aloes and Fairy Castle Cactus. His attempt at growing and caring for plants consisted of ones that were easy to maintain and only needed little care. Still, about a quarter of the plants were in a state of decay. Unfortunately, the one thing he didn't seem to have was a 'green thumb'.

Lucien's father informed him on more than one occasion that should there ever be a catastrophic disaster that had the potential to destroy the ecosystem and environment, an important skill to have was the cultivation and care of plants and animals. Farming, agriculture, and gardening would be essential to survival if ready-made goods were no longer produced or able to be acquired. And so, he had given it a shot, starting with these simple plants.

These specific types grew well in the artificial sunlight of OZI City and cultivating the Aloes for their medicinal properties was an additional benefit. In his line of work, burns, cuts, wounds, and sore muscles were commonplace; the soothing gel from the Aloe Vera plants was most helpful. Finished with that, he went through the living room towards the bedroom. Passing by the only decorations he had put up, a picture of his parents and his uncle, he suddenly noticed how they clashed garishly with the metallic colored walls. *Hrumph, home sweet home.*

Before he got any further into his own self-absorbance, he needed to do one last thing. With the sudden turn of events, he wouldn't have the time to supervise any additional training with the new troops. Due to his covert allegiance to The Hand, life just seemed to get that much more complicated. Activating his Sat-Com, he contacted the Reserve Division.

"Controller Stagg, please."

A minute later, a stern-faced man in full uniform appeared above the communications device.

"Well, well...looks like it's my lucky day. The man himself contacting *me*; must be important. How are you Lucien?"

"As always, Anderson, it could be better. How's that lovely wife of yours?" Everyone knew Anderson's spouse was a steel-fisted hard ass; the poor guy was always in a tiff about her. As such, it was Lucien's sworn duty to take a jab at him whenever time permitted.

"Hahaha. If Colleen's silent and not arguing, she's asleep! Other than that, we're all doing well...Now what can I help you with? Surely, you didn't contact me because you've got nothing better to do than give me grief...or did you?"

"No, I didn't. Listen, I'm going to need you to take over for the new recruits. I have some urgent matters to attend to. The thing is – I'm not sure for how long."

If anyone could be counted on to handle things efficiently, it was Anderson. He was the third best option beside Tom and himself.

"Do what you gotta do, I'll take care of it. Just send me the details through Freeband...And try not to be a stranger."

"Will do. Thanks and let me know if there are any complications."

Lucien ended the transmission and walked into the bedroom. *Today seems to be an abnormally hot day* he pondered, noticing the stuffiness in the room. Even with the sophisticated ventilation system running full bore and blasting cool air from the strategically placed shafts around the city, it could get downright sweltering here in the Cateton domiciles. He could feel the accumulated sweat starting to trickle down his back as his black linen shirt stuck in clumps, solid against his skin. Each time he moved his upper torso, it would come loose with a slight tearing sound.

Without waiting any longer for it to become unbearable, he removed his shirt and tossed it into the overflowing laundry hamper. Walking past the room, he caught a glimpse of himself and stopped.

Staring into the full-length mirror attached to the door, he could clearly remember how he received each and every one of the now scabbed-over scars that tore across his well-built frame. More times than not, things did not always go as planned in times of war and he was living proof of that. *I'll have to put that aloe to good use...*

Remembering that he had forgotten to stock up on the 'hard stuff', He strolled into the small, badly-lit kitchen and grabbed a cold beer from the refrigerator. Popping the aluminum tab open, he flopped down on the couch and took a thirst-quenching gulp of the bitter beverage. He couldn't get his mind off of Jenna Methis and the part he was playing in her deception. How had he managed to get her involved in all of this? Lies; manipulation; pain; death; these things had become a constant in his life and he was so tired of it all. The last thing he wanted to do was drag an innocent into all of this.

Sometimes he wished that he had stayed deaf, dumb, and blind to the oppressive truth behind The System. He could have lived a normal life...maybe even married a good wife and raised a loving family. He had been in love once, with a woman who should have been *the one*. Samantha Haggarty was everything he could have wanted in a partner: beautiful, playful, emotionally mature, and independent. They had dated exclusively for over three years during his time with the Seals and their relationship had progressed quickly.

Once he was promoted to his current position as High Commander of the OZI Catetons, things had gone downhill. Lucien was often away on mission after mission, having little time to spare for her. His biggest mistake was not explaining to her his reasons for doing what he did. In his mind, becoming an invaluable leader for The System was the only sure way to gain trust and gather much-needed intelligence for The Hand. To Sam, it was a life of loneliness and despair.

Less than a year later, Samantha called Lucien over to her Condo, stating they needed to have an important discussion about their relationship. Between tears of grief and bouts of anger, she had broken off the engagement. She wanted a husband who would be there for her and a family she knew he couldn't have. In Lucien's case, adoption was the only viable alternative and that was not the same for her. Even after they had split, he was sure that she would eventually have a change of heart and come back to him. She didn't.

He was heartbroken for months. He had trouble eating and sleeping, constantly trying to find some way to fill the hole where his heart had once been. Thankfully, his position kept him busy, allowing him to slowly come to terms with his loss. Three months later, he had written Sam a long heart-wrenching letter telling her that he would always love her and wished her nothing but the best. Internally, he hoped she would have a change of heart. He never did receive a response. Looking back now, he knew it was probably for the best.

Coming out of that long relationship, he would always have regrets. But he had purposely chosen this life for himself. Not because he didn't want the one he wished he had, but for the sake of a greater good. A brighter world of choices and freedom for everyone, including the family he might one day have. He could have chosen to reside in blind ignorance and idiotic bliss as most people of The New World, but his rigid sense of justice would not allow it...not for a minute.

It was his father's brother who had begun to open his eyes all those years ago. Slowly yet surely, he had been forced to come to his senses and take a deeper look at all the things he had always taken for granted. He was very close to nineteen when he'd last visited his Uncle Rowan Harper, who was well known as a phenom in Finance, both around the city he resided in and beyond it. Rowan, not quite good-looking with a mild case of acne and a clear appetite for sweets, was a fun-loving, caring man with a great sense of humor. He had never married nor been prone to it, so Rowan treated Lucien as more of a son that he never had instead of the arrogant nephew he sometimes was.

His uncle lived in New York, occupying a mid-sized brownstone home built sometime in the 19th century. Remodeled using a Gothic type of architecture, the home took on an eeriness all its own and stood out amongst the newer developments of the neighborhood. The place was a huge hit on Halloween for curious children to dare one another to approach as fast as they could, ring the doorbell and run like hell! Boy, his uncle hated that!

Lucien had seriously thought the house haunted himself, restlessly sleeping there when he needed to, through the sounds of creaking and strange bumps in the night. But he was always happy when he stayed. Rowan Harper, Financial Advisor extraordinaire, just so happened to be an excellent cook and made the best buttermilk flapjacks that side of the St. Lawrence.

Lucien recalled their conversation clearly. He had saved up almost $5,000 from working his summer job at Wiener World and his naïve plan was to strike it rich in the stock market or invest in something worthwhile. After four long years of being dressed up as an enormous sausage in a bun, while ironically cooking in the sun, he'd earned a nice chunk of change. Reminiscing back on how ridiculous he'd looked in that get-up, he smiled to himself, thinking how *normal* life had once been. What a shame The System had changed all of that...

Lucien's plan was to approach the most knowledgeable person he knew who could teach him how to make money and Rowan Harper *was* that man. Contradictory to his position as a financial advisor, Rowan frequently went to great lengths to steer people he cared about away from the monetary machine. He was an expert in his profession, but did not want to take advantage of good folk to get ahead. Lucien had knocked on the door that day and not getting an answer, made his way into the back garden, knowing he'd find Rowan watering his prized tulips.

"Well look who it is," Rowan said, looking up as Lucien approached, "If it isn't my long-lost nephew. I haven't seen you in a while; where've you been hiding?"

"You know me, been working hard as usual."

"Ahh, that would mean sitting on the stoop and drinking a soda," he teased.

"Speak for yourself, old man," Lucien grinned, "I get the feeling you weren't doing much yourself back then!"

"Son, *in my day* things were different, I'd have to earn my beer. When I was a boy, your late grandma would send me down to the corner store with a *dollar*, and I'd come back with six cobs of corn, three potatoes, two bottles of milk, a wheel of cheese, a box of biscuits, and six ropes of sausage. You can't do that anymore; too many damned security cameras!"

Lucien laughed out loud. His uncle always knew how to ease the mood. "Listen, Uncle Rowan, I have a favor to ask."

"Why else are you here," he retorted, "Get out with it then."

Rowan had listened to him with mild amusement, not once interrupting, but at the same time anxiously waiting to go into a long, drawn out lecture. After Lucien had finished explaining his goal of investing his money in great detail that was exactly what he did.

"I love you, boy; but you are so damned *naïve*! Don't you realize what a complicated game you're playing? It's all a sham!"

"What's a sham?"

"The entire financial system, that's what. Take it from me and stay out of the game."

"But...*you* are a financial advisor; why would you even promote it then," Lucien pointed out.

"I needed a job and I happened to be good with numbers," Rowan winked.

"Uncle Rowan, you're gonna have to do better than that."

"Kids these days...Okay then, listen up, you may as well learn something. If you want to make money, you need to understand the principles first. There is one main central institution that has jurisdiction over the money supply and that, is The Federal Reserve. It's a *private* company that controls all the printing and distribution of America's currency. They print as much money as they can and then loan it to the government, with interest. The government in turn, taxes us in order to pay it all back. Think about that carefully son..."

"So what; I vaguely remember you telling me something like that, but what does that have to do with *me* making money and investing? I'd still end up ahead no matter how little I make," Lucien had replied with all the cocky sureness of an all-knowing teenager.

He should have come prepared for a lecture because at that point, his uncle went into an emotional rant on the drab, dreary principles of finance and all the things his nephew should know, but didn't. "You're still not getting it kid. All you know is what everyone else *thinks* they know...Let me try to illustrate this for you. I'm going to use the United States Dollar as a base unit...Let's take a 100 year stretch...say from 1913 to 2013.

You keep on believing you are *making* money, right? Unfortunately for modern man, a small calculation called the Inflation Rate was invented. Take this for example - a gallon of milk in 1913 was sold for 35 cents. The average cost of a gallon of milk in 2013 is $3.50. Now take that same rate and apply it to other foods, housing, utilities, energy, and just about anything else a human being could want or need. Guess what you have now one hundred years later? Close to a *2,000* percent increase – due to Inflation!"

"And?"

"And what dipshit?" Rowan always had a flair for vulgar mannerisms. "Come on now. You are paying a helluva lot more than you should for the same damned gallon of milk...and most everything else! Not much has changed about that milk; it still comes from a cow; you still get a gallon of it; it's plentiful and readily available at most any location– so *why* has the price jumped so much?

Lucien had taken some time to think about that and come up with what he had thought was a very clever retort. "Okay Uncle, I get it. But when prices go up, so does the Minimum Wage. So that evens things out, doesn't it?"

The big man laughed. "And *that* is exactly what most people believe! According to the now defunct Bureau of Labor's bullshit calculations, the real minimum wage back in 2015 should have been $10.55 an hour. It never even got close! But here's the reality kid - Had the actual standards for minimum wage kept in stride with the combined total economic growth and inflation rates, the true minimum wage in the year 2015 *should have been* somewhere around the *$21 an hour* range!"

"What?!"

"My point exactly. Our so called government calls it 'Inflation'; I call it a crime! A con started long ago by convincing the general public that worthless paper distributed as IOU's from the Banks had the same value as physical coin."

Lucien remembered being infuriated about the revelation. "Why the hell aren't we told about this?!"

"The same reason why subjects as important as credit, finance, or budgeting isn't taught in school. How else can the captains of industry and government maintain social order? They need to condition the masses for jobs like menial labor; we couldn't get by without someone to pick up our trash or run our manufacturing facilities. Bee hive democracy is not so different from human democracy, we all need our 'worker-drones'. More so, they don't want us to think for ourselves, question the sociopolitical order, or communicate articulately. It's a system of control, designed to keep us uneducated and docile."

All of Lucien's dreams on 'striking it rich' had come crashing to a halt that day, but it was also his first step into seeing the world for what it actually was. He remembered being resentful of his uncle for weeks after that conversation until he took the time to finally reflect on it. Instead, he should have thanked him for opening his eyes to the greater truth. Regardless, that day, his sullen mood directly reflected his sulking form as he wandered towards the door in defeat.

"Hold on a minute Lucien. Before you go, let me broaden your mind a bit more. The knowledge I can pass on may as well be good for something..."

"Seriously...there's more?!"

"Listen, you are my brother's son and I love you. I want what's best for you and sometimes, that happens to be the *bluntness of honesty*," Rowan offered, objectively, "This wasn't meant to ruin your day. Let's consider this your first life lesson, but *learn from it*...don't shut it out. I know that with you youngsters, hearing and comprehending are two very different things. Do you understand the point I am trying to make?"

Lucien picked up his black flak jacket and put it on, but then sat down heavily on the small stool beside the entryway. "I get it Uncle

Rowan, I do...you did the right thing. It's just *not* what I wanted to hear."

"These things rarely are Lucien," he agreed.

"I see that. And yes, I think I get what you're saying about finances. Basically, it's continuously costing us more money now to purchase what we used to for pennies on the dollar. But at the same time, we are making much less than we should be, so it's putting us in 'a hole we can't climb out of'."

"That's right. The 'hole' as you say is the common situation most of us find ourselves in sooner or later. Our debts continue to increase, while we are forced to obtain credit and loans from the Banks in order to survive and support our families. It is perhaps the greatest legal racket in human history!"

As a quick-witted teenager fast approaching adulthood, he accepted what he was hearing with little question, however – verification was not denial and although he realized the answer even before he spoke, he asked anyway. "Okay, I agree – that's bullshit...But doesn't paying your debt off *build* your credit?"

"Kid, I can do this all day; this *is* my thing, you know," Rowan laughed good-naturedly, "You've got to remember the Bankers put this system into play in the first place. You think these government bailouts of these banks have benefited the people whatsoever? Hell no; the only thing they got in return was a $78 billion debt at the taxpayer's expense! Nothing is fair for you and I and don't you forget that. Let's take-"

"Nevermind, I think I already have the answer to my own question...if I bought a stereo for $200.00 on credit, I would eventually pay more just so I can have it *now* versus waiting until I can afford to buy it later...it's stupid, we all know that - but we've accepted it as a way of life. And yes, I should know better…"

"That's the *purpose* of credit, Lucien. Don't be so hard on yourself, we've all been setup and conditioned for failure before we were even born! If that doesn't push your buttons enough, the *banks* keep more and more of your money and use it to make millions on a daily basis. And in return they give you a measly ½ percent in interest back, while they keep the remaining 99.5% they earned from investing *your money* in the first place! Eventually, we all end up as literal work-horses, struggling to pay back everything we borrowed with no end in sight."

Seeing that his nephew appeared to be comprehending everything, he continued. "Listen son, the *banks* have created a debt that only exists as a computer entry, but they want you to secure that loan with an asset and then repay it with interest and slave labor. Does that make sense to you 'cause it sure as hell does not to me! Unfortunately, we're stuck living in the world that was created all those centuries ago. The human race has had an invisible 'yoke' placed upon its shoulders for far too long and we've forgotten the reality of our existence. We are...programmed for acceptance if you will, you understand?"

On that note, Uncle Rowan had gone to the dilapidated mini-fridge in the adjoining living room and retrieved two cold beers. What started out as a bad day ended up as *almost* a good one. That was the day he was offered his first alcoholic beverage. His friends were all into drinking and partying; he on the other hand was kept too busy by his father to have experienced that yet. "I know you're not old enough, but after everything you've had to endure today, I do believe you could use one. But you tell your Dad about this, you're a dead man, got it?!"

Lucien had grabbed the bottle in earnest, twisting off the cap and quickly taking a deep gulp right before...spitting it back out in his uncle's face. Rowan looked like he was about to murder him!

"What the hell, Lucien," Rowan yelled in disgust, as he tried in vain to wipe the dripping liquid from his face, "It's not Kool-Aid for Christ's sake...What is this your first time?! I thought kids your age were into that sort of thing."

"Why didn't you tell me this-" Lucien began.

"Don't be such a fricking baby," Rowan said, with a grin.

"Seriously," he coughed out, as he made a sour face. "This tastes like – what's the word for it - oh yeah – *shit*! How the heck can you drink this with a straight face?!" Handing his uncle a towel, he added "Sorry about that, I didn't mean to-"

Rowan laughed heartily and pulled him into an embrace, patting him on the back of his shoulder, though quite a bit harder than usual. "My fault, no harm done. Damn Lucien, when I was your age I was drinking stuff that would make your balls shrink and grow hair on your chest," He stopped suddenly in his train of thought. "Not that I'm encouraging anything, mind you..."

"You know Uncle Rowan," Lucien said sarcastically, "that explains a whole lot of things."

"Aww, shut up!"

Placing the half empty beer on the table, Lucien stood up. "I gotta go."

"Just think about what I've told you and do what's smart with that money of yours. And for God's sake, remember what I hammered into your head last time you were here about those *so called 'taxes'*."

Uncle Rowan was a wise man, always going into exceptional detail about what he believed was wrong with the financial system. His last lecture two weeks back had been about the FED and because he secretly admired his uncle, Lucien tried to remember his lessons well.

According to Rowan, most people believed that the Federal Reserve System belonged to a branch of the Federal government; the common assumption being the Treasury Department. The FED however, was *not* a Federal agency at all; it was a tax-exempt Central Bank owned 100% by its member banks! They worked hand in hand with the U.S. Bureau of Engraving and Printing to print however many of each bill was required at whenever times those might be.

Now here's the kicker and what Rowan was trying to make clear to him – The Taxes we pay are actually *paid directly back to the Federal Reserve and the Members who own it* and NOT to pay for government expenses and services as we are all led to believe! In fact, the Treasury charges the FED 2.3 cents for each note they print and then lends this new money to the government at face value, plus interest and in addition – requires the government to create a bond as security for the 'loan'! The old adage was true: *the rich get richer as the poor get poorer* and *that* was bullshit!

"Thanks for the advice Uncle Rowan...and for the beer," he replied as he turned to leave.

"You take care of yourself Lucien. Say hello to the old man for me."

From that moment on, Lucien had harbored doubts about many things he used to take for granted; it was the first time he'd questioned his country's socio-political rule. All these events were happening behind the curtain and our own government was the 'wizard', pulling the strings! Problem was that no one seemed to be the wiser...at least not enough people to do something about it.

Lucien enlisted with the Navy soon after, following in his father's footsteps. It wasn't a choice he made willingly, but he didn't see many other options available. He soon found that the armed forces provided him with an opportunity to investigate the inner workings of the 'political machine' and its far-reaching effects on society.

The things he witnessed became a foundation for his current beliefs and to this day, his disgust with affairs of state remained a festering wound, not easily forgotten. Laying back in his bed, he closed his eyes and drifted off to a better world.

Jenna stood in the kitchen washing the remaining dishes in the sink by hand. With just her and Collin in the home now and each of them working long hours, there were very few plates and utensils. There really was no need to use the Auto-wash and the calmness of physically doing them by hand added a much-needed tranquility to her chaotic environment. Lately, the fighting and arguing between her and Collin had lessened, but mostly because she was not there to participate in it.

She'd come to the conclusion that Collin was a difficult man to reach. He usually blamed everyone else, but himself for the problems in their marriage. He 'redirected' his anger and sadness, lashing out at her for small things that hardly mattered. It was okay to be disappointed in things that don't go your way; even jealousy is acceptable in certain situations, but to constantly 'point the finger' and blame everyone other than yourself for these issues was simply cowardice!

Not that she didn't have her own faults and personal inadequacies, but her husband sometimes lived in a 'fantasy world' of his own making. One where everyone else was the cause of their arguments, but him. Oftentimes she felt as if it was pointless in even trying to communicate with him; it usually amounted to little more than a catalyst to an unprovoked fight.

Jenna understood that most people in today's society refused to take responsibility or accountability for the problems and issues in their lives, but she never thought that *Collin* would be one of them. She felt like she didn't really know him anymore...he had changed so much! She had read somewhere that it was common for a man and a woman to meet and for one or the other to put up a false facade to portray an aura of perfection.

It wasn't as if someone who was dating a beautiful woman would say, "Hi, I'm Paul. I'm very attracted to you and hope we can move forward with this relationship. By the way, I wanted you to know that I am controlling, I have anger issues, and sometimes I piss my shorts in my sleep." No, there was a little part of our minds called the Ego which equated admitting our faults to weakness and failure. And Collin's was in overdrive...

The problem when it came to most relationships was that once that 'perfect' person was finally comfortable enough with the other partner, that false semblance of self drops away like a second skin. It revealed the real person beneath the multitude of built up layers; faults, personal struggles, and all. 'Surprise; we're already married and now you're stuck with me!'

And that was the reason why most relationships failed; there was no honesty or trust to begin with; not with each other and not with ourselves. Sometimes life itself was a mere illusion, driven by the failures of society where others could not accept a person for whom they really were. Either way, Jenna was certain that nothing would resolve itself if both people were not willing to meet in the middle.

Her mind drifted to thoughts of Lucien Bovier again – was he also prone to such inadequacies? *What are you thinki-* At that moment, Collin walked through the door. He hung up his coat, dropped his bag on the table and grabbed a beer from the fridge. "Hey," he replied and went into his office, shutting the door behind him.

Asshole! Couldn't he at least act like we're married?! The strain on this relationship was getting worse every day. As usual, she kept her thoughts to herself and began the tedious chore of drying the dishes. Just then, the home monitoring system they'd installed for Cole began to go off in a series of beeps. All other thoughts vacated her mind as she raced to Collin's office. When she got there, the look on his face told her everything she needed to know.

"He's slipped into a coma," Collin said, wide-eyed with fear.

CHAPTER 8: Vantage Pointe

Twenty-three days later, the meet between the High Commander and Doctor Methis had been lined up. During the wait, Ayla had insisted he get a crash course on the finer points of her research. He'd taken to it reluctantly at first, but the more time she spent with him, the better understanding of the project that registered. It was quite extraordinary!

For the last twenty-two of those days, Lucien had been struggling with the deep, gnawing guilt he felt over his decision to withhold the bonding process risks from Jenna. He was hoping that the good Doctor had taken this time to genuinely absorb the dire information about The System he had disclosed to her. If she didn't, things would only get more complicated from here on out.

He was also praying that she didn't get cold feet once he told her the truth of her situation. Not to mention, he *was* a leading member of The Hand. How would she take *that*?! Whether it was the guilt that he carried inside or the ever-plaguing doubts he had of something going horribly wrong, he resolved to stay true to himself and allow her to make her own decisions. Although he *could* still help those decisions along. Either way, he was determined to be upfront with her and hope for the best.

After dressing in something a bit more professional, he clipped his MIR-30 to his side hip-pack and checked to make sure it had a full charge. The Mini-rail Ion revolver was a specialized handgun given only to Catetons and bodyguards of high-ranking officials. These firearms were coded to each individual Global Identification Chip so that only the designated user could operate them. It was a dangerous weapon that generated a beam of heavy ions produced from a plasma made of inert or reactive gas. In short, it could bore a hole the size of a small dinner plate into a human body within a matter of seconds.

Lately, with his time focused on training the new recruits, Lucien hadn't fired it in some time. He'd still kept it in good condition regardless of the infrequent use; consistent maintenance could prove the difference between life and death. The gun may not be rusty, but *he was*. He preferred his fists to most weapons anyway.

Somehow he felt it would give his enemy a fair, fighting chance and he despised taking a life if he wasn't forced to.

All Cateton soldiers were schooled in the Israeli self-defense system called Krav Maga, it was part of their standard training. This Old World martial art consisted of a combination of techniques sourced from boxing, Muay Thai, Wing Chun, Judo, Jiu-Jitsu, wrestling, and grappling. Although the Art was an effective and dynamic self-defense and fighting system, the basic core principles were contradictory; encouraging it's practitioners to avoid confrontation, but at the same time to finish a fight as efficiently and quickly as possible.

Lucien was quite confident in himself and his abilities in a brawl - weapon in hand or not. It was too bad others didn't see it that way, countless deaths could have been avoided if they'd all shared the same mind-set. The training provided by The System was extremely valuable, but a MIR-30 strapped to his person put his mind at ease and it was always better to be safe than sorry.

He left the building and walked out to his Panzer. Getting behind the wheel, Lucien backed up into the paved street and headed for the security checkpoint. It was located on the other side of the city and the only main road in or out of the Sub-terrestrial. Once he passed the surveillance grid, it was another mile upward through the long twisting road to the surface.

From there he could take the Cateton Private Expressway, which was a System-sanctioned road that held no speed restrictions. Normally he would have taken the Hypertrans, but the Panzer was a formidable weapon in itself; he had a feeling he'd be needing it. Besides, there was nothing quite like driving really, really fast.

The meet was set for 6:00 that evening at the Belmont Building. On the 25th floor of this skyscraper, there was a restaurant by the name of - whimsical as it may sound – The Vantage Pointe. The chef-inspired food here he heard was incredible, but in truth he chose it for its unique characteristic of enclosed, sound-proof booths and enforced privacy.

The owners of The Vantage Pointe, Earl Michael White and Donald Franklin Spice were millionaire business partners who had decided that the public needed something far more interesting than a mere restaurant; they needed - a vision. To that end, The Vantage Pointe catered exclusively to people with secrets and preferred seclusion.

From political conspirators, to shady characters dealing in stolen goods, to rich, lonely wives having extramarital affairs; these were their favored clientele. No cameras or recording equipment of any kind were allowed inside and the entire place was swept every few hours for bugs or other listening devices. The restaurant's well-armed personal security detail stood guard at the only entrance in or out of the building, scanning the G-ID chips of everyone who entered. The privileged paid well for their privacy and exclusivity and so did The Hand of Light.

Pulling into the venue, Lucien popped an Alertisol; the drive had been long and exhausting and he needed to stay sharp. And a stiff drink should ease his sense of foreboding. He SIGHED. *Maybe not the drink...* Before his death, Lucien's father was an alcoholic. Whether that was from being ousted by the other Families or from loneliness and despair, he would never know. Fritz Bovier was a quiet man, spending much of his time shunning the people around him.

He was always more concerned with teaching Lucien his stock and trade than much of anything else. Drinking had become more of a hobby than a pastime and that part of him was passed onto his son. Lucien was fairly confident in his ability to keep in control of his penchant for alcohol, but the latest turn of events were pushing that restraint to its limits. ..He turned the engine off and hopped out of the truck. *It's now or never.*

Entering The Vantage Pointe, Lucien scanned the main room, taking into account every detail. Lined along the outer perimeter were the Privacy Booths, and nestled sporadically in the middle were long tables reserved for large parties. He noted the layout of the area; instinctively planning on how to get around the security in case it came down to it, and what available items he could use as weapons.

You are a single-minded idiot, he told himself as he finally focused on what was right in front of his face: a stunning vision of beauty in white. Not just any vision, but a gorgeous display of a woman at her finest. Doctor Jenna Methis smiled radiantly as he approached the table and walked inside the glass covered booth.

"I thought I should dress the part," she teased as he took her in from head to toe. The snow-white dress hugged her curves as if it was attached to her skin, flowing from her ample bosom down past her slim hips. She wore black high heels which matched nicely with the same dark shade of the grommeted leather belt that draped her mid-section, and the ornamental hair-piece that held her long golden tresses in place was an additional touch of finesse.

"Well, it's definitely a change from your lab coat." *Seriously? Did you really say that?* A stupid comment...and embarrassing at that. *Come on Lucien, you can do better than this...*

Jenna raised her eyes, but said nothing. She was admiring him with equal appreciation and somehow that made him more nervous.

"What I mean is - that's a nice dress." *Stupid **and** tongue-tied.* What was it about this woman that made his heart skip a beat each time he was near her? *This is business, get a hold of yourself!*

"Why, thank you Commander; you don't look too bad yourself," she laughed, gesturing to the seat across from her.

The situation was not as awkward as it should have been. During the past three weeks, Jenna and Lucien had been conversing with each other daily by secure Holo-chat, establishing a decent cover - Ayla's idea, not his. She said it would seem unusual not to know anything at all about Jenna, that it would build a sense of trust and familiarity between the two. It was unconventional, but made some sort of sense; after all, a person would be more responsive to someone they knew and it would be that much easier to gain their trust.

The meeting location was equally important and this is exactly why they'd chosen The Vantage Pointe. Should any inquisitive person ask why they were meeting here today, their actions would show this as nothing more than a new and flowering relationship – an unplanned rendezvous. Although Doctor Methis was married, most of her co-workers had never seen or met Collin in person. Due to the classified nature of her work, only those with high-level clearances were allowed in the vicinity of Psy-Gen Global. They would simply think Lucien was her husband.

If someone she knew walked in, which was very unlikely in this place, they would explain it away as a business meeting. Even then, if instead the assumption went the other way and this was pointed out as adultery, then meeting at The Vantage Pointe with its 'private exclusivity' gave the charade all the more credence. Since Jenna was at the lab more than anywhere else, she had the opportunity to create any one of these scenarios.

Jenna seemed to be perfectly at ease in playing her part; Lucien on the other hand was a bumbling mess of high-strung nerves. *What is the matter with you*, he scolded himself, *just breathe*...His training unfortunately did not consist of being a 'lady's man', that was Tom's forte, not his. If he didn't get a grip on this situation soon, he'd turn into a drooling, blundering idiot! *Too late for that; **now** I could use a drink.* He waved down a liquor cart and ordered a beer for himself.

"And for you, Ma'am," the attendee asked.

"Martini, please, with a twist of lemon."

Jenna watched him with amusement. For all his past bravado, the soldier before her had turned into a scared little boy! The sense that he was attracted to her too was making her feel a bit guilty; there was something about this man that sent her own heart racing! Perhaps it was the intrigue he brought into her daily routine or maybe the growing divide between her and Collin...Whatever it was, she had gotten to know a lot about him in a very short time and it was both refreshing and exciting.

The routine chats for Jenna had started out as aggravating at first, constantly taking her away from important endeavors, but *eventually* she had begun to enjoy them. She found herself actually seeking out the periodic distraction and of course, it was nice to be able to 'vent' her stresses and issues with work out on somebody other than a fellow employee! Restricted from talking about her research due to its classified nature, it was difficult to burden that alone.

She could not discuss much of anything with Collin, but the High Commander was already aware of the sensitive nature of her experiments and he provided a much-needed outlet to get things off her chest. In fact, she was beginning to feel quite comfortable around him; *perhaps more than she should be*. Their conversations had spanned from the horrors of The System to the possible hope of what the A.I. could provide Cole; if it could be accomplished he may have a fighting chance! Either way, he *was* interesting to talk to…

As they'd become more acquainted with each other, Lucien had delved into stories about his personal life. Jenna couldn't help but smile as she thought of his latest tale. He'd attended a school called Sawgus High, an enormous place, holding over 3000 students! So big in fact, that they had to build additional bungalows that soon stretched past school lines and into the large open fields owned by neighboring farmers. It was the night before April Fools Day and Lucien, with two of his friends had jumped the large security fence that wrapped around the school.

Dressed all in black, with tubes of Sure-tight rubber cement in each hand, they had squeezed ample amounts into the door locks of the classrooms. The next morning, all the student body sat gathered around the football field, while the janitors tried in vain to get the rooms unlocked. After two long hours, the principal had no choice but to cancel the rest of the day and send everyone home! It was the best prank of the past five years and Lucien and his friends had lived in infamy from that day on.

It was hilarious, and these were the small things that she appreciated about him; he was not as uptight as she had once thought. Strange attraction or not, Jenna strived to remain passive and professional. It wasn't supposed to go like this and the last thing she needed was to ruin her relationship with Collin! The guilt that tore through her for having these unspoken feelings threatened to overwhelm her.

Lucien sat across from her, drinking his beer in silence when an uppity Maître de, dressed much like a butler stopped at their table to greet them and pour water into the tall crystal glasses. *Damn, that's one ugly son-of-a-bitch; his mother must have been a Saint to take him around in public*…Even as order automation had become the norm, most up-scale restaurants still employed a 'front of house' person to look more presentable. These people also acted as the waiters to serve distinguished guests. *This guy* probably scared off more customers than made them feel welcome.

As the gentleman poured the water, Lucien noticed his rough, calloused hands. Something about the way this man carried himself put him on guard immediately. Suspicious of a possible threat, his quick hand reached for his holster. *Stop it!* Not the hands of a waiter...then again – he could have been a builder before this. He prepared to act, but the unusually ugly man simply asked if they needed anything else and left them in peace. *You have got to get over your paranoia,* he told himself, *you're a trained soldier – keep it together!* Jenna eyed him suspiciously, but remained composed.

Lucien took another look around the room. All around them, rich couples dressed in extravagant clothes, single older gentlemen in business suits, and even a few important diplomats dined on aromatic and fragrant smelling dishes. His stomach rumbled and his mouth watered in anticipation. Everything looked and felt on the up and up. *Relax Lucien.* He was in the company of a beautiful woman and all he could think was how he was going to react in case of an emergency! *You **are** an idiot!*

"Interesting place," Lucien said, forcing himself to get a grip and come back down to reality. Almost knocking over his glass of water, he grabbed a gold-embroidered menu, coughing to distract Jenna from the obvious folly. "I have no idea what to order."

Jenna placed her hand on his and his heart fluttered a beat. "Don't bother; I already took the liberty of ordering for us."

And I'm the chauvinist? That's good, because he had no clue where to start in a place like this. "Great, thanks."

"Are you alright," she inquired, "You're acting so...*odd.*"

Face to face and in person with the good Doctor and she could already see right through him. *Some Commander you turned out to be!* Although he had become quite friendly with Jenna during their conversations, it was a big difference between a Holo-screen and being physically here, right beside her. Why did he find it so difficult to speak intelligently? His stomach was in knots and his palms were sweaty. *Maybe you should start with an apology.*

"Sorry, a lot on my mind lately...Listen, I have to apologize for the...absurdity in of all of this," he began slowly once their privacy was confirmed, "and I'm sorry that you were forced into acting as if we were – you know. That wasn't my idea and if it wasn't necessary,

I – Actually, I don't know *why* it was necessary!"

She shook her head and laughed. "You don't have to apologize to me. After pondering for weeks about everything you've told me, I believe your people have no choice, but to do things with a certain amount of *weirdness*…And by the way Commander – strange as it may seem, I didn't mind our talks…I really enjoyed hearing about your life, it was a nice distraction from mine."

He flashed her a brilliant smile. *If only we weren't in the situation we are in* he thought, *things may have been different.* Then again, she *was* a married woman. But what a woman she was: beautiful; intelligent; sexy; she even had a great sense of humor…*Get your damned head on straight!* This was strictly business and the things they were about to discuss could have a profound effect on the world itself. Sometimes, feelings just got in the way…*Get on with it.*

Before he could continue, the privacy buzzer sounded to signal someone approaching and the enclosure parted as an elegant dinner was served. The mouth-watering main course consisted of a delicious spinach stuffed flank steak with flame-broiled lobster medallions. An orzo rice pilaf adorned a portion of the platter complimenting the roasted asparagus spears lying beside it. They were drizzled in garlic butter and a single chipotle cheese puff finished off the chef's creative genius.

Neither Jenna nor Lucien took more than a moment to savor the steaming aromas rising off their plates before diving ravenously into the gourmet meal. Lucien was pleased indeed that Ayla had picked this place for the meet; the mouth-watering delicacies here were amazing!

For a moment, he could almost imagine it was a real date. *What?!* He was having a great time and suddenly became aware of how long it had been since he was out with a beautiful woman. But then the reality of what he needed to tell her hit home. He had been anxiously trying to get something out for some time now; the closest thing between an apology and the truth that he could muster. He understood now why he was so nervous; he was afraid she would hate him after this…But she had a right to know, no matter the repercussions.

"Thanks for understanding how this all went down…" He paused a little longer than he should have; she knew something was off. "So...I want to discuss a matter that-" he began, cautiously as tiny beads of sweat began to form across his forehead. *No, that didn't come out right – be honest!* He started over again...*with the truth.* "Listen, I haven't been completely up front with you and I am *so sorry*...more than you know. It's about the B.I.O.N.E.X. procedure; the process, it's-"

"*Dangerous*," she stated bluntly, cutting him short, "I know." The surprised look on the High Commander's face spoke volumes. "Come on – I may be new to this, but I'm not *stupid*! You don't think that being a scientist I wouldn't investigate this on my own; that I would blindly stumble into the unknown without facts and research to back it up? It's what I do Commander. And if you're wondering how I found out, I may have forgotten to tell you that I have a level-5 priority clearance. *The emulation process*...it's the only way to create a true Artificial Intelligence, isn't it?"

Shit, a level 5?! He hadn't been briefed on that...*Damn it, Ayla!* "Yes," he answered, "From what Doctor Lockwood explained - in order for it to become self-aware, it needs a human counterpart; more of a *consciousness*, if that makes sense. The B.I.O.N.E.X. Emulation should provide that."

"I'm curious; If that's all you needed, you could have gone to anyone with this, *why me?*"

Tell her. "To be honest, Jenna – it *had* to be you. Your scans provided us with a compatible match for the A.I. Matrix, and that's a *rare* find! There was only one other person we could approach and he would be very difficult to get to. "

"I see," she said, after a moment of contemplation.

"This...process has never been tried before, I want you to know that."

"I understand...It's experimental and there are obviously going to be risks... but yes, I'll still do it."

Did she really say 'yes'?! He'd been expecting the opposite. For the fifth time in his life, Lucien was at a loss for words. He certainly admired Doctor Methis, but knowing the dangers and yet still willing to risk her life for a greater good was something on the verge of chivalrous. He had no idea how he should react or what he should say, so he remained silent and allowed her to continue.

"Once I did my research on the matter and discovered the low probability of success, I won't lie to you – I would have pushed you off a cliff had we been standing near one and most likely made the effort to drop a large boulder on that handsome face of yours. You know, for good measure – just in case the fall didn't kill you," she continued in a pleasant, but eerie tone, "But I took into account everything you'd told me and I thought about my son. Even if I could keep him alive for as long as I could - whether they found a viable cure or not or should he somehow miraculously recover – I thought to myself - *what kind of world would he be living in?*"

Jenna gently reached across the table and took Lucien's hands in hers, green-flecked eyes, a cross between turmoil and elation. She came to the sudden realization that she genuinely had some feelings for this man; what type of feelings or how strong, she couldn't say. She loved Collin with all her heart, but she knew that if given time with Lucien to get to know him better, she may very well fall for him in a different sort of way. There was something about the man that pulled at her heart and sent sensations of lust and confusion rattling about her brain like some biological pinball machine. *Damn it Jenna; what the hell did you go and get yourself into now?*

"Lucien? You still in there?"

He'd been sitting like a dummy just staring at her, lost in the physical touch of her smooth, velvet-like hands atop his. He shook his head as if waking from a dream. Suddenly, he wanted to stop her from going through with it! "Yeah, yes...I'm okay. I don't know what to say...you truly are a brave woman, but are you sure about this? There may be other options out there that we've overlooked..."

She quickly noticed her hands were lingering on his far longer than they should have and pulled them away in embarrassment. "Uhm, sorry...Just hear me out, alright? Now that I know these things, I can't just sit here and do nothing; I *have* to do this! I understand the dangers involved and I want you to know, *I'm okay with it*," she insisted fervently, "I also believe I can help lessen those risks."

Lucien perked up at that. *"Lessen the risks?"*

"Yes, let me show you." She pulled out a mini HOL-COM from her purse and quickly punched in a few commands to place it in privacy mode; it overrode the projection and only kept the information she brought up limited to the screen.

She placed it between them and drew a few sketches with a finger onto the rendered image of a human brain. "Here, look at this...the problem comes from the brain overlap sequence which presents a chance of a 'short-circuit' to the host during the emulation process. However, if we can keep the two consciousness from joining without internal interference, I think the imprint would be contained on the metaphysical level and not the physical one!"

"Uhh...okay. Plain English please."

"Sure...sorry. What I mean is – it lessens the chance of electrical feedback."

He studied the screen for a moment. *That may just work!* Ayla had never thought to consider it. "That's ingenious," Lucien exclaimed, "and it would boost the chances of a successful procedure substantially! Are you're sure you've thought this all through?"

Exiting from and closing the HOL-COM, she placed it back into her black leather handbag. *What is with this guy?* First, he gets her to commit to the emulation and now he's trying to convince her *not* to do it?! She tilted her head to face him. "Listen, all the things you've told me about The System...it scares the hell out of me! I'm not going to ask you to betray your people and tell me what it's going to be used for, but if this is what you need to change the way things are, then so be it. And if you can help my son with his care or if what you say is true, and the A.I. could possibly find a cure to his condition, I will do *whatever it takes!*"

He nodded. "And your family, what of them?"

"I spent the weekend with Collin you know, dancing at the Regula Company over in Hillsborough. We toured the vineyards and shopped at the Vellagio and ate at one of the new restaurants there. I needed that time with him...things haven't been so..." she said, lost in her own stray thoughts, before abruptly coming back to the present.

A wave of jealousy shot through him as she spoke about her time with Collin. *Like I needed to hear that...*Why *wouldn't* she have someone in her life, she was a great catch! He wondered what her husband must be like...hopefully he was an asshole. Maybe he could-*What the hell is wrong with you?!* He shouldn't be thinking this way!

She's willing to go through with it and you are getting what you wanted – this could save countless lives! Besides, she'd already made up her mind...Lucien gazed at her in reverence. This woman was determined to do the right thing and he had to let her...so he decided to help her in any way he could. She looked so sad...

"Are you alright," he asked, as she wiped a teardrop from her eye.

"It's just that...We've been going through some tough times as of late," she continued, "To be honest, Collin and I have been on the verge of a split for some time now. I-"

This must be hitting her harder than she'd let on. It was odd, hearing her discuss her marital problems with *him*; someone she didn't know well... "Jenna, that's really none of my business," he broke in. As much as he wanted to know, he couldn't afford any more distractions.

She wiped a tear from her cheek. "Sorry...you're right. I don't want to bore you with my personal problems. I don't have many people to vent to...actually, I don't have anyone."

Okay, what am I supposed to say here? "Listen, relationships are tough. I'm hardly an expert on the subject, but I do know when someone is hurting. I just don't know if I'm the right person to talk to about this, that's all." And the last thing he wanted to do was play counselor to her marriage, he was not cut out for that...

Jenna cleared her throat and regained her composure. "No, of course not. This is business; I didn't mean to-" *What is the matter with you, Jenna. You barely know him. Why would you tell him that?*

In truth, the short holiday with Collin had been a disaster. They hardly spoke a word to each other in private, but managed to fake it as a couple in public. Sharing her personal life with Lucien wasn't something she'd planned on doing, it just came out. He was so easy to talk to and too much of a gentleman to listen and take advantage of her emotional distress.

"It's fine," he said, a bit too quickly.

Jenna felt strangely hurt by his lack of support, but didn't force the issue. Instead, she changed the subject. "I haven't seen Cole since I've been back. I want you to take me to him...just in case something goes wrong I want to be able to..."

"I understand, of course I'll take you."

Lucien was scared for her – no, *worried* about her, but at the same time, he needed to keep her focused. He resolved to do everything in his power to keep her family safe, even as he knew what needed to be done. "I promise you Jenna – no matter what happens, my people will see to Cole's care and safety and your husband's as well; you have my word."

I wish he would have said everything is going to be alright, she thought. But she *knew* the risks; in fact, she had studied them for weeks and more by dumb luck than research, stumbled upon a safer alternative. Regardless, knowing that her family would be cared for should she not survive, helped alleviate her mounting doubts. She could trust this man and before she went through with this, she had to see Cole one last time.

Lucien felt torn between his allegiance to The Hand and his concern over Jenna's safety. Whatever the final outcome was, he would have to live with it as well. *Stay focused on the objective!* "Before we get off track, I promised you something and I brought it with me as requested." And hopefully he could steer this conversation away from her depressive outlook.

He reached into the rugged military-style Switchpack he had carried into the restaurant and pulled forth a small carbon-cooled chamber, handing it carefully to Jenna. Her face lit up as she eagerly accepted it. Searching the room for prying eyes, she turned her body towards the corner of the booth in an attempt at concealment before she opened it. Inside was a custom-made Adaptive Interface Module. She was familiar with the device: it was a storage unit for high-level computer code.

"It's the A.I. Matrix."

She grinned at him, good-naturedly. "Wow – thanks for clearing that up, I just assumed it was a super-secret black-ops nasal spray."

They both shared a good laugh at that and then she reached into her purse and took out what appeared to be a tiny tube of lipstick. "It's *not that I don't trust you*, Lucien, but I have never even met anyone in your organization. You promised me a solution to the hive-mind failure so I brought a particulate of the Nano-swarm with me."

Another bout of guilt tore through him as he thought about his deception. *But, what the hell was he supposed to do?* She never would have agreed to help them for nothing in return, at least that was what he'd assumed *back then*...should he tell her? He'd already lied to her more than once; revealing this would most likely destroy any trust that was remaining. *Better leave this one alone.* He just hoped the A.I. Matrix would remain intact long enough..."You don't have to explain," he stated, as he waited patiently, immersed in what she was doing.

Jenna pressed a hidden switch on the Bio-suspension Atomizer. She scanned the A.I. Matrix and encoded the data into the Atomizer. It made a soft sound, releasing a needle-thin capsule into her palm. She pushed the Atomizer back onto her hand and it sucked up the cartridge. Bringing her sunglasses down over her eyes from above her head, Jenna ran a perfectly manicured index finger along the side of the dark frame and immediately, the right lens lit up with a subtle reddish glow.

The optic sensor showed the individual nanobots swimming in a viscous substance. A small jolt of electricity shot through the fluid and within moments, the nanites began to cluster together. A few minutes later, they were still intact and they hadn't destroyed themselves. It was *working*, they were beginning to bond with the A.I. Matrix! Although it would not replace a 'queen', they would be able to accept individual programming simultaneously versus having to do it for each separate action. It would save an enormous amount of time and eventually bring her one step closer to her ultimate goal!

"I can't believe it," Jenna exclaimed, "Its functioning exactly as you said it would! Thank you!"

He smiled back at her. "You can see this through those glasses?!"

"You have your Tech, we have ours," she smiled to Lucien, as he looked on, clearly impressed, "You can thank your friend, High Commissar Riordan for this little piece of hardware; it's similar to a spectrasope, but allows me to view the subatomic behavior of the Nanites! This one is a modified version of what we call a Cryton Spectralyzer. It's-'""

The Spectralyzer! How did it get- He was familiar with this device, although it looked very different from what he had seen years ago... *And Riordan?* Why the hell would he..."*I know* what it is," Lucien interrupted, frowning deeply, "Riordan *gave* this to you? What did you tell him?!"

Jenna returned a funny look. *Why is he so angry?* "No – Lucien, I didn't tell him anything about this – nothing. I only sent in a spec request for this device. *Why*...what's the-"

The Privacy Buzzer sounded again notifying them of another possible intrusion to their conversation. Each booth had an auto-lock and manual over-ride switch in case customers seriously did not want to be disturbed. Lucien knew he was too late as their much-too-ugly Maître de came forward with a tray of decadent looking pastries and bite-size cakes.

"Dessert will be served Sir; we have mini Red Velvet Fusions with a chocolate eruption sauce or if you prefer – German Chocolate Linzer-"

Without waiting for further explanation, Lucien grabbed his belongings and herded Jenna roughly past the surprised man and towards the exit of the restaurant. "What are you-"

"We have to go Jenna. Now!"

Steering her through the exit and into the velvet-inlaid, glass elevator, he kept watch for possible signs of trouble. His gut told him something was wrong. Three other occupants were already inside, talking loudly amongst themselves. Lucien stood beside her in silence, warning her with a shake of his head to keep quiet. The external shaft of the Belmont Building's lift was an amazing achievement.

On one side, there was a 25-story tall circular aquarium with several types of exotic fish swimming frantically about; the onboard onlookers followed their every movement in awe, pointing and gasping at a group of brightly-colored marine life. The opposite side of the lift opened up to an expansive view of the city. Lucien didn't have the luxury of admiring either of these things as his attention was directed to the street below, looking for anything unusual.

As soon as the elevator hit the first floor, he took Jenna by the arm and led her towards his Panzer, strategically parked in the lot outside. He was happy to have brought the formidable machine, it was an armored all-terrain, military vehicle. The Panzer Mach-5 was capable of plowing through extremely heavy snow, mud, or water; it was strong enough to go through a four foot thick concrete wall and remain relatively unscathed.

Being as this was the Commander's transport, it was weaponized with ion cannons which were retractable within the vehicle itself. Powered by a prototype hydro-magnetic fuel cell, it topped out at speeds a little over 200 miles per hour and included all the bells and whistles: Infrared surveillance equipment, a night-vision modulator, on-board communications and holo-navigation.

Once they got in, Jenna could not keep silent any longer. *"What the hell* was that all about?"

Starting the Panzer by scanning his G-ID chip across the ignition-guard, Lucien placed it into gear and sped towards the highway with an irritated look on his face. "Listen Jenna; what we are doing here is of the *utmost secrecy*. The members of The Hand of Light are not known to *anyone* in the general public and sometimes not even to each other. If those people are exposed, The System will not hesitate to neutralize us as quickly as you would an insect in your home. We *cannot* afford to be discovered!"

"Okay Lucien – but what the hell does that have to do with *anything*," she screamed at him, and then came to a sudden realization. "Wait a minute, are you saying...you said 'we'! *The Hand of Light?!* You Son-of-a-"

She turned to him suddenly, hitting him on the shoulder with a clenched fist. "You Asshole! Are you telling me that you are a goddamned *terrorist*?! All this time...all the things I told you!?"

Jenna pushed against him, almost causing him to crash into the vehicle beside him as she tried to unsuccessfully pull the handle to open the door. "Stop the truck, damn it!"

He grabbed her roughly by the arm. "Are you crazy woman?!" He quickly pulled the Panzer off to the side of the road bank. Still holding her arm, he turned her to face him. "Look – everything I've told you is *true*! You yourself have admitted that things are *all wrong* in this world; you not only accepted that, but I thought you *understood* what needed to be done here!"

A Cateton who was also a rebel? What had she gotten herself mixed up in?! "Come on Lucien - that was *before* you were a member of The Hand! All this talk about The System makes sense now! You're *murderers*...all those people at the Executive Bureau-"

"Don't be a fool!"

"*A fool?!* How dare you; they were human beings who died in that fire! Are you so callous that-"

"*Yes, they did*...but you still don't get it! All those people you're worried about, *they are The System*, Jenna," he corrected angrily, "*They* are the killers. All those cowards hiding underground, why do you think they are there? They're scared of rebellion! They've *destroyed* democracy and freedom as we know it and they did it *willingly*; they've planned this for centuries, don't you realize that?!"

"*Centuries?* You're starting to sound like one of those nut-jobs in The Slums...It doesn't excuse the fact that people were killed," she countered, looking away from him, "*And you* – you're a terrorist?!" Being a Cateton was one thing, but a member of *The Hand*? She'd heard stories about these people; they were responsible for extremely violent acts and the destruction of numerous System satellites!

"There's a saying Ayla used to tell me when I posed the same question - one person's terrorist is another person's freedom fighter - it's all a matter of perception. I consider myself the latter and I can tell that you are mistaken about The Hand. Do you *truly believe* that The Amalgam would have in their employ, anyone who disagreed with their goals, their tactics, or their views?! These people have been scanned, interrogated, and tested for their loyalty. They-"

"You mean like you have?"

Lucien sighed deeply. "Okay...I'll give you that. All I can say is that these people are the epitome of evil; the ones that can look you in the face and smile as they slit your throats. Whatever you may think of me, The Hand has used extreme care in making sure that the primary targets are taken out with the least amount of loss to human life. I won't justify it, I don't believe I can. But I will tell you that we are *not terrorists*; we have always fought *for the people*, not against them. Now, will you please remove your hand from the door?"

She obliged, but the fear in her eyes betrayed her unspoken thoughts. He should have told her everything from the beginning, this was exactly what he was afraid that would happen. *"Look at me*, Jenna. Do you think I'm the type of person who would so callously take an innocent life?! I'm a soldier, *not a murderer*!

I should have been honest with you from the start; I see that now and *I'm sorry*. The targets we've hit have been mostly vacant and as far as the Executive Bureau building, we just couldn't wait any longer. The NAS Chip would have destroyed any semblance of free will we still have left! The world would have gone back to the days of legal slavery...we couldn't let that happen!"

They sat in silence for almost a full five minutes. Jenna couldn't believe what she'd just heard! The man she'd gotten to know over the past few months was part of the *resistance*?! Yes, the NAS chip was a total violation of human rights – even she knew that - but that didn't justify all the people who were killed in destroying that technology!

What else was he lying about? She didn't know how to feel about this, but if she ran, what then? He would only track her down and then there'd be hell to pay, who knew what he would do to her! She had to act calm, allow him to relax, and then..."Alright," she finally said, "I'm...still trying to *process* all of this...I can't say I agree with your methods, but I won't argue with the results. But you people-"

"Then let's just leave it at that," he snapped.

Doctor Methis seemed to have calmed down enough to at least acknowledge the bigger picture, Lucien thought...or else she was just biding her time to escape! After a few more moments of silence, she snorted and shook her head in irritation.

"I'm sorry I kept that from you, Jenna...I have certain obligations."

"Yeah, that helps," she rolled her eyes at him and then looked out the window at the highway signs. "You mind telling me where we're going?"

"I made you a promise and I intend to keep it. I'm taking you to see your son."

"And then?"

"Then we meet up with Ayla."

"For the procedure?"

"Yes."

"So soon?"

"Jenna, we don't have any more time to waste."

What a jerk! "Fine, but I still don't understand *what we are running from?*"

Lucien put the Panzer back into gear and pulled out into the highway. "As far as I know, the Cryton Spectralyzer has just *one function* – to view the recombinant bonding behavior of a Nano-swarm. It was developed by the Dagon scientific team and there are only *two* known to exist!"

"And? What does that-"

"Once our Nanotech research stalled, that device you have was confiscated by the Global System Defense Front. For some reason, they didn't want us to continue with our work. If it wasn't for Kallen's research...never mind - it doesn't matter. Just believe me when I tell you that sooner or later, they *will* be coming for us!"

She finally grasped what he was getting at. "And the High Commissar heads that division..."

"Did you truly think Riordan would have simply handed you something this *specific* and not asked twice about what you were going to use it for *unless* he already knew? I *know the man*, Jenna - he's Black Ops – If Riordan is involved in this project, you can bet he is *weaponizing* your Nanotech! Rest assured he would never have allowed you to take anything from Psy-Gen without keeping an eye on you, especially something as valuable as that!"

Jenna nervously twirled at a stray lock of blonde hair as his meaning sunk in. "And you think...he might have someone following me? But if he knows about the A.I., does that mean he knows about *you*? My God – that's it, isn't it?" Had they found out Lucien was a member of The Hand? That meant his entire organization was in danger! And if that was the case – *so was she*! No wonder he was acting so strangely.

Deep in his own thoughts, he barely registered what she was saying. The trust he had tried so hard to build was broken, that much was evident. If she opened her mouth, The Hand would be in grave danger and that would leave him with limited options... Lucien had no desire to hurt her, but he also couldn't- *Damn it!* He should have been honest with her from the start!

A loud horn interrupted his thoughts as he narrowly avoided a collision. The traffic was horrendous! An old man in a rusty, blue pickup truck cut him off as he tried to merge into the left lane. *What is wrong with these people?! This doesn't happen in the Ozarks, people actually know how to drive there...*The ancient bastard flipped him off as he passed by. *Yeah, yeah you old fart, hope you have a stroke before you hit the next light*! *Stay focused Lucien!*

"Commander?"

"What," he snapped, coming out of his trance.

"Do they know about you? Does Riordan-"

That was a good question..."Now that I can clear my head, no - I don't believe that he does; I've been building my cover since after the Seals. We could have met at The Vantage Pointe for any number of reasons and nothing about the Nanotech was discussed in public, except in a very secure location." He steered the Panzer onto Highway 25, which led directly to Princeton Memorial Hospital and re-checked the rear view mirror for the 7th time. "But something doesn't add up and I have to protect my organization's identity and my people; I can't take that chance!"

"I understand."

If there was even a remote chance she would talk, he had to disappear! He couldn't cause this woman any harm...it wasn't her fault – *it was his*! "No, you don't Jenna...After I have the B.I.O.N.E.X. scan, you and I must go our separate ways. We cannot be seen together again, nor can we take the chance to converse through Sat-com, Freeband, or Holo-chat. If Riordan is onto you, we may all be in danger...I've enjoyed getting to know so much about you in such a short time and I was sincerely hoping we could stay friends, but-" He stopped short to focus on his navigation.

For some reason that comment really hurt and Jenna's heart sank, like a heavy stone to water. *He's just going to drop me once he gets what he wants...What kind of silly thought is that? You sound like you're back in high school again and your prom date just dumped you!* His words irritated her, but she knew deep down it wasn't like that, at least she hoped not. After a few minutes of silence, she placed her hand on his thigh. "Why can't we? *Remain friends*, I mean?" Great, she was going from one extreme to the other, her emotions were in utter chaos.

"You know why...it's too much of a risk. As much as I'd like to, there are too many others involved who *cannot be exposed*. I'm sorry Jenna...I truly am."

"Me too," she replied quietly. *Now leave it be!*

Her touch sent tingles down Lucien's spine and he tried in vain to ignore them. It was not what he wanted either, but he had a larger responsibility to the Cause. Even though something about this woman made him feel like a pudgy, naked, winged child had shot an arrow through his heart, he knew he had to let her go.

Where the hell did that come from; do I have an obsession with her or something? He buried his feelings and steered the Panzer through the Bolivar Exit and towards the visitor parking lot of Princeton Memorial. They pulled in between two large non-descript vehicles, camouflaging the truck effectively from plain sight.

"I didn't mean to go off on you like that," Jenna mumbled, under her breath, as they parked.

Ignoring the comment, Lucien stepped out of the truck, and walked around to open the door for her. "We're here, let's go see your son."

CHAPTER 9: Assassin

Walking up towards the front entrance, Lucien scanned the immediate area for any sign of trouble. A food stand was adjacent to the main path, offering up a variety of delicious smelling foods to the hospital staff. All around him people were talking, eating, and smoking. A loud siren was heard in the distance and he watched as an ambulance pulled into the E.R. Even though it was a clear day with blue skies, the air around them smelled sickly.

*Incredible detective work – it **is** a hospital – congratulations Dipshit!* His body relaxed as the tension in his clenched fist gave way; he was feeling a bit sheepish…There were no clear signs that they'd been followed so he let Jenna lead them through the entrance and towards the middle annex. Patients in hospital gowns milled around the main visitor's foyer, having conversations with family and friends. He and Jenna walked past them in silent retrospection.

As they took the elevator to the 7th floor, Jenna felt a strange sense of loss that she couldn't explain. Was it for Lucien…or could it possibly be for Collin? Perhaps this is for the best she thought, things were getting a bit too complicated for her to handle. *Anyway, what the hell are you thinking – you are married with a child, and besides that – you've only met this man in person twice!*

But at the same time, she had gotten to know Lucien quite well and he was a *good* man. *Oh enough already, the best you can compare this to is a strange dream about online dating.* Besides, wasn't he a terrorist?! She was doing this all for Cole, right, maybe even the greater good? So why did she keep feeling as if she was cheating on Collin every time she was with Lucien?!

The doors opened to the Intensive Care Unit and they quickly made their way to Room 702. As they quietly stepped in, Cole Methis gently stirred, somehow aware of their presence in his room. The place looked much the same as it had the last time Jenna was here, except for an ebony vase overflowing with pale yellow roses.

No, there *was* another difference – this time Cole *wasn't* dying! It was only two weeks until his 19th birthday and here he was – laying like a slab of meat in a damned hospital bed in the ICU! Her heart strained whenever she thought of how something like this could have befallen someone so pure and innocent, it just wasn't fair! *God, I feel like crying.*

She'd come here to spend some time with Cole before she underwent the B.I.O.N.E.X. procedure and just looking at him lying there placed doubts in her head. If something went wrong, would she ever see him again; would he be alright without her? She knew that Collin would take care of their boy as best he could, but she had the nagging feeling that if she died or worse – suffered irreparable brain damage - Collin would be completely lost.

She'd thought long and hard about her choices and if one person could make a difference, then she may as well try. After all, who knew how long Cole had left. At the very least, he would get the best medical care possible...and be protected. It had been so long since she had heard Cole's sweet voice and as she took his hands into hers, it only confirmed that today could be the last few moments she may have to spend with him. Peering down at her son, she prayed for a miracle

At 6'2", his thin frame took most of the bed, feet almost pushed against the footboard. His sandy blonde hair was disheveled and dirty, but on better days, it matched his fierce blue eyes perfectly, painting a picture of a strong, handsome man. He had been a slender child most of his life, but laying for so long in that hospital bed, he seemed to have wasted away into little more than skin and bone. She brushed a lock of hair from his face. It hurt her so badly to see him like this. *Please Baby, wake up!*

"Oh Cole," she sighed, "Can you *hear* me?"

There was no reply except for the faint sound of his chest rising and falling. She stood there in silence, holding his hand in hers.

Lucien watched the boy for a moment. "What happened to him, Jenna?"

Fresh tears fell from her eyes as she spoke. "H-He lapsed into a coma some weeks ago, we don't know what happened. What he has...it's a disease called Spinal Muscular Atrophy, he was born with it...there is no cure."

Lucien felt even worse than before. "I'm...sorry, I didn't mean to bring that up."

"You know, he was the Captain of both the football and basketball teams…and a phenomenal student…he had a future once."

Lost in his own thoughts of the pain he may be causing this family, it took a moment before Lucien realized she had replied to his question. "Uhh...no. That's quite an accomplishment; I'm sure you are very proud of him."

"I am...I miss him so much; he doesn't deserve this!"

He could do nothing more than watch. What more can anyone do for a mother whose son is dying right in front of her? The boy looked frail and weak. He wondered how he would feel if this was his son lying there. Not that Lucien had one, but he was sure he would be heart-broken if he did. A silent prayer went through his head as he turned away from the sad sight before him.

After almost an hour of contemplative silence and little talk, Lucien gently placed his hand on Jenna's shoulder. "I'm sorry, but we have to go."

"I know," she replied as she bent over to kiss Cole on the forehead, and then followed Lucien towards the lift. She felt almost hollow, like there was an emptiness inside her. As they boarded the elevator, she felt physically ill. She put her arm out to steady herself and grab the handrail. A sudden jolt almost knocked her over!

As Jenna pressed the button for the lobby, the closing elevator was abruptly stopped. It happened so fast from there that she scarcely had time to even register much more than the loud bang that followed. Something was wedged in-between the doors and she heard herself scream as she recognized what is was. It was not one of the customary Ion-cannons that were the weapons of choice for the Catetons, but the long smoking barrel of a Smith and Wesson 500 Magnum, a gun belonging to The Old World!

Her father had been an avid gun collector, an odd hobby for his pacifist nature...regardless, she recognized the cannon by sight. These guns were outlawed as it was extremely difficult to trace weapons that were not pre-coded to a person's G-ID chip; even the ammunition you could only get on the Black Market.

This 'beast' in particular was an extremely dangerous weapon, one that fired a .50 caliber bullet and was once rumored to be one of the most powerful handguns in the Old World. Someone had fired at them! And whomever it was not only wanted her or Lucien dead, but he wanted to make certain someone would notice!

The first bullet had blasted a hole the size of a small melon through the back wall, narrowly missing both passengers. Jenna was frozen with fear, but Lucien reacted immediately, slamming the emergency door open with a fist and then charged at the unknown assailant.

Unprepared as he was to see the High Commander - alive and coming at him - the powerful tackle brought the attacker down hard against the solid tile floor. Managing to somehow kick the dangerous weapon far enough away, Lucien picked himself up, backing away slowly, even as he came face to face with...the ugly bastard from the restaurant!

"Oh, come on," he muttered under his breath. *That'll teach you to ignore your instincts!* Who was this man? He had followed them and tried to kill them! *But why wait to do this at the hospital? Because it made sense*, he answered himself. If this guy would have tried anything at the Vantage Pointe, he would been shot on sight.

He heard a scream come from the elevator, signifying that Jenna was still in there. *What is she doing; why hasn't she run?!* He didn't have much time to observe more than that as he focused his full attention on the assassin before him. Fists flying in a blur and in utter silence, the man came at Lucien hard and fast.

The blow meant for his nose whizzed by, close enough that Lucien felt his hair ruffle with the force of it. From the corner of his eye, he saw his opponent's right foot begin an upward trajectory. He raised his hands to block, but too late – Lucien was struck painfully in the jaw, sending him reeling at least three feet onto his tailbone.

Seeing his opening, the stranger immediately pulled out a viciously serrated Light Blade and went straight for Doctor Methis. Dazed and aching, Lucien forced himself back onto his feet, only to see the man brutally stab Jenna in her side! Luckily, the knife went in at an awkward angle, preventing the blade from going in too deep. The cruelty in the man's eyes shone bright like a predator going in for the kill.

She screamed in pain and shock as he reached his arm up and back to bring the dagger down yet again – this time for a killing blow!! Lucien launched himself at the man and seized his arm in the middle of the downward stroke. He hauled him backwards by his throat and knocked the knife from his hand.

"Jenna, **RUN – NOW!**"

Frightened beyond belief, she needed no coaxing to do exactly that. The dull throbbing pain along her side began to grow in intensity with every tiny movement she made. Jenna spun around quickly, holding her dripping wound in anguish and tripped...over the still-warm, but lifeless bodies of two I.C.U. nurses; their throats had been slit from one end to the other!

She was painfully shocked to find one of them was Florence Henderson! But Florence was Cole's nurse...*Oh my God – Cole!* He was alone and helpless; she couldn't let this man get to him! Bleeding profusely, she forced her heart-rate back down until she finally had a semblance of self-control.

Purposefully calm, she could now hear the shouting and screaming all around her as the remaining staff ran for their lives in every direction. She struggled with her instinct to go with them, but she knew she had to get to her son! Turning towards the ward, she noticed that somehow, a fire had started and it was spreading quickly. Wafts of black and grey smoke were drifting across the 7th floor, forcing her lungs into a coughing fit. Adrenaline took over as she forced herself to keep moving.

"Ughh"

Lucien hit the wall face first, his chest taking much of the brunt. The man was obviously well trained and he knew how to fight. Using the wall as leverage, he swung himself around just in time. The assassin had retrieved his own knife and was staring at him through murderous eyes. Luckily, he'd armed himself before coming into the hospital. Lucien reached behind his back, unsheathing his own Light Blade and the two met in a clash of glinting steel.

Lucien swung the blade in a tight arc, but was blocked by a forearm. Using his left hand, he pushed against the man's elbow, twisting his foe downward as he brought his knife-hand towards his head. It would have been a killing stroke, but the man went with the movement, narrowly avoiding a brutal slice. The killer turned his entire body to the right, striking Lucien with an elbow to his side. He went with the blow and they both came to face each other once more.

"Who are you," Lucien demanded, "What do you want with her?!"

His only response was an ugly, crooked smile as he came at Lucien yet again. Blocking a backhand thrust with both forearms, Lucien countered with a hammer fist to the crease of his assailant's elbow, at the same time, bringing his knife-hand down. The man grunted in pain as the blade opened up a shallow wound across his chest. Using the same hand to go in for a stabbing thrust, he was deflected by a quick block as the man used his free palm to strike Lucien's throat.

Tumbling backwards, he tried to regain his breath as he anticipated the man's next move. But instead of continuing the attack, the killer turned and ran the opposite way. Disoriented from the smoke and the pain, Lucien forced himself to stand up and ran after him. He needed to take this butcher down before he could get to Jenna!

Stumbling down the hall and into Room 702, Jenna was relieved to see that Cole was unharmed. Still lying in his bed, he was oblivious to the events taking place around him. Hacking uncontrollably from breathing in the black soot, she shut the reinforced hospital door, locking and barricading it with the visitor's armchair. *What the hell just happened?!* Someone was trying to kill her, she knew that much. *But why?* Who did this? Deep down, she had a gut feeling she knew, but she pushed it aside immediately. *Not now.*

Jenna winced in pain as her side grazed against the leaf of a nearby Weeping Fig. Investigating the damage, it didn't look good; somehow she had to stop the bleeding! The blade appeared to be a shallower stab than she had originally thought. Any deeper and it might have punctured her kidney; she would have died faster than she could have saved herself. She grabbed a small towel and placed pressure on the wound, taking a moment to catch her breath.

Not more than a few minutes later, there was a loud slam against the door and an angry growl came from behind it. "Arrgh; I will get in eventually! You can make it so much easier on yourself if-"

"Go to hell, you sick bastard!"

"You're *going* to die bitch! Of that, I have no doubt! Open the door and I promise *I'll make it quick.*"

Shit, what now?! Frantically Jenna searched the room for something...anything she could use to defend herself with. Finding most of the cabinets locked, her eyes settled on the purse on top of the small end table; *her* purse! She was so distraught with everything that had happened to her, she must have forgotten it there.

Limping to the table and quickly dumping out its cargo, she scanned around for anything she could use as a weapon, preferably something sharp. *Why didn't you listen to Collin and get that weapons scan authorization?!* A small bottle of Hydroneurontin tumbled out with the rest. *Thank God!* She quickly swallowed a few pills for the pain and resumed her search.

Another powerful bash to the door caused the worn armchair to jump as if it had a life of its own. A few more of those and he was getting in! What had happened to Lucien, where the hell was he?! The only items from the purse that were of any real benefit were a nail file and a pair of clippers. What the hell was she going to do with those, clip his nails and hope for a bleeder?! She laughed to herself in spite of her worsening situation.

As she clutched the nail file in her bloodied hand, she noticed the Atomizer laying amongst the scattered contents. *Idiot, you'd lose your own head if it wasn't attached!* She had a sudden revelation...*The Nanotech* - Jesus, could this be what they were after?! It made sense that the same ugly man from the restaurant was the one trying to kill them.

A near-functioning Nano-swarm was invaluable to many mega-corporations, competitors or otherwise...especially for military applications - *Riordan!* Her intuition told her this may be what was going on here; Lucien was right! But how did they know if she'd even succeeded; had he been spying on her? With one hand, she picked up the Atomizer and placed it back into her purse. Maybe she could somehow get it to the High Commander before...

Suddenly, the monitoring alarms attached to Cole's torso began to go off. A red light on one of the machines started blinking on and off as another beep joined the chorus of grating noise. *Oh God, not now, why now?!* She struggled to her feet and watched his body convulse; his heartbeat was getting weaker, something was terribly wrong!

Jenna struggled to her feet and took Cole in her arms, frantically shaking him, hoping it would bring about some kind of response. "Cole? Come on baby, please...wake up!"

The frame on the door splintered as the murderer crashed into it again. He was in a rage and the entire situation was making her lose focus. Smoke was now starting to trickle in from beneath the door and the air was getting hotter. Jenna forced her breathing to slow down to keep her frantic emotions from consuming her.

"I *will* get through! And when I do, I'm going to flay the skin right off your bone!" The raspiness in his voice made it all the more terrifying as the drifting smoke altered his speech.

"You *won't* get that far," she heard a familiar voice say in the distance. *Lucien, he's still alive! Thank God!*

The High Commander stepped out of the shadows as the killer turned away from the door, acknowledging the soldier's presence. The same questions were going through Lucien's head even as he struggled to assess the situation. *Who sent this assassin after us; is he here for Jenna or me? How did he find us? Is this about the Nanotech? Does he know about The Hand?!*

The look on the man's face was etched with a coldness that sent a shiver down Lucien's spine; he was determined to do whatever it took to get through that door. This time however, Lucien was ready for him. He had to put this guy down fast; the air around them was getting harder to breathe as his mind calculated his next move!

He charged the stranger before he had time to react and their dance of death continued once more. Luck was against him as the man stepped smoothly aside. As he flew past, he grabbed Lucien by the shoulder with one arm. Turning inwards, Lucien used a straight hand to come behind his wrist and break the hold, throwing an elbow to his face. Swiftly kicking the man at the knee caused him to stumble.

Following through with a hard palm to the chest sent the killer sprawling backwards. The man recovered quickly and came back with a wide swing. Blocking with his left forearm, Lucien reached his right hand up and around the stranger's arm, swinging downwards leaving the man's face unprotected. Another elbow to his nose brought about a flow of gushing blood.

Behind the barricaded door, Jenna prayed that Lucien would gain the upper hand. She quickly weighed her options as the grunts and struggles were heard outside. If she opened the door, it would expose both herself and Cole to immediate danger. If she didn't, Lucien may be killed! But Cole was dying...*she* may be dying herself from lack of blood! If the killer succeeded in getting through, she resolved to protect her child. There was no doubt that they would die horribly as he had promised and she could not bear to witness her son's suffering at that murderer's hands.

If he broke through...*when* he broke through, she was too weak to defend herself, much less Cole. And that was if he didn't pass away in the next few minutes! Besides, what chance did she have against a murderous thug? Even if she could fight, she had lost too much blood. Should she somehow get past the killer, there would still be no hope for Cole. There were no doctors or nurses to save him; they were all gone...or dead. There was only *her*. *Think, Damn it!* The incessant beeping of the machines wasn't helping...her head was pounding, her pulse racing. *Why is this happening?!*

Cole's heartbeat had slowed considerably and his face appeared paler. She had to do something *now*. Her Sat-com registered no reception was available so she reached into her handbag and fumbled through the side pocket for the HOL-COM, her hand brushed against the Atomizer. Maybe she could contact Collin, but what good would that – *Wait* - the Nano-swarm!

She played a scenario out in her head. *Could it really work?* Jenna already had the programming code, including the restoration protocols! Frantically, she opened the HOL-COM and uploaded the directives to the Swarm. Hypothetically, they were capable of repairing and rebuilding organic tissue! They might be able to save Cole; maybe even heal him! It was untested - which meant there was a very good chance it could kill him - but he was *already* dying.

Theoretically, it was possible; scientifically it was a foolish risk! In the next few minutes, it wouldn't matter anyway, she had to try! The door behind her slammed hard again, creaking against its frame. Weak from a loss of blood, Jenna reached for the Atomizer and fumbled for the injection switch. She forced herself up, kissing Cole once more on the forehead, tears in her eyes.

"I love you baby, always remember that."

She tore open his hospital gown to expose his bare chest. His heartbeat flat-lined and as the alarm began to go off, signaling cardiac arrest, she injected her son with the Nano-swarm. The last thing she heard was the door bursting open before darkness claimed her for the last time.

CHAPTER 10: Rebirth

Cole Methis slept...and dreamed peacefully. For what seemed like ages, he'd been stranded in a surreal world that did not seem to be of his own making. As always, he was walking through an endless meadow, passing by people he knew or loved: family members, friends, school-mates, and other acquaintances.

No one spoke to or with him; it was a strange scene that kept repeating day after day. They recognized him as well and each time he came closer, their blank faces would light up in knowing smiles and phantasmal hands brushed against his, in comforting gestures of love and friendship. It was strange, but tranquil in a way.

He wanted to stop and speak with them, to share experiences, maybe even gain some insight as to why he was here. But each time he tried, it was as if his feet had a mind of their own. It felt more like he was on a moving walkway that followed a specific invisible path through this beautiful meadow that seemed to go on and on and on.

As long as he'd been here, he had become accustomed to the strange 'rules' of this place. In fact, he never tired, he never became hungry or thirsty, and he did not remember the last time he had stopped walking and slept. *I **must** be dreaming...nothing else makes sense.*

Still...the tranquil beauty of this place was a sight to behold! A gentle breeze swept along the golden path he walked. The thick, lush grass was a strange shade of dark green, it was almost blue in the rays of the much-too-close sun that hung in the cloudless sky. The thick, brown-grey trunks of immense and ancient Redwoods dotted the landscape. Stretching up into the heavens, the giant alien trees towered over the entire meadow in an eerie, but stunning spectacle.

Red, showy tulips and pearl white lilies were scattered around the tall, green grass and white, snow-capped mountains rose grandly in the distance. Birds sang melodious songs all around him like they were somehow trying to communicate. The steady rush of a distant, but unseen waterfall filled the silence of the meadow in the constant rhythm of a meditative symphony. It was...*perfect*.

All in all, Cole thought to himself, *not a bad place to be.* But the nagging question was *'where am I'?* How did he get here and why couldn't he leave? As beautiful as it was, he couldn't get over the fact that something was wrong; he shouldn't be here...Today was just like every other day, although something was different in the air; he couldn't quite place it-

"Arrrgh!" He collapsed to his knees, a sharp stab in his chest almost taking his breath away. He slowly forced himself back up.

What's happening?! Cole let out a scream as another bout of anguish threatened to overwhelm him. Gradually the pain subsided and...he could feel his legs again! *What the-* Suddenly, his senses sharpened ten-fold, causing his head to spin with vertigo. He could distinctly hear the rhythmic flapping of the birds' wings; even the roaring of the cool breeze was like a hurricane to his ears. He could see the insects on the leaves as if he was standing right there!

The drum-like beat of his heart pounded loudly in his ears. He clutched his chest as he stumbled onto the worn green path. His body felt incredibly weak, as if it hadn't moved in months, his arms and legs were numb. But with each step he took, it was flooding with newfound strength and he quickly regained his balance. Something was happening to him!

Out of nowhere, Cole heard a thunderous clap and the ground beneath him began to shake violently, opening up fissures in the once peaceful meadow. The skies darkened as black clouds rolled in, the giant trees swayed in the distance, and he heard the animals crying out in fright. He was thrown furiously off his feet with a great heaving of the terrain, as if a gigantic mole was burrowing underneath the ground. *What the hell?!*

Dazed and confused, he looked ahead as he forced himself up with unsteady hands; the entire meadow was cloven in two! An enormous gaping hole ran down from the earth as far as his eyes could see, with no apparent end in sight. Cole heard the scurrying of insectile legs and within moments, what appeared to be tiny white spiders crawled up from the breach in multitudes of hundreds...maybe thousands! *Now would be a good time to wake up!*

His heart was beating so fast that he started to hyperventilate, feeling on the verge of going into a seizure. He tried to back up, but wasn't fast enough! On eight spindly legs, they came at him, swarming all over his feet and quickly scurrying up towards his face. *Oh God* – they were heading for his mouth; they were trying to get *inside* him!

Cole screamed and frantically tried to brush them off of his body, but his hands just went right through them as if they were not even there – *that's impossible!* Too late - he could feel them crawling into his mouth, down his esophagus, and into the pit of his stomach! He began coughing and choking, gasping for air. Suddenly, he was inside his own skin – seeing infinitesimal events happen simultaneously as if peering through an electron microscope.

Things took place in the blink of an eye! The miniscule spiders began to descend into his bloodstream, ferociously biting through the membranes of his cells, then being absorbed by the bacterium itself and growing into a bloated sack. Moments later, the entire cocoon burst, sending forth a mutated version of the intangible insects.

These new monsters appeared to be a cross between a metal-like construct and some biological form of life. Comprehension flowed into him as he understood what he was witnessing take place before him – the birth of a new virus!

Each new cell they bored into created multiple instances of the pathogen until the infection had spread throughout his entire body. His strange, transparent sight then ventured into the brain area where he saw a new form of spider infecting the brain stem; this one was a deep red and did not seem to be reproducing. Instead, thin glowing tendrils of a wispy substance connected it to all the others like a sophisticated network of nerves.

Suddenly, an electrical current was discharged from the red mechanical hybrid. Intense pain shattered his thoughts as millions of other spiders were given new life and as one, fought his own mind for dominance! He opened his mouth to scream and found that he could not control his own actions. Something was invading him, a presence of some kind that wrestled for mastery of his conscience; *something intelligent.*

A sense of drowning...or being smothered overwhelmed him, only to be replaced by something much worse. Cole felt as if small portions of himself were blinking out of existence and being replaced by a strange new life form, given omniscience. He found his own mind enticing him to give in to whatever was attacking him, to allow it to envelop him in its cold, dark embrace. It *wanted* him to stop fighting for survival as he had his entire life; to give in and finally...be free.

Cole felt himself sinking deeper and deeper into oblivion and an unusual calmness filled his being. His mind swirled into a black hole of confusion and fear, coalescing into fragmented thoughts. He would soon stop being such a burden to his family and his mother and father could go on with their lives...His mother would...be so...*angry*.

Why did he think that? Shouldn't she welcome it, wouldn't she be happy? NO! She would feel betrayed...sad...hurt. He was *giving up*, taking the easy way out. Whatever it was inside of him was wresting control of his emotions – because he was too scared to thwart his own fate! It felt like his mind had splintered into a million pieces and was slowly being put back together like a child's jigsaw puzzle.

His parents had been scared as well, but they were there for him through every good and bad thing that had happened in his life; they had cared for him even when the Doctor's had said it was a lost cause! They hadn't given up on him, they never would. Then *why* was he so inclined to quit? Why was he so unwilling to try? *He had to fight!* He had to force out whatever had possessed him, take back control of his mind! And he had to win...or lose himself forever – he was certain of that.

And so he did - Cole fought back with every fiber of his being; with every emotion he had held trapped for so long: love, hate, desire, and most of all - anger. After what seemed like an eternity, he felt the strain on his mind give way...Cole sensed that the presence was aware of what he was doing...more than that – it was *afraid*.

It had falsely lulled him into surrender and tried unsuccessfully to...*replace him*. There wasn't another word to describe it. Slowly, yet firmly, his confusion became clarity and his fear was replaced with a sense of purpose. The frightening sensation of being consumed into nothingness seceded. He could breathe again…

He pushed, pulled, and clawed himself out of the dark pit he had fallen into and with every inch he took, the entity retreated until he had pushed it back upon itself. *It knew*...It understood that for it to survive, it would need to submit to him – completely and utterly. To feel any semblance of emotion was confusing to it; as alien as it was to Cole. The invader did not comprehend how to process these strange new feelings...or combat it. Opening its mind up to him, it grudgingly allowed Cole in.

A long, single, continuous drone started from afar, becoming louder and louder as it broke into a chorus of static-filled noise. Suddenly, Cole was...somewhere else and he was not prepared for what he witnessed. The blackness opened up into zigzags of color: black and green lines forming themselves into grids.

The scene that flashed across his mind reminded him of a giant circuit board. He was formless, moving blindingly fast as if he was riding an electrical pulse. Ahead of him loomed an enormous silver sphere with a glowing orange center.

At first, it seemed malevolent, but that must have been what only his human mind registered. Whatever was moving him was aiming his bodiless form straight towards it. This thing was...alien, but strangely welcoming. It was *watching* him, it knew he was there. It was...*intelligence made manifest*. The orange middle suddenly blinked open, resembling the eye of a predator and he shot through it and back into the darkness. Cole felt a tingling in the back of his head, an almost physical sensation.

It began like fingers softly caressing the nape of his neck and then became rougher, like sandpaper as it went. Instinctively, he knew it was the entity. But this time, it was not invading; this time it was...becoming a part of him – merging with him. It felt like his physical shell was a costume and something was putting him on...or maybe the other way around.

In an instant, a white hot glow grew outwards from the center of his mind, getting brighter and brighter until it enveloped his entire field of vision in bright iridescent light. There was a pressure in his head that throbbed with an irregular beat. It was not painful, rather his mind opening up into a greater consciousness. [WAKE UP].

As he took his first real breath in what felt like years, he knew he had won the battle - one he was certain only he knew he had fought.

"Doctor Lockwood, we're getting a reading!"

Cole stirred in the Med-Chamber, slowly turning onto his side. As his vision cleared, he could make out faces above him in the blinding light. He felt foggy and light-headed, but strangely alert at the same time. A sense of feeling flooded his body…he could move again!

"Holy shi– lie back son; Doctor Lockwood!"

He saw a pretty young woman in a lab coat running towards him, her eyes wide open in a look of pure bewilderment. She immediately began to take all types of readings from a multitude of strange whirring, beeping machines that were hooked up to his torso. *What the hell's going on?! Where was he? Who was she?*

The woman placed a warm palm under his sweat-soaked head and a mask of concern formed across her features. "Cole…Cole Methis, right? How are you feeling son, can you hear me?"

"Y-yeah…I-I think so." His voice cracked, his throat parched.

The woman held up her index finger in front of his face. "Follow my finger with your eyes, please."

Cole complied with her request, but *something was different!* As he shook off the fogginess in his head and his eyes adjusted to the light, he could see clearly now…in fact, he could see - *perfectly!* Cole took the opportunity to scan the room.

Not only did he notice the array of lighting that came down from the ceiling, but he could pinpoint the seams where the various parts of it came to fit together. Even peering into the Doctor's face, he witnessed the slight mis-aligned blemishes of imperfect skin. He could see each stitch of thread in the cotton sheets that blanketed him. *How odd…*

It was almost like when he used to sit in one place and stare at something until it focused into each of its individual parts. Except it used to take intense concentration before, now it was…*normal!* His eyes blinked furiously of their own accord and just as suddenly as it was brought on, it dissipated and his vision returned to normal.

He was in some type of surgical room, at least that's what it appeared to be. Robotic-looking machines were positioned around the spotless white tile as medical monitors took readings of all his vital signs. Small scanning implements were laid out on the table beside him and a large virtual screen showed his internal workings.

"W-Who are you," he sputtered nervously, "Why am I not in the hospital? Why do I feel like...Blechhh!" Bile spewed up from his gut and ran into his throat, finally ending up all over the scrubs of the young man who had spoken to him when he first woke up!

"What the hell, you little shit" the orderly screamed like a small girl, as he ran as fast as he could from the room, looking quite pale and sickly himself. As nauseated as he felt, Cole couldn't help it; he broke out into a fit of laughter!

"I...I'm sorry," he tried to explain, as he came down from his high.

The pretty Doctor or whomever she was, appeared to be amused by the recent turn of events, trying hard to stifle a grin. "It's okay, Archibald probably deserved that for something he's done in a past life. Glad to see you're feeling much better though. We thought we'd lost you, you've been out for some time!"

"Archibald; seriously?" *Of all the questions you could have asked...*

"I think that's what *he said* when he was old enough to know better," she joked. He liked this woman immediately; she was very kind *and* had a good sense of humor! "My name is Ayla Lockwood and you're not at Princeton Memorial anymore."

"Huh...then where am I?"

"You're in an off-the-books military facility owned by The Hand. We didn't quite know what to expect! You-"

"A what? The Hand of Light? The *terrorists?"*

"Trust me, you're better off without the details. You're *safe*; that's what counts. Better yet, you're *alive!"*

Cole knew very little about The Hand, but he did know they were responsible for multiple attacks on System-controlled sub-stations. They'd been labeled as terrorists, but so far the people here did not seem like the dangerous fugitives the media had made them out to be. It looked to Cole as if they had saved his life. Unless they wanted knowledge he did not have, there really was no reason for them to hurt him. *Relax!*

Either way, at this point he did not have enough information to make a determination if they were here to help him or harm him. His intuition told him the former. *Just go with it.* Cole rubbed his sleeve across his mouth, wiping away the remains of the rancid vomit. *"I'm so damned thirsty!* It feels like I haven't drank anything in months!"

She motioned to the orderly and he quietly handed Cole a large plastic container of water. He took it impatiently and began to greedily gulp down as much as he could.

"That's because you haven't," she replied. "Listen Cole, I am going to tell you some things you may not want to hear..."

CHAPTER 11: Shadows

A rough, calloused hand adorned with expensive gold rings breached the shadows as if it had materialized from thin air. The hand held a custom MIR-30, aiming it with precision at the head of the man cowering in the corner. It was dark in the room, but that did not belie the fact that the office was extremely large and spacious.

Works of art by prominent artists hung on the far cream colored wall, precisely placed in the shape of an inverted cross. The 15-foot tall windows, usually opening up to a grand view of the city stood partially covered by expensive Venetian blinds. It looked like the typical office of a top executive, except for the laid-in red and black tiles which were arranged in a unique star shape that aligned the middle of the floor.

A lone man sat at an immense mahogany office desk, barely silhouetted in the light of the last remaining rays of sunset. The man in the shadows waited patiently as if in deep thought; his suit-covered arms, the only sign that someone was behind the desk. He sat there in the dark, rubbing an ebony crucifix between his thumb and forefinger. Suddenly, he turned to face the other two in the room and regarded the whimpering man, cowering in the corner.

"*Come now Genarro,*" the man behind the desk drawled in a thick accent, "Tell us what we want to know and Michael will make this quick, *won't you* High Commissar?"

Genarro stared up at the barrel of the weapon in unveiled fear, pale as a ghost as he scrambled for the words to stay his execution. "Please Lord Lehovec...I beg of you!"

What a disgusting pile of rubbish! How was a man such as this admitted into The Amalgam's employ?! *Whomever vouched for Genarro must also be dealt with lest he or she bring more undesirables into the fold.* This pathetic semblance of a man could not even accept his punishment graciously; the spineless coward that had now replaced the once stoic man was definitive proof of that!

Lord Lehovec sneered with contempt. "I will ask you one last time.

How did they get past Cateton security? How did they know where to find and destroy the data? How did they bypass the Vault?"

"Sir, I told you," Genarro pleaded, his voice shaking in fear, "I have...no idea how-"

"You are in charge of the entire Cateton force for the Executive Bureau Building, yes?"

"Yes, but-"

This is getting nowhere; best to put him out of his misery. Lehovec nodded to the man holding the gun.

"Kill him and get the body out of my sight!"

"As you command Lord Lehovec," replied High Commissar Riordan ecstatically as he squeezed the trigger.

A loud, whirring hum came from the gun and Genarro's brain matter exploded from the base of his skull as his head flew back hard against the reinforced wall. The now headless corpse twitched with the last of its death throes as his red pool of life began to flow off the plastic sheeting and permeate through the lush white carpet.

"Do not displease me by being careless Michael," stated Lehovec, gesturing to the blood running its course over his office matting.

"Yes, Lord Lehovec." He quickly pulled up the plastic to quell the flow of the blood.

"On second thought, *burn the body*," Lehovec ordered, "What news of the 'Traitor'?"

The High Commissar appeared to be caught off guard. "I sent Kolschak to dispatch her. She was followed and executed at the hospital."

"Has Kolschak reported in then?"

"No Sir."

"And why is that?"

Riordan cleared his throat in hesitation. "He's dead, Sir."

"I see."

"But one of the targets has been neutralized," he put in, much too quickly.

"Rather messy, don't you think?"

"It got out of hand, Sir. It was the best option while they were both together."

The older man silently took some time to consider what he'd been told. "Hmmm...*And how did you know it was her, Michael? I did not divulge that information to you.*"

"I had my suspicions for some time Sir. I've studied her profile; I know her mannerisms; and she's made mistakes, but the brain scan confirmed them. It was *her*...I'm aware that you allowed Doctor Methis to continue her work unhindered, to gain the Polymer. It was well played."

But how did Bovier get mixed up in all of this? The only reason that was unusual was because the High Commander was the head of Ozi's Catetons; he was a servant of The System! What was he doing with *her*? If it wasn't for Methis' request for the Spectralyzer, her usefulness would not have ended. But it had proved her work complete and due to this, Methis and her son needed to disappear!

No loose ends; it was their way. Unfortunately, Bovier had been in the wrong place at the right time...And what would Lehovec think about him knowing Lucien on a personal level? Better not to complicate matters; all he needed to know was that Michael Riordan was of sufficient value to The Amalgam.

Lehovec grunted, a self-satisfied look appearing across his face. "Very well. And the research, how far was she?"

"I believe Doctor Methis had found a solution to our problem, but..."

"*But what*?! Let's have it."

"It is most unfortunate, Sir, but what knowledge she had, passed with her death. She did not keep anything on file; it was all up here," he said, pointing to his temple. "However, we believe that the High Commander of the OZI City Catetons, Lucien Bovier, may have somehow been involved. We have footage that it was he who eliminated Kolschak. I already had all evidence of the altercation destroyed. He could have been passed knowledge of the Radiose data, but *he is also missing.*"

"What do you mean, *missing*?!"

"I'm sorry, Lord Lehovec, but neither Bovier's Global ID Chip, nor the boys could be tracked. There appears to be some sort of interference when we attempt to triangulate the signals. However, we are keeping an operative stationed near the boy's home."

Riordan could see that his Employer was on the verge of a meltdown, the anger clearly evident on his face. It was best that he was not here to witness whatever followed this man's rage.

Amazingly, with no more than a few short breaths and a moment of contemplation, Lehovec brought himself down from the precipice of rage. The self-control of the man was impressive. He was silent for over three minutes, evidently lost in deep thought, his eyes closed in concentration. Michael knew better than to interrupt and so he waited patiently.

"I want you to initiate the *Overwatch Program*," Lord Lehovec commanded.

What; Now?! "Sir...we are hardly ready for the final phase. If you will give me some more time to-"

"I said – *do it!*"

The High Comissar stared at Lehovec in confusion, but who was he to argue. "Yes Lord Lehovec. Sir, you have *no need to worry*, I will make certain-"

Lord Lehovec's bared-teeth smile was intimidating. "Oh, but I *do worry* Michael. Your 'friend' Lucien Bovier and the boy have not been accounted for. I want them found and brought to *me*."

Friend? Did he already know? "Does that mean you want them alive, Sir?"

The malicious glint in Lord Lehovec's eyes spoke volumes. "I want them *able to speak*."

High Commissar Michael Trevor Riordan took the elevator from the sky rise down to the lobby, walked calmly outside to the atrium and emptied the contents of his stomach into the large terra cotta planter. He had come very close to being laid in the dirt beside Genarro; mistakes were not well tolerated by Lord Lehovec. Sometimes, the man's ferocity scared even him!

Still - there was much to be gained from serving him: wealth, power, survival, and eventually – a seat within The Elite. Besides, the Amalgam had taken him in after his stint as a Blackburn Cateton for the System. They had given him purpose and the chance to be his own man; he was now Lehovec's personal enforcer.

Although his position had made him both efficient and coldly calculating, Michael was a killer long before he was an assassin for The Amalgam. He remembered hearing somewhere that psychopaths were born, not made...maybe there was some truth to that.

It was ironic that at one time, he could have been on the opposite side of all of this. Back then, he may have fought against Lehovec's system of tyranny and been at odds with The System. But that was then...it was different now.

His life-long career in the armed forces had begun in the Old World, as a soldier for the United States military. At the tender age of 19, he was subsequently fighting in the war with Iraq and many other transcontinental incursions. Although he was seen as just and fair in his dealings with the enemy, he was considered antisocial by his peers and had a strong propensity for violence.

The way he was had nothing to do with his past. There had been no physical or mental abuse growing up; there were no traumatic experiences in his childhood; nothing strange had happened to him during his upbringing.

Once Michael joined up with the military, he was simply curious to see what he could do, and his brutal environment provided him with the opportunity to do just that. His superiors had preyed upon his already fragile state of mind and re-made him into a loyal soldier. They had put Michael in charge of his own team and unleashed him upon the unsuspecting world.

Throughout the years, he, along with the other brainwashed soldiers soon realized they were fighting someone else's war. Not for the 'freedom and democracy of our country' as suggested and widely-believed by the general public, nor for the purpose of finding WMD's, but for pure profit and greater political power!

There was a monumental difference in protecting one's country from foreign invasion and going to war for bullshit reasons. Furthermore, these conflicts between our government and foreign ones had nothing to do with *our freedoms* in any way whatsoever.

He began to realize that to the army, he was simply another pawn. One that was used for a specific purpose and then, when his use was over, would be discarded like garbage on the side of the road. It had happened with many of his former comrades and that disgusted him more than their bullshit excuses for going to war.

The stressors of war and his progressive disillusionment of what the military stood for became the driving force that forged him into the man he was today. Michael Riordan wanted something more for risking his life and he wasn't going to get it by earning it. No, he finally understood that if you wanted something bad enough, you had to take it, no matter the consequences.

By the time The System disbanded the separate military factions and transitioned them into the Cateton Global Command, he was a changed man. He didn't have much in the way of emotions anymore, nor did he strive to learn to recognize, control, or express any. As far as he was concerned, a man without the baggage of remorse was powerful and in his current line of work, this was a huge asset to have. He began to reach for higher aspirations and eventually found himself in the sights of The Amalgam.

After recognizing Riordan's 'special skill set', his superiors soon understood that they had a unique and single-minded psychopath in their employment. Someone they hardly had to twist to carry out their bidding; rather someone who was already...twisted.

He was a man who could be counted on to get the job done, regardless of how messy and bloody that may become. In less than five short years, he became the personal enforcer to Lord Magnus Lehovec, the High Seat of The Amalgam. The High Commissar was smart, violent, power-mad, and quite likely a sociopath. He was death, made flesh and blood and he fit right in.

Even now, a small part of him felt dirty...he *was* dirty; a 'wolf in sheep's clothing', a *traitor* to his family, his former comrades, and to much of the known populace of the world he lived in. And he was...okay with that. As much as he was disgusted with himself, he was bound to The Amalgam.

Yet, he reveled in the power and status it granted him; he wanted...no – he *needed* more! But the thought of doing in his friend, High Commander Lucien Bovier was a problem. The boy he could care less about, but he and Lucien had personal history.

He had seen the potential in the younger man during his time with Blackburn; Lucien was a natural born killer – the only limitation being his conscience. Riordan had taken Bovier under his wing and seized the already built-up military know-how and fighting abilities Lucien had gained with the Seals and expanded it to the next level.

Bovier had surpassed most of his expectations, but no matter what trials he put Lucien through and regardless of the harsh punishments he dished out, the bastard still held onto his damned moral compass! He had an indomitable will, that one; he couldn't be controlled. No matter - If Lucien couldn't see reason, he would make every effort to bring him onboard – *before he was given no other choice.*

The last time he had seen the High Commander, it was right before he had been recruited into the Global System Defense Front, which was little more than a pretense for the group of highly-trained assassins who served The System. They were completely loyal to The Amalgam and carried out their every command.

Whether that be executing their political foes to providing protection to high-value leaders such as Lehovec, these men were always ready for action. The missions he was sent on were highly classified and he performed them well and without any moral constraints.

So why was it that for a man, mostly devoid of emotion, Lucien Bovier was such a hard mark? For once, here was someone he would rather *not* kill. Perhaps, he thought because throughout his unstable, shallow semblance of a life, the High Commander was the only *friend* he'd ever had.

The only person he'd felt a kindling of love for; a brother in arms. His only other relationships consisted of little more than leading his men and following orders. Either way, Lehovec's plans were swiftly descending into chaos and it was up to him to take back control.

If that wasn't complicated enough, Lehovec had ordered the commencement of Overwatch! Even he knew the Program was not yet ready for the next phase. The subjects had proved...unstable at best. They had not perfected the process and he was afraid they never would. The Radiose Polymer was the key and now, that might also be lost to them.

All due to the constant barrage of attacks led by The Hand. The damned Rebels had accomplished the impossible by taking down the Executive Bureau Building! Soon, the other factions would rally up against them as well...But there was still a small window of opportunity to re-establish a sense of order...

But how had they done it? Whomever was responsible for the destruction of the Executive Bureau Building had not only gotten past the ample security, but also broken into the Vault! It was almost as if they had walked right in, as easily as going for a Sunday stroll. Lehovec was furious! Maybe it was best that he had kept the part about the IRQ Implant to himself. If Lehovec was angry now, what would he have done if he were informed about that?!

No, it was better to keep it under wraps – indefinitely. Regardless, the back-trace they had attempted led to the cloud servers of The Java Mill, a coffee shop which had close to 1900 locations that spanned across the globe. There was no point in spending valuable resources to hunt down a lead that couldn't be found. No, instead he'd have to do it the old fashioned way.

Katya Prulova boarded her private jet, a customized Hullstream H600 for the long flight to CABALA City. The central Hypertrans would have been much faster, but she preferred the familiarity and comfort of her own transport. National Republic Armaments had satellite offices around the globe and the one they were heading to was the second largest facility.

The meeting with Tom Quinn had gone well. It had been a little over a month since she'd seen him last, although she didn't miss him any less. They'd been together for over seven years; sometimes on, sometimes off. More akin to marriage actually, without all the commitments and work that you had to put into something like that. She truly cared for Tom but in their line of work - marriage, two kids, and a white picket fence were a fantasy you only dreamed about.

Opening her compact to fix her makeup before landing, she saw two jaded crystal blue eyes staring back at her. Brushing back her dark brown locks, she was shocked to see the distinct pattern of crow's feet forming around them. *You're much too young to look this old,* she thought sadly, *maybe a brow lift is in order...*

The trip had been exhausting and she looked forward to a strong drink and a long nap. Now, the flight to Kazakhstan would cast the additional weariness of jet lag upon her person. And then another tiring limousine ride to the base and finally a Hypertrans to her satellite office. Not that she minded coming back to the city though; Kazakhstan itself was a breath-taking, exotic place filled with deep mysteries and amazing sights.

It was the largest land-locked country in the world, with more than a 131 different ethnic groups living there. It was home to the Baikonur Cosmodome, the world's first and largest space launch facility and a large number of geoglyphs depicting swastikas, rumored occultish symbols, and other bizarre representations of strange designs!

Even in the Old World, most had never heard much about the place. During that time however, it was a little known player having access to vast natural resources, including major deposits of petroleum, natural gas, and minerals.

Along with strategic trade and transit routes, the one-time country had one of the world's best economies. Interestingly enough, Kazakhstan was also the number one producer of Uranium, having an excess of over 15 mines! The only downside was that radioactive or toxic chemical sites associated with former defense industries and test ranges scattered throughout the country posed health risks for both humans and animals. For CABALA city and its inhabitants however, being over two miles underground and encased in a protective dome, there was no need to be concerned about detrimental effects. To Katya, it was home.

"We'll be landing soon My Lady," Sophie Devereux said, interrupting her reverie, "Is there anything else you may be needing? A cup of ginger tea perhaps?"

As her personal attendant, Sophie was extremely well organized in the way she kept track of appointments, meetings, and expenses. As a person however, she was annoying, controlling, and arrogant.

"No, I'm fine Sophie, thank you."

"Maybe a Scotch and a crumpet then? Miss, you really should *put something in you.*"

"I believe Mr. Quinn has already taken care of *that*, Sophie," she laughed. But the younger woman only stared back at her with a blank look on her face, clearly not comprehending or appreciating the sexual innuendo.

"Ma'am?"

"Nevermind...thank you, Sophie, that will be all." *Why couldn't I have hired someone with a sense of humor? Was that too much to ask?*

Tiredly, Katya turned her gaze to the window. The golden sun was perfectly situated in the light blue sky, not blindingly bright, but strong enough for its rays to give the scenery below a grand symphony of darks and lights. *Up here, you wouldn't even know how polluted the Earth really is*, she thought to herself. She could see the majestic peaks of the Tengri Tag mountain range, home to Khan Tengri, the most northerly seven-thousander in the world.

For climbers, such as herself, this was a big deal. Other famous landmarks included the Charyn Canyon - much like the Grand Canyon in the United States - and the Singing Sand Dunes, a desolate, but serene place of wonder. She reclined back into her seat and took some time to meditate before they reached the one-time city of Almaty.

Katya's mother was born in Almaty and had spent her younger years as part of a center-right political movement, before becoming a liaison to the International Monetary Fund. *Here you go again, dredging up bad memories better left buried.* The IMF did not exist anymore, but according to their statutes, the organization worked to foster global monetary cooperation, promote sustainable economic growth, facilitate international trade, and most importantly - regulate exchange rate stability.

The Hand of Light was convinced that the institution had another goal entirely. Soon after Kazakhstan became the base of operations for the IMF, the world economy stumbled; not as disastrously as it would after the third World War, but enough so numerous regions had to declare bankruptcy.

These countries could not pay back their international debts and their individual currencies were becoming next to worthless. The International Monetary Fund, claiming its intentions were to meet global demands for more reserve currencies and to build a stronger foundation of global economy, took the opportunity to act in accordance to their goals.

A new form of currency, the Global Reserve Bancor Credit or GRB Credit was introduced to be a replacement for the now weakened medium of exchange that existed in those bankrupted countries. Any ward willing to 'trade in' their existing defunct banknotes for GRB Credits were initially given two and a half times the value of their old legal tender. Most would consider this too good to be true...*It was.*

After the third World War destroyed any hope of economic

redemption for most of the known world, other regions soon followed suit. The International Monetary Fund, indirectly owned by the same 13 Families who would eventually put The System in place, now had total and complete authority over these countries' wealth, well-being, and economies. The rumors were that they were putting into place 'puppet' Presidents, tyrants, or high-ranking officials to gain control of everything from each state's resources and politics, to dictating new laws and regulations that were to be followed unconditionally.

As all new currency was now controlled and distributed by the IMF, the people had little choice. They could either lose the ability to purchase food, property, and invaluable offerings such as medical care and insurance or join the status quo, and accept their hopeless situation. Ultimately, even the GRB Credits would become virtual and be integrated into the Global Identification Chip. Within a few short years, The System would soon be initiated and the powerful figures behind the veil would have something they had been striving for since the beginning – Control.

As far as Katya was concerned, the IMF had never been what they adhered to be! Was it not strange that almost every single Old World country which the IMF and World Bank got involved with ended in a crashed economy and a destroyed government? It was a brilliant process which accomplished this...first, they would open up capital markets, selling local banks to foreign ones.

Then, they established a free market system in which prices were determined by unrestricted competition between privately owned businesses. Finally, they opened these countries' borders to trade, forcing all industry into a state that the globalists fully controlled. This was the reason provinces like China could charge a 40% tariff on the U.S. while the U.S. could only charge 2% to them! It wasn't free trade; it was coercion.

The IMF was successful in destroying global financial stability, but that was not all. They were responsible for other lesser known deeds such as purchasing millions of tons of grain and burning them to keep the world prices stable. They spread rampant Communism, forcing people into class systems where they work and are paid according to their needs and abilities. They set monetary inflation and rates, driving average citizens into boundless debt. It was all a carefully orchestrated system of subjugational control!

Her mother, Alma Prulova had built her vast wealth upon the ambitions of the same powerful people who perpetuated The System in the first place and it was a legacy Katya resented her for. Soon after her tenure was complete, Alma obtained investors and started National Republic Armaments.

With the world-wide connections she had built up through her time with the IMF, her company already had vast distributorships in place. NRA grew into a dominant position amongst the smaller ones; buying them out and absorbing them into the parent corporation. Soon, they became the largest weapons manufacturer in the world and had remained ever since.

Katya was suddenly jolted from her seat as the jet hit some irregular turbulence, coming in low for a hard landing. Flying through these stormy skies was frightening enough without the added bruising to her own body. Once the plane came to a complete stop, she led the way through the cabin with Sophie in tow, struggling with several pieces of Louie Vuitton luggage. The portly chauffeur waved them both into the stretch limousine and off they went. Just one more stop to make before Katya could finally take a much needed breather – The Intra-Global Railway Station.

This complex network of underground tunnels ran from one Sub-terrestrial to another, spanning the vast distances between them. The passages could be used for many things: transferring equipment, supplies, foodstuffs, construction and manufacturing materials, and most importantly – Cateton soldiers, military-style vehicles, and weapons. The tunnels under Kazakhstan happened to be the common connecting point and mainstream transport site that led from there to all the other Sub-terrestrials.

Katya pressed a switch on the side panel of the onboard bar and a small refrigerated compartment released its valuable contents. She opened the elegant looking bottle and poured herself a glass of Chateau Lafite 1865, an exquisite and very expensive sweet red wine. She had read somewhere that a bottle of Lafite once sold for a record $111,000! She was saving this for a very special occasion and this was as good a time as any.

If she were discovered or caught, none of this would matter anyway. As she brought it to her lips, she noticed that the color was a light ruby red with just a touch of subtle brown. It tasted fresh and pure, with a hint of tannins still present. *Oh Tom, what a shame you aren't here to share this with me*, she thought to herself. Katya reached for a linen handkerchief and wiped the still forming beads of sweat from her forehead. She didn't realize how nervous she truly was. She had every right to be. After all, she had one more bomb to plant.

CHAPTER 12: Emergence

In the far corner of the isolated room, stifled sobs could be heard. Cole had been huddled there, hiding for what seemed like hours. Anger; fear; resentment: all these he could feel and acknowledge, but the deep down feeling of betrayal was something new. If his mother was dead, why hadn't his father come looking for him?

The sense that he was not being told everything permeated his thoughts. Times like these when the cold truth of reality overcame his memories, he would weep away his grief in what little privacy he could get. He judged it had been a little over two weeks since he'd woken up in that VR bed.

The first four days, he had taken the time to recover, both emotionally over the news of his mother's death and physically from being immobilized at Princeton Memorial. The next seven days, they had put him through one exam after another: physical fitness exams; endurance testing; multiple blood samples; a CT scan; an MRI; and constant medical diagnostics.

During that time, they'd hooked him into all sorts of monitors and machines that took everything from his vitals to God only knows what else! The rest of the time he had been isolated in this room, alone - except for the frequent visits by Doctor Lockwood.

She had taken several days to care for and get to know him on a personal level. Thanks to her, Cole was starting to feel more like a person rather than a lab rat. She was nice enough to talk to, but at the same time, avoided answering many of his questions. The days just came and went filling him with increasing frustration.

The interesting thing was that he should have been exhausted from all of this, but he wasn't. He had not felt tired for days since he'd woken up and the energy only seemed to increase as the days went by. Perhaps all that bed rest had revitalized him...or perhaps it was simply the boredom of being cooped up like this.

The kind woman had explained to him very little of the events that had led to him being here. The only facts he *was* sure of were that some psychopath had stabbed his mother and she had succumbed to her wounds in the same hospital he had spent the latter part of his life in. A friend of Jenna Methis - someone they called the High Commander had fought the killer and unable to save his mother, had chosen to liberate him instead. Her story however, still seemed to be full of holes.

Why would someone want to hurt him or his mother? What did they have against his family? Who were these people? Why had they brought him here instead of to his father? There must have been a good enough reason. Did they think him stupid? Were they looking down on him, manipulating events, trying to trick him? He didn't think so.

Why would they do something like that after going through all this trouble to save and rehabilitate him? That didn't make sense. And what was with all the medical testing? He was obviously fine, even better in fact than he'd ever felt before. Except of course, being hungry...again. What were they not telling him? Perhaps his paranoia was getting the best of him...

Either way, the red-hot anger that burned deep within Cole threatened to overwhelm him. He wanted vengeance upon the people who took his mother's life; whomever had done this deserved no less! But what could he do even if he should find them? He was barely into adulthood and had little, if any idea how to fight, nor was he capable of harming a fly, much less another human being.

And that was if he could escape this place he was trapped in. If he did, then what? He didn't know where he was, how to get out, or whom to contact. Thinking this way was a waste of time and eventually, he resigned himself to accept his fate...whatever that may be. *Not as if you have much choice in the matter anyway...*

Wiping the still fresh tears from his eyes with the back of his hand, Cole forced himself up and made his way to the quilt topped queen-sized bed. The spacious room they had put him in was a large rectangular shaped area with an expansive window facing east. It was not a personalized space by any means.

There were no other colors except for the standard black walls surrounding the cream-colored carpeting on the floor; no knick knacks were scattered around, no posters or framed pictures up on the walls, and no personal belongings anywhere in the closets, drawers, or in the room itself.

Besides the full length mirror hanging from the wall, the only other semblance of comfort were the Holo-View coming from the wall and a black and silver HOL-COM resting on the bedside table. The better assumption was that it was a guest room of some kind for in-frequent visitors...or maybe permanent *prisoners*.

Laid out on the mattress were a set of clothes: a plain white nylon T-shirt, socks, a pair of boxers, running shoes and an all-black Track Suit of some hybrid material. The first week he was stuck wearing only a hospital gown. Later he'd been given a pair of a size too-big green athletic shorts and a red long-sleeve thermal that had emblazoned on it in large bold letters 'YOU CAN'T FIX STUPID', overlaid on a picture of a hand with its finger pointing up.

It was courtesy of the gentleman he'd vomited all over. Maybe Archibald picked the ugly get-up on purpose, hoping to get even...or could be he was just an intense fanatic of Christmas. Cole was pretty sure it wasn't the latter.

Anyway, something clean and different was a nice change of pace. He quickly removed his old clothing and put on the fresh ones. The trousers were lined with a breathable porous, nylon fabric and the zippered jacket had hidden zippable vents in the back and armpit areas. There was even a dark green micro fleece cap and waterproof leather gloves, obviously optional for incremental weather. Being cooped up inside, he didn't really know how he could utilize those, but he was glad to have them nevertheless.

Once he finished dressing, he plopped down onto the small couch, trying in vain to relax. *Now what?* He was alone once again, with nothing to do. *How uninspiring; why didn't they put in a gaming system or something?* It would have been nice to have his Gibson acoustic with him; it had been ages since he'd played...he missed the course feel of the strings against his fingers.

More so, he missed the peacefulness that came with composing music. At any rate it was wishful thinking...these people didn't owe him anything. Cole lay waiting for a full ten minutes feeling lazy, going through some options in his head, but finding himself again at a loss for something to do. Maybe he should run in place and get some exercise? He could do some push-ups and try to re-gain some of his strength.

All that time laying in a bed should have literally wasted away much of the muscle in his arms and legs. But he felt physically perfect...powerful even, with an abundance of energy. In fact, he had noticed that he was quickly putting on muscle throughout his body without the benefit of *any* exercise!

Besides that, it should have taken at least three to six months to recover, even with rehabilitation and kinetic therapy. Instead he had not only regained much of his lost mass, but also added to it! *How is that possible?!* Even more bizarre was the fact that he was upright and walking! Yet two more questions for Doctor Lockwood it would seem.

Another thought hit him. Perhaps with all the lost time, he should get caught up on current events. After all, many things of considerable importance must have happened over the past few years. As a child, Collin had assigned him the daily task of reading up on a news article and reporting to his father what he had learned.

At first, he always complained and considered it a boring waste of time. Later, he found that there were benefits to that knowledge...It turned out to be a rather useful tool in impressing a girl's parents; to be able to carry on a conversation with his elders on topics kids his age usually weren't aware of. *Who knew?*

Regardless, he had a lot to catch up on. *You've got nothing but time, use it wisely.* "Viewer On. All news channels onscreen," he said, giving the voice command to the Holo-View. There were twelve channels in all, but a number of these showed unimportant things such as the weather or were in the middle of one commercial or another. "Channels 2, 5, and 23 please." He didn't really need to add the last comment, but his instinctive politeness was ingrained into him by his parents. This *also* was a nice little benefit to impressing most people.

Channels 2 and 23 were going on about the yearlong delay to the newest policies, rules and regulations set forth by the Executive Bureau due to the acts of terrorism that had sabotaged the building. *Holy shit! The Executive Bureau was bombed?!* Every four years, the Bureau tweaked existing laws or put into place new global legislature for the masses to assimilate and follow. Before he was hospitalized, he had heard in Policies class that this anniversary year, The System would be implementing the Neural Assimilation Chip.

It would replace and be an upgrade to the Global ID Chip. The new Chip would work much like the outdated Retina Scanner, allowing information and data to pass from one medium to the other, but unlike the R.S. someone could never falsify a cerebral network.

A person's mind was the world's most powerful biological tool and as every snowflake was unique, the same was said of the human brain. No longer would everything from bank accounts to identification need to be tediously uploaded and coded to the G-ID chip. Directly connected to the neural cortex of the brain, the new NAS Chip would instantly update all information the User processes in an expediently fast fashion.

As expected, rebellion and picketing had broken out by specific public watchdog groups, but were quickly quelled by the Cateton Militia. The insubordination came from the fact that the NAS Chip would not only make things far easier for The System, but The Amalgam would also be privy to every bit of personal, business, and private information of anyone they chose to investigate.

Information they could access at any time or anywhere they wanted! Of course, they had said there were fail-safes in place to keep this from happening, but no one believed their empty promises. *Thank God The Hand had put a stop to that!*

And stopped it they had. Perhaps they weren't the 'bad guys' after all...In a bid to create the software, hardware, and mechanisms for the Chip and keep them highly classified and safe, the Executive Bureau had gone to great lengths to keep most available databases, information, and blueprints stored in one single location. Common sense would dictate that storing invaluable information like this in one place would have been altogether foolish, but the Executive Bureau Building was the most *secure* location in the world! Severe paranoia probably played a part in that decision as well, no one really knew which divisions the rebels had infiltrated.

Who would have guessed that The Hand could break into and destroy invaluable System data in such an impregnable fortress! Not that they should, given that the Executive Bureau Building was heavily guarded with state of the art security and Catetons in close proximity who could be summoned within a moment's notice. There was much more to the building that met the naked eye!

The grounds themselves were weaponized with self-arming ion cannons and flying V4 drones, whizzing to and fro about the structure. If that wasn't impressive enough, the top-secret information that was kept there was located in a vault that consisted of a 25-ton blast door which required a 10-person retina scan to unlock. *And that* was after getting past motion and heat detectors, a laser system grid, and 5 feet of solid granite.

The place was deemed impenetrable, but somehow, The Hand of Light had infiltrated and appeared to have completely eradicated all this relevant data, bringing about a huge delay on the administration of the new Tech! *Nice*. The last thing he wanted was a microchip injected into his cerebral cortex! Regardless, these people must have access to a vast amount of intelligence to pull something like that off! But even with that on hand, it was probably an inside job or someone had tipped them off. That made the most sense.

Interesting as it was, he wanted to find out more on the world's current events. Channel 5 was a separate story entirely. One that he could relate to; since he was a young boy, he'd always been taught to care about the environment. It was a reality that most people chose to ignore. *Such a shame...*

The reporter was speaking of the increasingly erratic climate change all around the globe. The sudden and violent increase in everything from tornados, earthquakes, and hurricanes to weather changes gravitating towards the opposite side of a region's normal elemental spectrum. The drastic developments were quite alarming!

Heavy snows and freezing winds had turned the lands into a mini ice age in some countries, while in others - heat waves surpassed record highs, climbing as far up as 130 degrees Fahrenheit! So much for the Global Warming Deniers claiming this was all a hoax. Cole remembered a lot of this from Earth Sciences.

It was basic chemistry really: CO_2 absorbed and emitted long wave radiation; the Earth re-emits this energy as infrared radiation which then creates abnormal warmth. This in turn causes chaos with atmospheric currents and begins a domino-effect of frenzied weather patterns. *What a bunch of hypocritical, closed-minded idiots!* It was much too late for the world to start giving a shit about what they had done anyway. Recycling and conservation were nothing more than bandages meant to stall the inevitable.

All the pollution humanity had been putting into the atmosphere through manufacturing, the combustion of fossil fuels for energy, and industrial production had caused an overall increase in the planet's temperature. The release of CO_2, plus a multitude of other heat-trapping fumes into the atmosphere were causing all this strange and unnatural weather.

These Greenhouse Gasses had ultimately produced increasingly detrimental effects in the oceans of the world: rising sea levels; acidification; higher temperatures; and even slowing down the natural ocean currents! This would eventually affect the entire ecosystem; both on land and in the sea. The shame was that we did this to ourselves...

He abruptly lost his train of thought as he was alerted to someone knocking at his door. "Viewer off."

Cole got up and pushed the 'Entry Button' on the wall beside the door. They had not encoded his Chip yet for individual recognition. A very large and intimidating man with kind soulful eyes strolled right in as if he was walking into his own home. He was wearing a similar track suit to Cole's own, but his one was an off-grey version with a military insignia above the front pocket. He was sweating and breathing heavily.

"Hello Cole, I'm-."

Whoa buddy, didn't anyone teach you any manners!? "Yeah, hey...Is this *my room* or isn't it?" At least something was his...

The big man laughed out loud. "Yes, I suppose it is kid...that was rude of me. Sorry about that – my name is Tom Quinn." He reached out a meaty hand and Cole grabbed it in turn, shaking it briskly.

Okay, this is unexpected. He hadn't met this guy before; nine times out of ten, it was Ayla who was coming or going. "Good to know, now are you here to get me the hell outta here...or to *keep* me here?"

Tom strolled off to the far corner and sat in one of the chairs by the dark mahogany desk and then realizing what he had done, immediately jumped up, embarrassment showing on his reddening cheeks. "May I," he blurted out, gesturing to the chair before sitting down again. It was rather hilarious.

Smiling back at him, Cole nodded his head. "Yeah sure – go ahead." *What a doofus!*

"Okay thanks," he acknowledged, "So listen, how's everything going? Is there anything I can get for you?"

Well, he asked for it..."Sure, you can tell me why I'm being held here; that would be a good start."

He frowned. "To be honest, I don't know either; I haven't been briefed yet on your...situation. Doctor Lockwood sent me to bring you in."

"Bring me *where*?" Cole was getting tired of the secretive nature of this group. *If you have something to say, come on out with it!*

"To meet with the others."

What others? "Why is it that I'm not being told anything?!"

"Look son...I'm just following orders. I mean, I'd rather finish my workout, you know, instead of babysit some kid...I'd assume they would answer any questions you might have and-"

"You mean *answers to questions that I actually want answers for* or answers to questions that are completely irrelevant?! Why don't you tell me why you people didn't bring me to my father? Better yet, why the hell is Doctor Lockwood running all these medical tests on me, what's wrong with me?"

Tom scratched his chin searching for an answer that would calm him down. "Listen, I can't tell you-"

"Oh, *I'm sorry*," Cole interrupted sarcastically, "Am I asking the wrong questions here? Maybe you can tell me something a bit more simple, here's one I always asked my mother: why does a tampon commercial show two women playing tennis instead of what a tampon is actually used for, huh? *Why is that?*"

Understandably Cole was having a hard time adjusting. Tom would have probably demanded the same explanation. After all, the kid was in a strange place with people he hardly knew. If this was what parenting was like, he was glad he didn't have kids. "Relax, I'm trying to-"

"Aah, *As I thought* – no answer. Okay, let's try again. Here's an easy one: Why do hot dogs still come 10 to a package while the buns come in packs of 8? I mean after all this time, haven't they figured that out yet? And *why* do they *sterilize* needles to put someone to death by lethal injection? That kind of defeats the purpose, doesn't it?"

"Alright, I get it!"

"What, you don't like my questions? Let's take an orange for example: why is an orange an orange, but a lemon isn't a yellow – I mean who's the idiot that named the orange?"

"Look son..."

"Oh wait, I'm not done, Tom. And the *most unanswerable and inexplicable question of all* – is *Goofy* a frigging dog or *isn't he*?!"

Cocky little bastard! Tom was having a difficult time holding a straight face. *At least the boy has a good sense of humor!* He didn't know whether to laugh his ass off or punch the little shit square in the nose. He understood how Cole could be angry and confused, but he didn't have the right answers for him. No, it was better that Ayla dealt with this; she was the mother hen. "*Alright kid*, are you just about done?"

"No, not really. What is this place? Why am I here?!"

"You're better off asking Ayla. I'm not authorized to-"

"See, that's exactly what I mean. You people keep avoiding my questions! Can't you just give me one solid answer?"

"That's *enough*, come on!"

Cole backed away from him slowly. "No, I don't think so Tom...not until you people tell me *something; anything,* instead of running me around in circles!*"*

You might not have gotten a spanking when you were a child, but pretty soon – I'm going to give you a beating! "And as I've been *trying to tell you –* I can't answer questions I don't know the answers to! Now if you'd stop acting like a spoiled little brat and-"

"Screw you, you big dumb dope!"

The nerve of this kid! "That's it you *little shit,*" Tom bellowed as he forcefully seized Cole's arm in a vice-like grip, "I've had just about enough of this-"

"Let. Me. Go," Cole hissed as he twisted his arm out of the hold and pushed the larger man roughly with both hands, slamming them into his chest.

At six foot four, Tom Quinn was a large man, his upper torso rippling with muscle from years of hard lifting and a high protein diet. He was tough as nails and just as resilient, confident that he could overpower men larger than him and had proven that on more than one occasion.

He had survived many dangerous missions and was considered both fearless and brave by his peers. But as he was hit with what he could only describe as the same force of a grown man swinging a sledge hammer into his chest, the once forgotten feeling of cold fear permeated his being. He flew back at least five feet, landing hard on his tailbone. *What the fu-*

As he came out of his daze, Cole was leaning down next to him trying to help him up, a look of regret written on his face. "Tom...Hey...are you alright?! *I'm sorry!* I didn't mean to...I don't know what-"

The bruising in his chest hurt a little as Tom coughed out an apology. "No...*I'm* sorry...*hukh hukh*...What the hell did you...hit me with kid?!"

I didn't hit you with anything, Cole thought, *what the hell just happened here? Did I do this?* The only rational explanation was that it was a sudden rush of adrenaline. *Yeah, that's got to be it.*

"*Nothing.* I didn't hit you with *anything.* I don't know what happened, all I did was...*push you...*"

Tom wearily grasped the edge of the end table and pulled himself to his feet, meeting Cole's troubled eyes. "You know those *questions* you had, kid? I think it's about time we *both* get some answers!"

CHAPTER 13: Revelations

"Calm down Tom," Lucien cautioned, "You're not making any sense. That-"

"I'm telling you Lucien. I haven't been drinking; I'm not hallucinating; and I damn well am not an idiot so stop looking at me that way!" Tom unzipped his top and pointed to the black and blue bruising on his chest. "Take a look for yourself; it happened. Don't tell me I'm not making sense!"

Cole stood with his back against the wall at a loss for words. These two were like a married couple. Of course, he wanted an explanation just as much as Tom did.

"He's making *perfect sense*," Ayla interjected. Murmurs went around the room as all eyes turned to face her.

"And just what the hell does *that* mean, Ayla," Lucien prompted.

The lights from the room they were in made his head hurt as Cole struggled to make sense of the Doctor's words. Besides Ayla, Tom, and him, there was one other – the man who had apparently saved him...and brought him here – High Commander Lucien Bovier. It was hard to look at him...He somehow felt as if he had to show a respect he didn't yet feel while at the same time resisting the urge to speak his mind. *How the hell am I supposed to feel about the man who saved me, but left my mother to die?*

The High Commander in turn looked towards the boy and it brought back painful memories of Jenna Methis; it was easy to tell that the two were related. The same sharp facial features stared back at him, causing him to turn away. The guilt that tore through him for leaving Jenna bleeding on the hospital floor made his palms begin to sweat and his mouth go dry.

He had tried to save her and failed. Between the fire and the chance that other enemy assassins were in the building, he had no choice but to take Cole and carry him to safety. Already having checked Doctor Methis for a pulse and finding none, he took the only choice left available to him: save the boy. The intensity with which Cole glared back at him was a tell-tale sign that he blamed Lucien for his mother's death. Ignoring his own personal pain, he shifted his attention back to the conversation.

Tom was the first one to find his voice. *"What are you not telling us,* Ayla?"

The small statured woman calmly punched in a few commands into her HOL-COM and Cole's medical statistics and test results were projected to the middle of the table. "The preliminary tests I initiated showed extremely unusual readings even before he woke up, but I didn't want to say anything until I had medical confirmation."

Cole who was listening quietly to their conversation appeared incredibly confused as he recognized the holographic image as himself. "That's me, isn't it?"

"Yes Cole, it is," she confirmed, and then addressed the entire group, "What we are witnessing is what I consider to be a true case of *scientific magic!"*

"And that is?"

"I believe we now know what happened to the missing Nano-swarm, Lucien." The three dimensional image that was on the Viewer suddenly turned into a mass of individual microscopic machine-like biological components that formed the outline of a human body. There were billions of them, swarming over one another like ants over sugar!

The Commander got up from his chair and placed both his hands on the table, peering at the image. *"What*...what are you getting at? Are you telling us that it's *inside* him?!"

Cole suddenly felt like he was being examined by all eyes in the room as they turned towards him. "What are you people talking about?! *What's* inside me?! Why are you all looking at me like that, I got something on my face?!"

"Not *inside* him, more like *a part of him*," Ayla explained.

Tendrils of fear crept through Cole as he tried to make sense of what they were talking about. "Look...you guys are really scaring me now...Can someone please tell me what the *hell* is going on?!"

"Okay, Kid – *just relax*," Tom pleaded, "Everyone calm down, this isn't getting anywhere. Ayla, please explain." Directing his gaze at both Lucien and Cole as they both opened their mouths to speak, he held a palm up, "Let's hear what she has to say before we go into any half-cocked assumptions"

Ayla Lockwood exhaled deeply before she began. "I believe that Doctor Methis...injected her son with the Nano-swarm before she died!" Realizing what she said, then looking quickly at Cole, she felt embarrassed. "I'm sorry...I didn't mean to-"

"Its fine," Cole asserted sadly, wiping a fresh tear from his eye. "I'm...okay. I just want some answers... Please, go on."

Turning to face Lucien, she continued. "The B.I.O.N.E.X. procedure. We'd always assumed that Jenna Methis was one of our last chances at a viable match, but we never thought to consider *her son*! He shares her same genetic code and the neural emulations are very similar, so the bonding took without the need for the overlay.

But somehow, this happened from within him; my best guess is that the brain imprint we created the A.I. with recognized Cole's mind as a logical option. This proves that the Nano-swarm not only has a functional control protocol, but that it is as perfect an equivalent as we could have hoped for!"

What the hell were they talking about? What was a B.I.O.N.E.X. Scan?

"We *did* ask for English, right?"

Ignoring Tom's quip, Lucien's eyes narrowed. "So there are little robotic machines *inside* him; *who* exactly is in control?"

"As far as I can tell – *he is*," she replied and continued on excitedly. "The DNA scans show that the bonding is...or soon will be at a biological level. His blood tests confirm that his cellular matrix has been, for lack of a better word – *infected* - by a combined form of the Nanites and his original genetic code - a hybrid cell if you will. This was unforeseen; it is almost an impossibility for these types of cells to even be created much less function past a specific threshold! The mutation has spread throughout his entire body and is slowly becoming a part of his DNA. This is...*extraordinary!*"

"I see," Lucien pondered, as he struggled to find the words to express his thoughts.

Cole didn't seem to be taking this too well and why would he be? His face was ashen and he was shaking his head in disbelief. He suddenly felt like he *was* the science experiment.

"*Infected?!* Did I hear you right? What does that mean; am I sick?!"

Tom noticed Cole's agitation too. He poured something into a glass and placed it in his hand. "Here, take this; it'll calm you down."

"No, *don't take that*," Ayla blurted out, "Tom, that's *vodka*, you idiot!'

"Yeah, so?"

"So, he's not even 21 yet! Lucien – get the boy some water."

"Works for me," Tom muttered under his breath, downing the shot himself.

Taking the tall cold glass of water into his hand, Cole greedily gulped it down in a matter of seconds. He felt hot, nervous, and sick at the same time. *Maybe I should have drank the vodka...* He stood up from his chair and then thinking better of it, sat back down. *Calm yourself, Cole. You wanted answers, well here they are. Listen, learn, and then decide what all this means.*

"Please tell me...*am I sick?*"

"Quite the contrary," answered Ayla. "To be perfectly honest, the Nanites in your bloodstream will most likely prevent you from *ever becoming* sick. If they note an outside infection of any kind, they will literally analyze the viral or bacterium contagion immediately and create the correct antibody. You will not have to wait – like the rest of us – to build an immunity to the sickness."

"So they are *changing* me?"

"Yes, Cole, they are...The Nanites are affecting every system of your body, *improving them* as they begin to bond on a cellular level. Most likely, you haven't felt the need to rest much, right?"

Cole nodded, "Yeah, how did you know that?"

"I didn't. Everything I am telling you right now is nothing more than conjecture. The scientific community has never seen anything like this before; we have no concrete facts to back up a hypothesis so please, take what I am saying with a grain of salt. However – there are some very good guesses I can base off your medical results." She made a few gestures on her HOL-COM and motioned to the 3D data.

All three men were listening with rapt attention.

"The Nanites enhance all of your metabolic functions and prevent the build-up of fatigue poisons, such as lactic acid, in the muscles. Therefore, this will give you endurance and energy far in excess of an ordinary human being!"

Cole had a horrified look on his face. "What?! What do you mean *'ordinary human being'*? Are you saying I'm not even *human*?!"

"*Enhanced*," Tom corrected, immediately understanding the concepts she was speaking of. "You're still human kid; just a better version, that's all."

Cole rolled his eyes. "*That's all?!* Wow Tom, leave it to you to take something jaw-shattering and make it trivial."

"You know what I mean."

Even as he made the comment, a chill crept outward from within. These people were telling him that he was no longer what science would consider 'human', at least not text book. But did the Nanites make him *less than human* or *more than human*; that seemed to be the question that needed answering. One thing that was more than excellent was the fact that whatever he was, it was a helluva lot better than being a paralyzed sack of skin spending the rest of what life he had left in a hospital ICU! The benefits had been brought to light, but it still scared the hell out of him all the same!

What if it turned him into something else?! Or worse – somehow took control of his body; his thoughts; his consciousness...Then again, he *was* alive. His inadequate feelings suddenly turned into a strange sort of logic. *You feel better than you've ever felt before; more energized; alert; even stronger and faster than when you were leading the team! Find out more about your...condition before you start thinking crazy thoughts.*

"Sorry Tom, I'm still getting used to you."

Tom crossed his arms and tipped his head up, shaking it slowly while closing his eyes. "God, grant me the patience to keep from slapping the shit out of this boy."

They both looked at each other and shared a grin. Tom and Cole seemed to heading in a fast direction towards friendship, Ayla thought as she smiled back at them. At least the boy still retained all of his emotional sensitivity for personal interaction...The changes to Cole's physiology were fascinating and frightening at the same time!

One odd thing was that logically, the Nanites' very nature should have short-circuited his Chip! Instead, they had integrated themselves into it, which meant that it would no longer be considered an implant; it would be *a part of him*!

Lucien, who had kept relatively quiet up until this point finally cut in. "Alright, alright – let's allow Ayla to finish this up. I'm sure we all have many more questions."

"I assume you'd like to begin, Lucien?"

He nodded back. "You said Cole was highly resistant to disease. Does that mean these Nanites can also repair damaged tissue?"

"You mean like *regeneration*," Tom interjected.

"Well...sure, whatever you want to call it. It would stand to reason if they sense that a Virus is invading the body and then fixes it, why not a knife wound...or a bullet hole?!"

To that, Cole spoke up quickly, a wave of fear passing over his face. "Uhh...I'd rather *not* test that theory."

Ayla stepped in front of him in a defensive stance. "And he won't have to, *right Lucien*? Cole is not a *weapon*, he's just a boy."

"He's also not a *science experiment*, Ayla! Relax. I'm not saying anything like that. I'm just feeding into your hypothesis. So?"

Both Cole and Ayla appeared to let out a mutual sigh of relief and relaxed their postures. "Yes, my guess is that it is very likely possible." She looked to Tom, "However I wouldn't exactly call it regeneration; more like 'repair'."

"Okay, that makes sense."

"There is much more than that, Lucien."

"Go on."

"Cole's mutated cells have re-assimilated themselves into his neuromuscular, endocrine, and skeletal systems. His bones are now much denser than his original cellular makeup, allowing for increases in strength and resistance to injury! Most likely they may even enhance his reflexes, speed, and thought processes."

"So...you're saying I have superpowers," Cole cracked.

"Great, a smart-ass teenager a little past puberty, with super strength," Tom said sarcastically, "Just what we needed."

"He's special," insisted Ayla.

"Oh, so now I'm licking windows with the kids on the 'short bus'?" The two of them broke out into laughter as Ayla gave Cole a hard look.

"That's *not* funny!" One thing Ayla wouldn't stand for were any tasteless jokes about the handicapped. When she was young, she would help her mother care for children with multiple sclerosis; it was a heart-wrenching experience, but embedded in her a sense of righteousness that followed her through adulthood.

Disabled people didn't get a chance to insult the able-bodied; it wasn't a fair trade-off. They were the most vulnerable people in society and should be protected from *everything*. *Ooh, that just tears me up!* With his own past, Cole should have known better than that!

Her tone sobered them up fast. "I...I'm sorry; I didn't mean it like that," Cole said quickly, embarrassed at his careless comment.

"Enough," ordered Lucien, "Let's get on with it."

Ayla rapped her fingers on the table, clearly annoyed. Damned young adults; they never think before they speak! *He could probably use a little support after all he's been through.* But sometimes these cocky, know-it-all post-teenagers just needed a high five...to the face...with a chair.

"Anyway, neither one of those labels apply to you Cole. The fluctuations in added strength or other...abilities are dependent upon emotional stimuli, such as the anger you felt towards Tom earlier. The Nanites gauge how much adrenaline your muscles may need in different stressful situations."

Cole could not believe what he was hearing. "That's fricking awesome...I think!"

Everyone stayed quiet.

"That *is awesome*, right?"

"To be honest with you," Ayla replied, "I don't know. If you can't control it, you could hurt someone. It was a pretty incredible feat to throw Tom around like you did."

"Hey now," Tom said, "Let's not try to embarrass me any further."

Lucien was having a difficult time accepting this. In his world, rational explanations were more likely than science fiction.

"*Or*...it could simply be a *boost of adrenaline*...There have been many documented cases of hysterical strength. A mother lifting a 4 ton car off her daughter; a grandfather throwing a riding lawnmower off his granddaughter like it was a toy; In Quebec, a woman actually wrestled a polar bear to keep it from attacking 2 children," Lucien argued, "It's not so strange as we are led to believe...Are you sure what happened to Tom wasn't something like that?"

"*I'm sure*," Tom cut in, "He's just a *runt* who's half my size and he threw me on my ass like I was a rag-doll! You still doubting me, Lucien? This wasn't something as simple as adrenaline; this was...*power*; I felt it!"

"I hope that was a compliment," Cole muttered.

"I'm *not* doubting you; I'm only putting up a few rational explanations...we can't dismiss them either," he nodded in Ayla's direction, "Now, you were saying the fluctuations in strength are determined by his *emotions*?"

Tom responded instead. "She is, except in Cole's case, these chemical reactions react to internal stimuli instead of outside stimuli." He stabbed a finger at Cole. "And don't get so excited yet kid, there could also be side effects we have no idea about."

"That is true," Ayla agreed, "We don't have near enough data on this as we ought to and to reproduce these situations in a clinical setting would be unethical...and dangerous."

"Hey, I'm good if you guys are," Cole insisted. He wanted to know what he was capable of as much as they did. The benefit of a controlled environment would be much more useful than happenstance. He had a feeling however, that Ayla would be difficult to convince...and Lucien would want to use him as some sort of guinea pig to test Cole's 'military applications'. Maybe he should just let it be for now. "On second thought-"

"Its fine Cole," Lucien said, cutting him off, "However, I would appreciate the opportunity to speak to you later – in private. Whatever else this might be leading to can wait until-" A small beep sounded as a message was sent to the Commander's Sat-Com. He read it privately and gestured to Tom. "Excuse us please, we have to go – *now*."

Watching the two soldiers leave, Ayla reached out and took Cole by the arm, bringing him in for a hug. The motion took him completely by surprise. He had no idea what he should do and so resigned to leave his arms hanging at their sides.

"What was that for?"

"After all you've been through, I just thought you could use one," she said kindly.

She was right, he could. He felt his arms move of their own accord, wrapping around her and squeezing her back, as another tear fell from his eye.

CHAPTER 14: Soldiers

The communication was from Tech-Ops Malcolm Smith. The man was a genius in the fields of technology, computers, and electronics. Lucien had found him when he was just a 16 year old boy, breaking into ATM machines for some fast cash.

In The Old World, these automated terminals dispensed bills of currency to anyone with an available bank account. At that time, Malcolm was a homeless runaway and the account he had hacked into happened to be Lucien's! He'd seen some potential in the boy.

Instead of turning the kid into the authorities, Lucien had brought him home, given him a hot meal and a place to stay for the night. Malcolm had been on his own for years, struggling to survive in a world that could care less about those in his unfortunate situation. Lucien gave him a choice: either receive military training and come work for him or continue to scrounge for scraps like he had been, with a good chance of eventually ending up in prison.

The boy had picked the better option and Lucien used his connections to bring him into his fold. Within three years of intense training, Malcolm had come out of there with system intrusion skills that surpassed all others in that field. Eventually, he was placed under Lucien's command and had been with the High Commander ever since. The news Mal had just relayed to him was not good.

After reaching a far enough distance from the lab, Lucien explained to Tom, the reasons for their sudden departure. "They found Genarro's body; at least what's left of it. It was burned beyond recognition and dumped-"

Tom stopped abruptly, turning quickly and pushing Lucien hard up against the concrete wall. "You son-of-a-bitch! I warned you, didn't I?!"

"Tom, it was complic-"

"You can't keep using people like this; they're not pawns to sacrifice in one of your little games!"

Bringing his arm down in a chopping motion, the High Commander broke the hold and pushed Tom back with a show of force. "And you'd better understand the difference between *us and them*! You've been around these people so damned long, you can't remember which side you're on. Genarro was a Cateton of The System, Tom!"

Shaking his head, he took a step back. "That doesn't change the fact that he was killed *because of what we did*, Lucien!"

"*No*, he was killed because the people he worked for are sick, twisted sociopaths! If you want revenge, then save it for them, not me! Listen Tom...Neither of us had any idea this would happen. Yes, we cloned his G-ID chip and the Retina Scans, but the trail we left to Brenner was evident! I don't-"

"I get that! But, I warned you that he may be held responsible...and *he was*."

Bringing both his palms from the back of his head to the front of his face, Lucien tilted his head down and sighed deeply. He punched the steel door hard, then pulled his hand back in a yelp of pain. "Damn it!"

After a few moments of leaning against the wall, Lucien placed his hand on Tom's shoulder. "I'm sorry. You're right; it's my fault..."

A short while later, Tom asked. "What are we going to do about this?"

"What we always do – *we make them pay*."

The readying room was stock-piled with armaments, nano-suits, and most everything else a soldier would need to prepare for battle. The System Action Front [SAF] consisted of nine members, including Tom and Lucien. They were highly trained in espionage, infiltration, and various other combat situations. The numerous other militia teams stationed around the globe each had their own unique team name and call-sign.

Many of these former System Catetons had defected over to The Hand of Light over the years for various reasons, but mostly because their morals and ideals were in direct conflict with The System's goals. Extreme care had to be taken to weed out the possible spies from the revolutionaries.

As such, each convert or new member subjected themselves to a brain scan, interrogation sessions, and a pulse monitor coded to their G-ID Chips. This team however, had been carefully screened and selected by the High Commander himself. He trusted them with his life.

As they stepped in, most of the men had already locked into their Nano-suits. The Suit was as far as they'd come to an actual breakthrough with the Nanotech. They were designed to provide both flexibility and protection to the wearer.

It was a light-weight polymer of Nanites that could solidify to absorb everything from hard impacts to bladed weapons. The hardening of the Nanites also offered some enhanced strength and durability for the soldier it was equipped to.

The only significant weakness being that it was not an automatic defense feature of the suit; rather, the user had to very aware of his surroundings and external threats in order to press the composite button at the precise time of vulnerability. The barrier lasted only 15 seconds at a time before reverting back to its hybrid material.

If it wasn't timed perfectly, a soldier's anatomy could still be damaged. Although the body was protected for the most part, the head still remained a vulnerable target. As such, watchful eyes and sharp ears were still the favored defense against most enemy perils.

Prelate Terry Williams welcomed Tom and Lucien immediately and bade them get prepared while he updated them on the mission. "We've gone through all the data from the IRQ Implant on Commander Genarro. There are two hits that came up: something called the Overwatch Program and a Doctor Magnus Lehovec. The term 'Overwatch' was not familiar to our operatives. However, we did discover that Lehovec was once a world-renowned geneticist for many years before he was let go from Suncore Genetics-"

"I remember that incident; it was on the Global News Network *years* ago, big scandal," interrupted Weapons Master Fred Reed,"

There was a huge lawsuit against the company. The bastard was conducting research on children!"

"Are you serious, on kids," interjected Specialist Henry Wright.

"He's right," Tom explained, "Lehovec was looking for a particular variant on the MAO-A Gene. It's also known as the 'Warrior Gene' because it is associated with feelings of violence and rage."

"How the hell do you know so much about this Tom," asked Henry.

"He's a genius, remember," Lucien offered, with dripping sarcasm.

"Anyway, that specific gene regulates serotonin, which in turn regulates your mood," he said, smoothly brushing aside his leader's wisecrack, "People with low activity of the orbital cortex means that they have less normal suppression of behaviors that have violent tendencies. According to behavioral principles, these people are what we have come to label as 'Sociopaths'!"

Malcolm Smith whistled low, in surprise. "That's crazy! So what was this asshole doing with children?"

"He was looking for ways to genetically modify their tendencies *for aggression*," Tom answered, "He was mutating their genes! I believe he was trying to breed soldiers with an inherit will and aptitude for war. Last I heard though, he was sentenced to three consecutive life terms at Folcrox. I would've done worse than that if you ask me."

"Well, apparently he's been freed and we've tracked his work to a company called Psy-Gen Global," Terry informed them, "It's-"

What did he say? "You've got to be *kidding me*," Lucien angrily interrupted.
"Why...what'd I say?"

"That's the same company Jenna Methis worked for! You're telling me that this Lehovec is employed there as well?!"

"Not employed; more like 'off the books'. Three years ago, 1.5 million credits were transferred from a Psy-Gen company ghost server to the Warden of - guess where?"

"Folcrox," Tom stated bluntly.

"Believe me, we had to do some digging to find this information, but we still don't have much," Terry divulged.

"That's an understatement," snorted Ortega. Carmine Ortega was the demolitions expert and the oldest member of the team. Employing modular and innovative bomb design, he was known for his skill at making an explosive into anything else: a golf ball; a dinner plate; even a teacup if he chose to. He was loyal to an extreme and a idealist. "I'm surprised we pulled up anything at all, it's like this guy's a ghost!"

"Why not talk to the Warden," asked Tom.

"We've not only approached him, but the prisoners who knew him as well; no one is talking! We've put them through the standard interrogation techniques...and even used unconventional methods. Something about this man, Lehovec scares the shit out of them!"

Lucien couldn't believe what he was hearing. *How is this all related?* Had Jenna been hiding something? *No way, she died saving her child.* She had been as against The System as he was. Regardless, her morals were impeccable. *God rest her soul...*But Riordan on the other hand, was he somehow involved in this? He was sure of it! There *was* something here...

"What's the Op," Tom asked.

"Rand has ordered us to bring in this Lehovec guy. We have about 30 days to plan the mission, infiltrate Psy-Gen, and retrieve the package."

"Bring him in for what?"

Terry thought about it for a moment. "You know...I couldn't really tell you. If I had to guess, it's got something to do with this 'Overwatch Program'."

CHAPTER 15: Re-education

He was sitting in a clean, white-tiled room. The padded walls reminded him of a cell inside a mental institute for the criminally insane! *It wouldn't surprise me if someone came in here with a straitjacket; this looks like a loony bin. Do they think I've gone crazy?*

A strange looking device with hanging electrodes sat atop a small, metallic table. There was nothing else inside the room except a chair on either side of the table, recording equipment, and a bottle of water. *Oh boy...*

As Cole's mind wandered further down a path of anxiety, the electronic door made a swooshing sound and he looked up to see a man in a white lab coat walk in. *Any more white and I won't remember what color used to look like.*

The tall, thin man appeared to be in his late forties; a kind face, beginning to show the etches of wrinkles that were starting to take shape, and a receding hair line. He wore a button-up shirt adorned with a pocketful of tools and carried a HOL-COM in one hand.

"Good Morning, Cole, I'm Doctor Rutherford. I'll be performing a series of tests today. Please bear with me, we may be here awhile."

Great, more tests! "Yeah, Hi."

The doctor took the seat opposite from Cole and began to punch in a few commands into the portable computer. A holographic projection took shape above it, displaying an image of a transparent human body.

"Now, if you would kindly remove your shirt."

Cole complied and the man attached the electrodes to his chest.

"You're not into some type of kinky torture play, are you," Cole joked, "because I want to warn you that my nipples and electricity just don't mix."

He smiled back at him and shook his head. "Don't worry, I'm not that kind of guy."

A doctor with a sense of humor, will wonders never cease!

"These are going to monitor a number of your body's physiological responses while I administer the tests."

"What type of tests?"

"Mostly psychological...and a few others."

"So you're some kind of Shrink?"

"Nope, just the operator. Now take a deep breath and relax."

Doctor Rutherford made a few gestures and a purplish array of light appeared in front of the HOL-COM. A geometric figure formed within the haze.

"What you have before you is called the Halstead-Reitan battery. It's going to show us if you have any neurological impairments. All you have to do is decide whether the picture reminds you of the number 1, 2, 3, or 4. Then-"

"I've heard of it; you think I have brain damage?"

"Cole, with what's happened to you, we need to be sure. Please, continue when you are ready."

It took less than half an hour for Cole to go through all 208 pictures. Next came a floating board containing ten cut-out shapes which he was supposed to place in their appropriate space. The same procedure was repeated using both hands and then he was then asked to do it blindfolded. Rutherford took him through a number of other evaluations that were based on logic, memory, and a host of other boring exams.

Halfway through the day, they brought him a plateful of oven baked chicken, steamed vegetables, and a lemon pastry. He was ravenous. Finishing the entire meal in record time, his stomach at least seemed to be functioning properly. Throughout the process, Doctor Rutherford talked very little, taking notes on his HOL-COM as he kept tabs on Cole's progress. There was one scientific procedure after another and by the time they were finished, it was already late into the evening. *This sucks!*

Finally after another hour, Rutherford stood up and took the electrodes off. Cole breathed a sigh of relief. Any longer and his ass would have fallen off from sitting in the cold metal chair for so damned long.

"Now that wasn't so bad, was it?"

"It was about as fun as the time my dog crapped in my lunchbox. Next time, please – send me a warning in advance."

Rutherford laughed good-naturedly. "You're free to go, Cole, thank you for your time. I'll send the results to Doctor Lockwood...and it's been a pleasure, young man."

"Nice to meet you as well."

He didn't waste any time getting out the door.

"How are you doing today, Cole," Ayla asked as she entered the room. He was lazily sprawled on the chaise lounge, patiently waiting for her to arrive. *Typical young adults...*

Cole had a smirk on his face, no doubt ready to spit out some smartass comment as usual. The boy had an interesting sense of humor, but she appreciated it nonetheless.

"Well...I've had a horribly busy day converting oxygen into carbon dioxide, but other than that - no complaints here."

She laughed, heartily. "Regardless of the past injuries to your body, I see that your sarcasm has remained intact."

He grinned back. Ayla motioned to the rubber mat and Cole took a seat, crossing one leg between the other. He was refreshed from a great night's sleep and was eager to get started.

"Are you ready to try this?"

"I'm ready."

"Okay, now close your eyes and relax. Focus on the pulse."

Listening to the tick of the metronome, Cole focused his concentration on his breathing to match the rhythm of the device. Doctor Lockwood was convinced that to better use and direct his Nanites, he had to reach and be comfortable with the four brainwave states of consciousness. Gamma was associated with a lift in mood and well-being; Alpha was a calm, relaxed state of mind; Theta was for relaxation and body healing; and Delta was linked to altered states as well as a healing of both the body and the mind.

In addition, these techniques were designed to help him manage his emotions, regulate stress, direct his focus, and even increase energy when more was needed. Unbelievably, he was picking it up perfectly...*as he was learning it! I could get used to this.*

Of course, he *was* in a peaceful state of mind. Perhaps it was easier to relax now that the Doctor had offered him a few pieces of much needed information. The question that had gnawed at him since he'd been here was why they hadn't taken him back to his father after his mother's death. He was informed that until The Hand figured out who murdered his mother *and why*, they didn't want to risk Collin Methis' life...or his.

Someone out there was after his family; for what, he didn't know. Doctor Lockwood promised him that as soon as things calmed down and the situation was deemed safe, The Hand would make contact with his Dad and inform him of the status of his son.

Until then, however, she made him promise not to try to connect with him in any way. Not only could it expose the members of The Hand, but it would put too many people at risk, including his father! He didn't want that on his conscience as well. These people had saved his life and he owed them that at the very least.

What he did know was that soon after the incident at the hospital, Collin had filed a missing person's report with the Cateton Agency in Illinois. That alone had made him feel like crap. Cole could only imagine the pain and confusion his father must have gone through with all that had taken place: his Wife's death; a missing son; no explanation for either.

Emotionally, he wanted nothing more than to go home and tell his Dad that he was alive and well! Logic however, dictated that it would be smarter to stay 'missing' than expose his father to possible dangerous elements that could very well end with his life. These people had already murdered his mother; he sure didn't want the same to happen to his father! Reason had won in the end.

The other piece was more of an interesting discovery than anything else. Cole was eating much larger meals and more frequently than he could ever remember doing before. At first, he was convinced it was simply his body trying to recover from all the trauma. Ayla however, had another explanation.

She theorized that Cole's increased appetite was due to the energy the Nano-Swarm utilized when performing specific functions. He didn't know enough about the scientific principles of how this was done, but it made a certain kind of sense. Besides, who was he to argue with the results?

Case in point, he had not rested much in days, yet he still retained the vitality and endurance of a man who had been in a deep sleep for a full eight hours. All of his metabolic functions had been enhanced, therefore requiring more food for energy.

He was told that he would feel hungry soon after a feat such as the strength he had used to push Tom, or perhaps even with Lucien's theory of self-healing. Cole was both scared and fascinated with his new abilities and craved for the chance to test them out. For now though, reaching the various brainwave states was taking up most of his concentration.

Watching Cole slip so easily into a meditative state, Ayla was clearly impressed. It had taken no more than a few short hours and already he was learning how to enter the four states of consciousness at will. His intelligence was increasing every single day and who knew what other abilities his Nanites had in store for him! Although the constant ticking of the metronome was close to driving her mad, she forced herself to be patient as she waited for him to come out of his meditative trance.

Instead of putting the poor kid through further testing, she had decided to teach him – as well as she could – to harness the power of the Nanites. The amazing thing she had noticed about Cole was that the processing power of the Nanites had bestowed upon him *true* eidetic memory; he had total recall of everything he learned, saw, or read, down to each minute detail!

She surmised that it was more to do with the nanotech's ability to store data rather than Cole's cellular mutations. Strangely, his instant recollection mostly consisted of the things he'd learned once waking up at this outpost. *I'll have to look into that when time permits.*

She watched the boy closely, taking notes on her HOL-COM. *That's it, Cole, you're doing great...*Glancing at her Sat-Com for the fifth time, Ayla's face flickered with annoyance. There was so much to do and such little time...*You're beginning to sound like Dad*. As far as she was concerned, the worst invention in human history was the clock! She was especially resentful because it had robbed her of a father and the sad thing was - he hadn't even realized it.

Professor Daniel Lockwood had his entire life mapped out to the minute; there was no deviation from his schedule. Due to his obsessive nature with time, he had missed many important moments that were dear to her, even a few of her birthdays. Growing up, Ayla was determined to be as impulsive as she could be, trying hard to do everything at a moment's notice. It was mostly out of spite and sadly, it had not fazed her father one bit. Either way, thinking on a deeper level and one way or another, everyone's lives were ruled by the damned clock.

Everything people did on a daily basis was based one way or another on time. Unfortunately, trying to constantly manage and monitor time only led to greater anxiety, as it had done to her father. In fact, all the hang-ups on time just led to more questions regarding it: 'What time is it?'; 'How much time do I have left?'; 'What time do I have to be there?'; 'What time does it start?'

It was a vicious circle and she wanted no part of it; it certainly didn't help with her anxiety – perhaps that had more to do with it than anything else...Whatever the case, it was *her* reason for introspection. During meditation, time was meaningless; it simply did not exist. To pass this knowledge on to Cole, she felt, would be a true benefit and this was why they were here today. Now if only she didn't have to sit here for hours on end watching him master it.

Suddenly, someone spoke directly in front of her. "Are *you* meditating or am I? Maybe I should try my hand at teaching instead!"

Ayla jumped at first, then calmed down after noticing it was only Cole. "You snuck up on me, you little shit!"

He was bubbling with excitement. "I've got it down, Ayla; I've learned all four states! It just kind of...came to me. "

Sometimes his excitability overtook his focus; Cole's maturity seemed not to have caught up with his age. He had that innocence that was expected of a child. Then again, much of what he now experienced was probably new to him, given all those years of wasted youth.

He must have missed out on quite a lot while he was comatose in that ICU. *How sad...*But his exuberance in every small accomplishment was delightful. The boy had a great personality and a kind heart. At times, Ayla felt like he was the son she'd never had and was completely fine with that. Sometimes, she wished he was.

She smiled up at him. "Most things will. Your Nanites allow you to perform complex calculations and process vast amounts of data at an incredible rate. With their technological aspect and storage capabilities, you should be able to retain most of the information you learn both mentally and visually."

He looked at her with a raised eyebrow. "You know, sometimes I think I'm speaking to a robot"

"Yeah, yeah – heard it all before! It's the way I think," she answered with a grin, "You know, Nerd-speak. Anyway, it *is* pretty cool, right?"

"Cool? This just keeps getting better and better," he replied, rubbing his hands together in anticipation for whatever was coming next.

"Don't get too carried away, Cole. You will still have to practice and study whatever you learn. Your brain will know *how it's done*, but to perfect the lesson, form or rhythm and to commit it to muscle memory takes constant usage, just remember that. You'll be learning at an accelerated pace, but practice will *always* make perfect."

Twisting the cap off his water bottle and taking a big gulp, he nodded his head towards her. "Fair enough; I need *some* sort of challenge, right? And what will you be ordering me to do next, Ma'am?"

Ayla laughed and threw him a towel. "Your *orders* are to get some sleep, young man! We have a visitor coming tomorrow. Her name is Katya Prulova and she is very excited to meet you."

CHAPTER 16: Doubt

At first, it seemed to be an evening like any other. He left work, drove to their favorite Mediterranean Cafe and picked up some of those delicious savory tapas, snuck a cigarette and went back to their spacious condo in the downtown suburbs. He and Jenna had decided against a residential home until they found the perfect one with all their expectations. Tiringly, he took the elevator to the 15th floor, turned into the east hallway and walked into the condo.

He draped his coat around the dining room chair and caught the news, searching from one channel to the other, hoping to find the report he was looking for. Pulling up a chair, he began to unpack the fragrant smelling short eats. Only then did he notice the vacant seats around him and broke down in a fitful of tears. Reality hit him like a ton of bricks: he had no one to return home to. *What had happened to them?*

Collin Methis didn't know how much more of this he could take. The only two people in his life that truly mattered were gone, as if they never existed in the first place. It had been months and no one had contacted him with any news on the investigation of his deceased wife and missing child. Things didn't add up. It was odd that Jenna had been to see Cole without him; they always went together. *Why would she do that?* She hadn't even told him about her plans to visit.

A frightening thought came to mind that Jenna's past had finally caught up with her. But that was difficult to digest; they had been extremely careful and it didn't make sense for them to take Cole. What possible reason would they have to kidnap or harm a sick kid? Before lapsing into a coma, Cole had found it incredibly difficult to move his limbs scant inches, much less stand up and walk away! That meant that someone had *taken* him. Whether that person saved him or kidnapped him was what needed to be determined.

The fire had been all over the news and many who had lost loved ones were in the process of legal action with the hospital. Collin knew better than to expose himself and instead, was focused on finding his missing son. The first few weeks had been fraught with grief and heart-wrenching loss. He couldn't eat; he couldn't sleep;

and the fluctuations between anger and sadness took an emotional toll on his psyche.

Not much had changed since then, other than being able to finally stomach small amounts of food. The sleeping pills helped some, but the sporadic bouts of sleep that came to him were more from utter exhaustion than the medication.

The false hope that his wife was somehow still alive was blurred by the DNA evidence that was found at the scene. If she was alive, he knew that she would have found a way to contact him. But the burned out wreckage of the hospital floor was such that not many escaped unscathed. Jenna was gone and he would need to find a way to cope with that.

What hurt most of all was the way they had left things: in a bitter state of anger and resentment. Collin had always pictured marriage as a wonderful experience, filled with joy and happiness. And it was; for a time. Lately, it had all come crumbling down...

He knew he was at fault for most of the problems and arguments that tore their relationship apart, but the disease that had claimed Cole affected him both body and soul. Collin could not get over it, and so had taken out his frustrations on his wife. He suddenly felt ashamed that he had allowed his grief to ruin his life. There was nothing he could do about it now. The only thing he did know was that he needed to find Cole. *But how?*

Ayla was sitting at her well organized desk going through the latest updates to Cole's medical status when she noticed her Sat-Com glowing beside her. The subtle blue pulse signified privacy mode. Looking down, she saw that it was a call from the High Commander. *Oh, great!* She got up from her chair and began to pace back and forth as she answered. Anytime Lucien contacted her in 'private', the news was not usually very good.

"Ayla, are you alone," came his gruff voice on the other end.

"Einstein is in the next room working on some labs, otherwise –

yes."

"Huh? You have a colleague named '*Einstein*', you're kidding me, right…Nevermind, listen, I didn't have a chance to talk to you about my concerns before I left."

"Concerns?"

"Yes, about Cole."

"Ahh, I see…You're wondering about the Nanites…"

Ayla had been meaning to speak to Lucien herself, but time was always short with the man. She never knew when the next mission would be calling him away at a moment's notice. She should be used to it by now, but it was still a major inconvenience.

"I am and I'll just get to my point. Is the boy *dangerous*?!"

"You mean - is he *unstable*?"

"Call it what you will."

"He's just a kid, Lucien. He-"

"That's beside the point. I understand that, but I have an entire team I have to look out for! I can't have a 'loose cannon' standing around without some expectations of what may or may not happen. You are well aware of the scenarios we've run with the Nanites…"

Ayla sighed in frustration. "If you are asking me if the Nanites will get loose somehow and turn the world into 'grey goo', I couldn't tell you. But this is *not* a situation where they are free to do what they please, as far as I can tell, Cole is in control of them…or soon will be. They seem to be a part of him, not a separate entity swimming around in his bloodstream. From what I can see, the 'security protocols' do not apply to him!"

There was a moment of silence before he spoke again. "Fine, then what *does 'apply to him'*?"

"I can only tell you what we have found from the medical results. He appears to be in perfect physical condition. As for his abilities, we would have to conduct the proper testing in a controlled environment. Don't get me wrong, I see where you're going with this - you're worried about the emotional trauma he's been through..."

"I'm not just talking of his mother's death. That boy's entire life has been turned upside down over the past few years. All these things compounded over time would have an effect on a person's mental stability, would it not?"

"Why don't you be a bit more specific?"

"Is there a chance of him losing control and endangering my people; is that specific enough?!"

So *that* was his concern... It definitely warranted a sense of caution, this was true. If her assumptions about his abilities were even partially correct, Cole could be turned into a very dangerous weapon! A weapon capable of feats normal humans could only dream of.

Then again, all soldiers go through some type of emotional trauma fighting in wars and conducting missions. PTSD was a real physical threat once these men and women came home and tried to re-integrate into their everyday lives. The fact that Cole had a lot of baggage without ever being in the field did indeed create doubt, however there *was* something that helped alleviate those fears.

The difference was that Cole had an exceptionally high I.Q. and according to the medical results, also had a high capacity for Emotional Intelligence. 'EI' was the ability to identify, use, understand, and manage emotions in a positive way.

It was an adaptable skill that could be used to relieve stress, communicate effectively, empathize with others, overcome challenges, and even defuse conflict. From what she had seen thus far, Cole had the potential to use this to his advantage. He was young and still had streaks of immaturity in him, but with time and practice he would be able to overcome most emotional obstacles. She was sure of it.

"There is always the possibility of *any one of us* 'going off the deep end'. It's the precautionary measures that are necessary. Cole has already mastered the four brain wave meditation techniques and seems to be able to identify with his emotional states. He very well may have dramatic outbursts like what happened with Tom, but given patience and direction he should be just fine."

"That's hardly a guarantee," Lucien pressed.

"And *that's* the best I can give you! I wish I could say for certain that there is nothing to worry about, Lucien, but I can't. None of us has seen anything like what he has become...or is becoming. The only thing we can do is keep a close eye on him and help him cope with whatever comes his way. I have faith in him to do what's right. He has strong morals and knows the difference between right and wrong. What we *can* offer him is guidance."

There was another short stretch of silence before Lucien spoke. "I hope you're right."

"Me too."

"When you think he's ready, run him through all the usual field tests and send me the results. Run a neurological diagnostics as well to be on the safe side."

"We already have. He passed with flying colors."

"Freeband me the results. I'll be in touch."

The transmission ended and Ayla was left to her own thoughts.

CHAPTER 17: The Hidden Truth

The smell of crisping bacon and the sweet spice of cinnamon woke him up from his deep slumber late that morning. Warming rays of sunshine shone down on Cole through the large picture window, almost blinding him as he blinked open his eyes. He must have slept right through the alarm as it was still going off. Week after week, all these new experiences were taking a toll on his body and it was obvious that over the last couple of days, he had overdid it – again!

Even with the recuperating benefits of the Nanotech, if he didn't keep his body energized, he could relapse into a weakened state. Cole had learned that the hard way not long back. Like an idiot he had tried to test his limits and pushed himself too far in training, without resting or eating for days. He had eventually collapsed and gone into a state of hibernation for nearly two days. Ayla had come down on him like he was still some petulant child and it was probably lucky she did; who knew what could have happened!

"I'm surprised you didn't put yourself back *into a coma*," she'd said, "and if you keep that up without giving your body the energy it needs, you may end up overloading the Nanites!" It was a lesson learned that didn't need repeating...

He was still a bit groggy, but a few plates of food should fix that right up and he would be good as new. Getting up out of bed and putting on his black track suit, he made a pit-stop at the bathroom before heading off in the direction of the kitchen. Hearing the sound of voices as he got closer, he paused to take a look at who was conversing.

Doctor Lockwood was sitting in a chair across from two new arrivals. The first could only be Katya Prulova, striking blue eyes with shoulder-length dark brown hair; she was sipping from a steaming cup of morning tea. *What is it with these people and their tea?!* Prulova appeared to be a stately woman, dressed in a long-sleeve black mini-dress adorned with intricate geometrical patterns that ran all along it. Her black stockings ran into a pair of off-white fur boots and a ruby pendant hung from her slim neck.

A Lynx-fur Russian hat and a matching fur coat were draped on the chair beside her. Cole didn't have much in the way of fashion sense, but simply taking into account the way the elegant woman was dressed and how she conducted herself, he knew this was a very important person who was used to being in charge.

Katya sat next to a much younger woman who looked to be in her early 20's. Whomever this woman was, she was striking! She was a pretty mixture of eastern and western features. High cheek bones highlighted a round face cascading in a waterfall of rose gold locks, her greyish blue eyes were dark circles against her fair skin and her sharp nose and full lips added a certain amount of flair to her already gorgeous looks.

Seeing that she was also dressed quite fashionably, he immediately regretted not having anything else in his wardrobe except the same damned black track suit. He'd have to bring that up with Ayla, much sooner than later. *At least I'm not still wearing Archibald's clothes...anything's better than that.*

Ayla looked up as he walked in. "Ahh Cole...late morning; I see you took my advice and slept in for a change."

"Just following orders, Ma'am," he answered with a smile.

Katya immediately stood up and took his hand, shaking it politely with a firm grip and then gesturing to the younger woman. "Very nice to finally meet you, Cole, we have all heard a lot about you," she said in a thick European accent, "My name is Katya Prulova and this is my daughter, Yelena."

It was a different scenario altogether being this close to her. Cole stood in a stupor, staring at Yelena. Maybe he was drooling, he wasn't quite sure...but this woman was simply exquisite!

"Uhhm...I'm sorry; he doesn't get out much," Ayla said, covering for him. *Oh, Cole, put your tongue back in your mouth....*

He hadn't needed to apologize as Yelena Prulova stared back at the young man before her with equal appreciation.

Katya laughed with mild amusement. "It's okay, no need. She has that effect on people...*young men* especially."

Cole reddened noticeably and stepped forward to take Yelena's hand. "Hi." *Good Lord, you're beautiful!*

"Hello," she replied back, with a smirk.

"Grab yourself a plate and get some breakfast," suggested Doctor Lockwood.

"Don't have to tell me twice," he muttered under his breath and followed his nose towards the table.

The display laid out before him in a buffet-style conglomeration was more than he had expected. There was of course, the savory, mouth-watering bacon that had woken him up, but in addition, there were freshly baked cinnamon rolls, scrambled eggs, toasted bagels, and heaps of home-made waffles and pancakes.

A bounty of fresh fruit: golden apples, perfectly ripened bananas, succulent pears, and berries of all kinds were piled neatly around the rest of the table. *Real fruit! How did they get their hands on so much of this?* Only the wealthier Citizens could afford something like this! *Isolated or not, I'm beginning to like this place...*

Just in case *anyone else was hungry*, Cole grabbed *two* plates and made certain to take generous portions of everything. Joining the three women back at the table who were again deep in conversation, he sat in front of Yelena and began eating ravenously. Cole's eyes flitted back and forth between his meal and the ravishing young woman across from him. He forced himself to turn his attention to the conversation at hand to keep from looking like some drooling pervert. He looked at his heaping plates. *Either that or she thinks you're a gluttonous pig...*

"-things have already been prepared," Katya was saying, "Although I have never had to do it myself before. It was a strange experience..."

"I'm sorry Katya; you were the only one we could reach fast enough with the sufficient clearance and contacts to get through the Monoliths."

The woman nodded in acceptance. "I must say however, it was rather exciting to get back into the field again, after so many years in the corporate world."

Catching Yelena watching him, Cole sputtered and coughed through his last mouthful. Normally he didn't mind being stared at, but a beautiful woman admiring him from directly in front of him made his heart flutter in nervous excitement. He recovered and found that he had brought attention to himself. Both ladies stopped talking and were looking at him. *Keep...on...chewing.*

"Are you alright," Ayla asked assuming he was choking on his food; which he was, only for the wrong reasons. He nodded back trying to catch his breath.

"How are you liking it here, Cole," Katya asked.

What could he say to that? *Sometimes, I feel like a prisoner; I still don't know what I'm doing here and I'm scared as hell about what's happening to me...* "Uhmm, I'm...doing fine I guess. I...don't-"

Katya was peering over her nose at him like a mother would to a child who's done something wrong. "You appear to be very confused with all of this," she interrupted, "Come now, you must be wondering what's happening around you; who we are, The Hand of Light, I mean."

"I...uhh..."

"Katya, I'm not sure if Cole is ready to-"

"Nonsense darling. I'm sure the young man is smart enough to be informed exactly what our reasons are for what we do. If you ask me, he should have been briefed sooner."

Yes, I should have. From piecing together what little information Cole had been freely given, he surmised that The Hand of Light was fighting for what they believed to be freedom from despotism. He readily agreed that things had gone sour with The System; it was broken even before it was initiated.

The way individual thought and expression had slowly decayed into blind allegiance and ignorant hatred of anyone who 'rebelled' against the mandated way of life was an abhorrence. The past few years of his own so-called existence had literally been tied to a hospital bed at Princeton Memorial and he didn't know or remember much of what had been happening while he was sick. *If they're willing to share, I'm happy to listen.*

Most everyone at the facility was very discreet with what was said openly. They went out of their way to keep conversations 'hush, hush'. However, he *had* learned a few items of note: there had been four attacks throughout the years on System strongholds and political bodies. These raids had been strategically planned and aimed at targets that considerably stalled, damaged, or stopped System progress throughout the globe. It seemed to be the aim of The Hand of Light, but he was sure there was something much bigger than that going on here.

When he first woke up at this place, he had considered these people terrorists. Now he was pretty sure that was not the case at all. Either way the truth turns out with what she was about to say, he didn't have much choice in the matter. The Hand was giving him the help he needed to figure out what had happened to him and hopefully control the Nanites; maybe even reunite him with his father. At the same time, these *strangers* were turning into...*friends*?

While he was pondering his own thoughts, Katya took the initiative.

"You must be at least curious..."

So much for staying quiet..."I am, but I assume you have your reasons for keeping things to yourself...All I know Ma'am, is that you fight for a cause that you think is just. I don't believe I understand exactly what that is, but your methods have branded your organization as 'terrorists'! I have no idea what is happening even now; I woke up and the world-"

"Forget what's happening *now,* young man. The question you *should* be asking, is *how* all of this began in the first place."

Behind him, the squeal of plastic wheels rubbing against the smooth floors disrupted his train of thought as the clean-up crew began to place used plates and silverware on the carts beside them. A large, muscular man who looked like 'Mr. Clean'; bald with an earring in one ear directed the other two. Cole had seen him a number of times around the installation; he was the head maintenance man and took care of his many tasks with the utmost pride. Sealing the long trays of food with plastic wrap, they busied themselves with their duties.

Realizing this was taking more time than she cared for, Ayla finally spoke up. "Ahem...Mr. Sims, my colleagues and I in the middle of an important meeting. Would you mind delaying this for a few hours?"

The man gave her an irritated stare and then motioned to the other two. "Paula; Ernesto, come. We have been dismissed." He turned sharply and led the others out, leaving the carts and ignoring the leftovers.

"Where do we find these people," she asked Katya sarcastically.

"My Dear, you really must learn to be more appreciative. '*These people*' are well versed in everything you *do not* know how to do, and that means everything from boiling water to using proper manners. Be thankful they are here, otherwise we'd all starve; the only thing you know how to cook well is toast."

Everyone had a good laugh at Ayla's expense. The two women had clearly known each other a long time and they interacted like good friends. But for the life of him, Cole couldn't figure out if this was a serious conversation or an inside joke.

"I deserved that. I didn't mean to refer to *anyone* in a derogatory way, you know that."

"I know, my friend. We are all certainly under a lot of stress. Besides, even I understand you can sometimes be *such* a bitch."

Doctor Lockwood flashed a look of exaggerated hurt. "A bitch?! Why you old minx, shall I take that as a *compliment* or punch you in the nose?"

Waving off her small tantrum, Katya continued as if no interruption had taken place and turned her attention back to Cole. "Now, where were we..."

"I don't understand, Ma'am," Cole went on, getting back on track, "How *what* began?"

"Cole," Ayla interrupted, "What she is about to tell you, will change everything you think you know of the world. I've put you in a tough situation and I apologize for that. You're still an innocent in all of this, but if you want to go down this path, I won't stop you. I can only warn you that you won't like what you hear."

Maybe she's right, but... "I appreciate that, Ayla," Cole responded gratefully, "You've given me a new lease on life, but I still don't have a direction on how to live it. I thank you for all that you've done, but *this* is beyond me. I didn't ask for any of it and if you want me to comprehend things, I need to know what I can." Turning towards Katya, he proceeded. "I'm ready to listen."

The boy speaks quite eloquently, Katya thought to herself. An intelligence beyond his meager years lay hidden beneath his eyes. It was more than just the Nanites enhancing his mind; this boy was born of an extraordinary intellect...

"Then let me begin with this. The rumors you've heard about The Hand are completely untrue! We are not anarchists, neither are we *terrorists*. The Amalgam has portrayed us as murderous criminals, but they do so to keep you from the truth. There is a much darker agenda to their goals than you and I-"

"Let me tell him, Mother," Yelena ventured, interrupting her thoughts, "I think he needs to hear it from a different point of view."

Katya laughed and gestured back with an open palm.

Acknowledging her mother's agreement, Yelena began. "What do you know of an organization called The Illuminated Ones?"

He'd heard of them. "They are the ones who inadvertently started the War; or at least someone who was a member of that group did. From what I can remember, they were some type of cult. I don't know much more than that." he replied.

"*Why* do you think they spearheaded the War, Cole," the elder Prulova interjected.

He took a gulp of air and scratched his head. "What are you saying...Ma'am? That the War was started on *purpose*?"

"Ahh...Handsome *and* respectful," she mused, "how refreshing...but please – call me Katya."

"Yes, Ma- I mean... Katya. You said the War was *planned*?"

"I did...but it goes far beyond that." She motioned for Yelena to continue.

"Listen carefully Cole, what I'm about to tell you will shed light on a great many things. Think of it as a 'history lesson', it may help you wrap your head around things...The War *was* a planned event, but the path of The Illuminated Ones began centuries ago during the times of the first Crusades, from roughly 1095 to 1291. It -"

"Wait a minute; you're telling me that what is happening now started with a catalyst that took place almost a thousand years ago!?"

"Yes."

He shook his head in disbelief. "That's hard to accept...but go on."

"It is said that during that time, the King of Jerusalem enlisted the aid of nine Knights to protect Christian Pilgrims as they travelled back and forth from the Holy City. These Knights soon gained notoriety for being a highly trained, well-equipped fighting force. They called themselves the Knights Templar.

Once endorsed by the Catholic Church in 1129, they quickly grew to an Order of 15-20,000 members! As their Knights became the most powerful military faction of that time, the non-combatant members used some of the first financial techniques to garner enormous wealth across Europe. You could accuse the Templars of being the first early Bankers of the modern world!"

"Wow, and I thought Ayla was the only 'robot' here," he joked. Seeing frowning faces peering back at him, he quickly changed the subject. "You used the word 'accuse'. Is that because you disapprove of the old financial system? Was that such a bad thing, everyone wanted to make money before Credits replaced our currency..."

"Think about it Cole," explained Ayla, "The Bankers destroyed the Old World's economic system; printing worthless money, handing out bad loans, and forcing people into debt! It was part of the plot in which The System was initiated in the first place. You know the saying 'With wealth comes power, but power most times turns into corruption'? It's usually the norm, we've seen it throughout history!"

"Fair statement. I remember reading about that in my father's 'Public's Truth Journal'; it said the banks were to blame too, I just don't understand why...Now, I know very little about the Knights Templar and the Crusades, but how are *they* at fault for any of this?"

"Wealth and power go hand in hand, it's the underlying reason why most wars are fought in the first place," Yelena answered, "It wasn't so different with the Templars...What was considered wealth in that time was very similar to today's perception. The Knights gained control of large tracts of land, farms, and vineyards and were involved in everything from manufacturing, imports and exports, and other economical bounties.

They developed a system of banks that allowed religious pilgrims to deposit assets in their home countries and then withdraw funds in the Holy Land. It was quite an amazing achievement! At the height of their influence, the Templars held enormous financial sway and served as the primary lender to European monarchs and nobles. They managed to establish power over some very influential people."

Then why gamble it away..."All that wealth and influence at their disposal and they still risked it all by fighting in the Crusades?! Their beliefs must have been strong to risk losing that advantage... "

"They were...The Templars believed that they fought, converted, and killed *in the name of God* and that by doing so, they were saving the souls of the conquered. For them it was not murder, rather the path to righteousness!"

Cole was confused. "And what, they were doing them a *favor*?! These Templars were *Christians*, but killed people because they believed in a different religion and thought that it was justified?"

"It was a combination of distorted faith and xenophobia of foreign cultures. More so, it was a perversely warped devotion to the Will of God."

"What you're saying is complete hypocrisy, that doesn't make a lick of sense!"

"That's *exactly* what I'm saying, faith has been twisted into an ideology of separatism and discrimination; we still judge others by their individual beliefs, religion or otherwise. Many wars have been fought over these things in their time *and ours*. People have always used God or some higher power as an excuse to kill, segregate, or destroy entire civilizations, is that not right?"

"I suppose that's true," Cole conceded, "but how can any religious person believe that God would approve murder *of any kind*, regardless of the justifications. It goes against the very fundamentals of Christianity!"

"Much more twisted a perception than that actually," Katya elaborated, "You have to understand that in those days, the common folk believed that a man of the cloth dictated if a person's immortal soul would burn in Hell or be saved in Heaven! That priest or representative had absolute command of his peers and even of some folks in very prestigious circles. Basically, he was considered by commoners to be the next best thing to God; on this Earth anyway. The same could be said of the Church."

"Regardless of that, the Templars were indoctrinated in their ways for ages," inserted Ayla. "It's like growing up in a cult. Eventually, they break your will to the point where what you once would never accept or consider doing, is now second nature."

"Given time, most people eventually realized the truth," Katya continued, "Wealth and power, combined with the Knights' secretive initiations and practices eventually bred jealousy and mistrust throughout the land. The veil was pierced and public perception of the Knights soon changed amongst accusations of murder, corruption, and accepting bribes. The commoners saw that the Templars were performing acts that were considered *against* the Christian ways and soon rose up in defiance."

"Mother is right," Yelena agreed, "To give you more of a historical account, it was King Phillip IV who sped along the scrutiny. Struggling from significant debt owed to the Templars, he used the general outcry of the people to his advantage. Together with the Church - specifically Pope Clement, who was a relative of Phillip's

– they called for their arrest and persecution. The Knights were hunted down like common criminals for many years after.

A great number of their Order were caught and tortured into giving false confessions of heresy and other unspeakable acts. The surviving Templars who were not executed fled underground and outraged by the betrayal of both God and Church, turned against them. Ironically after being trained and indoctrinated by the Roman Catholics, the remaining Knights strayed to the opposite end of the spectrum, diving into the occult, mysticism, and other black arts."

Cole raised an eyebrow. "Black arts; you mean like satanic practices and such? Isn't that a stretch for Christians who were firm believers in God for all those years?"

"Look at it this way," Ayla appealed, taking a sip of her tea, "The Knights Templar fought and killed *in the name of God*. They wholeheartedly conceived that if they struck down a non-believer, they were guaranteed a place in Heaven. What happens if everything you were ever taught to believe; your ideals; your morals; your way of life – turned out to be nothing *but a lie*?!"

"You'd probably lose it, maybe go insane. They'd feel betrayed and abandoned...I see what you're getting at."

"Exactly. But more so, their *convictions* changed," Yelena asserted, "Their once strong Christian faith gave way to darkness. They blamed *God* for deceiving and persecuting them. After all, everything they had done was in His name and was approved by the Church. Guilt and shame for their prior actions delved them further into degeneracy. Some stories agree that they turned away from God because they were forsaken by the Catholic Church. Others say that they formed secret societies and went into hiding so they could infiltrate and destroy Christianity as retribution for their betrayal."

"And what do *you* believe, Yelena," asked Cole.

The beautiful woman cleared her throat before she spoke. "I believe that it was a bit of both. Think about the secret societies and the shadowy groups that existed in The Old World...the way they integrated themselves into government, religion, and other organizations; it's like they were following the step by step design of the Templars."

"Do you really think that?!"

"Perhaps," she acknowledged, "But whatever the truth may be, we will never know. As for the Order - they went into hiding and remained out of sight and mind for over 400 years. At first, it made sense that they went underground to avoid persecution, but I have done extensive research on the Templars and I don't think that was their only intent. I believe that their ultimate goal was something else - they wanted vengeance! It was far easier to corrupt Christianity from the inside out, especially if no one remembered they existed at all. It was in this way that they spread their teachings to other religions."

"The greatest deception the devil ever pulled was convincing the world he didn't exist," Ayla recited. "It's the reason evil people have absolute power: because they don't believe there will be a judgment upon death for the atrocities they commit."

Cole's father had once said that some people are *born inherently evil* and just don't realize it until later on in their lives. Most did not believe in life after death, therefore, they did not believe in God. It made sense that a person's actions could be overlooked, especially if they had no higher power to fear. But how can these Templars who were indoctrinated into Christianity all their lives simply abandon their beliefs just like that. It was a crushing blow for Cole to hear something like that.

"400 years is a long time to remain undetected, don't you think," Cole speculated, trying to ignore his internal thoughts, "How would they have kept their ideals and beliefs intact all that time?"

Katya acknowledged his question with a cough. "You *are* an attentive one, aren't you? There are several ways to spread a belief system, but to change one's views, all you really need is 'doubt'. Fear and uncertainty can often times lead to skepticism, more so in those whose faith is weak. It's a similar concept, except in this case – the individual or group of fanatics infiltrate each religion from the inside out and subvert the members to their cause."

"Sounds more like a 'Corporate Takeover'," he pointed out, humorlessly.

"Perhaps it was in a sense, but it *is* an interesting way to change the views of the majority," the mature woman answered.

"They've been working towards the goal of corrupting Christianity for centuries, it's not a new onjective," Yelena stated, "Worse yet, the Templar's corruption has spread from one religion to another."

"How's that," Cole asked, intrigued.

"In 1666, an offshoot of the Jewish Kabbalah was led by the false prophet Shabbetai Zevi, consisting of many of the same doctrines of the Templars. His movement was made up of much of the known Jewish population at that time, but this group too was fractured. It was actually what created the division of the Jewish people into the sects and factions that exist today.

Later still, they became to be known as Shabbatean Frankists and their leader was replaced by a man named Jacob Frank. Convincing his followers that the overthrow and destruction of society was mankind's salvation, Frank sought the annihilation of every known religion while preaching Luciferian radiance. Their far-reaching power came in the form of a wide network of inter-family relationships brought about through incest and other prohibited sexual unions. Aside from that, we see the similar paths converge."

"So, you're saying that the Templars purposely indoctrinated themselves into other religions and groups in order to disappear?"

"It seems to me that their goal was to stay hidden in plain sight, yes. But more so, they were able to strategize their plans from within and sway people to their cause. It was a stroke of genius. Either way, they accomplished what they sought to do."

Cole had a begrudging respect for their methods. It made sense to have 'agents' in multiple places. They could study their adversaries, gain information, and even learn their movements and practices. It *was* a tremendous advantage to have!

"Do these Shabbatean Frankists still exist," he asked.

"According to history, they eventually disbanded, but that doesn't mean others did not carry on their objectives. In fact, on May 1st 1776, a former Jesuit by the name of Adam Weishaupt, financed by International Bankers - formed the 'Order of the Illuminati'. Many of the practices of the Shabbatean Frankists were transplanted into-"

"Hang on a minute, I'm not familiar with the different terms in 'Religions'; what exactly is a Jesuit?"

Ayla answered for her. "A Jesuit is a member of the Society of Jesus, a Roman Catholic religious order. I have my suspicions that Weishaupt was not a true Jesuit, rather an infiltrator! Until The System abolished separate religions, they were one of the largest organizations within the Catholic Church. In the 1500's they were literally referred to as 'Soldiers of God' because many of them had military-style training and led armies to recapture lands for the Church."

"They sound like the Knights Templar!"

"Indeed they do! There are proven lineal bloodlines from both the Jesuits and the Freemasons. You might say that they are the 'more acceptable' heirs to the Templars. If you're wondering why I'm bringing up these other sects - to understand the Illuminated Ones, you need to first see how these various Orders are related."

"This is crazy," exclaimed Cole, "It's like a conspiracy over a conspiracy over a conspiracy!"

"More than you know," Yelena concurred. "It gets deeper as you dig through history...The members of Weishaupt's Illuminati were mostly made up of 'Freethinkers', which was a very unusual philosophical viewpoint in that day and age.

The basis was that opinions should be formed on the groundwork of logic, reason, and knowledge through sensory experience rather than authority, tradition, or principles; religious, political, or otherwise. Literary men, reigning dukes, rich industrialists, and many important and authoritative figures were all members of the Order during this time. By then, they had many of their people in influential positions of power.

Weishaupt believed that there were only a few among us destined for 'Enlightenment', chosen to guide and *rule the world*. He and his associates infiltrated many lodges and orders, such as the Freemasons, gaining followers, sympathetic to their cause. Similar to the Sabbatean Frankists, their goal at that time was to overthrow all political and religious institutions and replace them with members of their own Order. This was to establish a base of power and most importantly – a system of control."

"You said something about Freemasons; I've heard of them. What's their relationship with the Illuminati?"

Yelena took another sip from her teacup on the table and purposely placed her hands, palm down on her lap. Cole noticed that she had a habit of fidgeting if she didn't do so. Perhaps she had a certain level of anxiety. "Well...again we have many of the teachings of the Templars intertwined into Freemasonry. They-"

"But they are *not* a religion," Cole argued, "Neither is the Illuminati."

"That is true, but you don't have to be a religion to have the same beliefs and goals."

"Fair enough..."

"I'm just trying to give you another way to see things, Cole...Freemasonry does *not* recognize a supreme being and their members are required to hold that belief. The Masons were led by a man named Brigadier General Albert Pike of the Confederate Army. He was a racist, a Satanist, and a top ranking Freemason. Pike took the Templar's philosophies to a whole other level! He was also a genius who believed that to bring about The New World Order, three world wars were necessary."

Cole leaned his body closer towards her in interest. "What exactly would three World Wars hope to accomplish, other than killing a whole lot of people?!"

"I thought the same thing...but according to Pike, the first World War must be brought about for the Illuminati to overthrow the powers in Russia, to bring about Communism and weaken Religion. The second World War must be a war between Fascism and Zionism in order to strengthen Communism and spread it to other parts of the globe.

Finally, the third World War will be fought between the way of Islam and political Zionism so they could be coerced to mutually destroy each other. In essence, they would be forced to fight each other to the point of complete physical, moral, spiritual, and economical exhaustion. He believed this would start a social cataclysm which would eventually bring about the destruction of Christianity."

"Wait a minute. When was the first World War fought?"

"I believe it was around 1914," Ayla affirmed.

Turning back to Yelena, Cole asked, "And when did you say this man, Pike made these declarations?"

"He wrote these objectives in a letter to a man named Giuseppe Mazzini in 1871," Yelena replied.

Cole shook his head in confusion. "So how can a man predict three World Wars exactly like they happened *before* any of them even took place?!"

"Interesting point," Ayla commented.

"According to the histories, Pike claims he had a vision from Lucifer himself," answered Yelena.

"Perhaps it was not a prediction at all," Katya countered, "For all anyone knows, they may very well have been a *blueprint!*"

At that point, Cole felt as if his head would burst. He rubbed his temples with both hands. There were an awful lot of facts mixed in with possible conjecture that ultimately ended with some abhorrent truths. It was frighteningly fascinating how all these single events were coming together...

"I don't even know how to wrap my mind around all this, this is so *confusing*! These events that took place and how all this seemed to have begun with the Roman Catholic Church is so *bizarre*. The rational part of me strays towards doubt, but I have to admit, there's too much that fits together!"

Yelena gave him a small smile and nodded in agreement. "Yes, well most people are ignorant to the truth; they have no idea what is going on behind closed doors. The majority of Catholic worshipers are God-fearing folk as are most of the people in all other religious sects. They innocently follow the Church's rigid doctrines without understanding the theory or history behind these practices; after all, these things are *not* common knowledge... It's like parts of a complicated puzzle that appear to have no relation at all, until you start putting together the pieces."

"So the Church is *not* to blame?"

"Throughout history, they've definitely made their share of mistakes - but no. Those like Weishaupt and his followers were the ones who orchestrated these hidden agendas and corrupted their rituals and beliefs! ...Here's something you may find interesting. What is odd about the year in which Weishaupt formed the Illuminati," asked Ayla cryptically.

"What do you mean; what does the year have to-"

"1776 is a *significant* year, Cole," Katya cut in, "It was the inception of the government that existed throughout the third World War. Many important events occurred during this time: the Declaration of Independence was signed; the Articles of Federation were proposed; the Great Seal of the United States was created; and most importantly, the 1st Congressional Committee was formed-."

"Well sure, but as you said – it was the inception of government, why wouldn't those things happen?"

"Let me finish...the Congressional Committee was created by the following Founders: Thomas Jefferson, John Adams, Benjamin Franklin, Roger Sherman, and Robert Livingston. All five Founding fathers were Freemasons! Each man was either a member of the Illuminati or sympathetic to their cause; the exact details of what they supported however, are still shrouded in mystery."

These pre-formation events were common knowledge, but the revelation of how everything seemed to be related once again took him completely by surprise. "And you're saying that this Weishaupt established the Illuminati that very same year?"

"I am," Katya declared, "and I for one, don't believe in coincidence! His Order, the Illuminati gradually became an openly destructive Luciferian cult and grew into one of the most feared & powerful shadow governments in history. Their objective is simple: to create a one-world government, a one-world religion, and a one-world currency. This would, in effect, give them absolute power through the total and absolute control of church, economics, and politics. ”

“Yeah, I get it, but-”

“No Cole, I don't believe you do. Everything we've told you: the manipulation of religions; the relationship between the Illuminati and Freemasonry; the three World Wars; the Roman Catholic the Church's decrees; all of it – *they're all connected!*

One begets the other and they all share similar patterns. These events may not seem related, but they all lead to the same conclusion! A wolf in sheep's clothing is still a wolf no matter what it appears to be. The Illuminated Ones *are* the Illuminati and the Illuminati *is* The System; do you *understand that*?!”

Suddenly noticing her heightened emotions, Katya calmed herself. “I'm sorry...I did not mean to come off on you like that.”

Cole was taken aback by her sudden outburst. His first reaction was an angry retort, but on second thought it was probably a good idea not to piss this woman off...*ever*. Cole pulled at his fingers below the table in silence for a few moments, taking it all in. “No, you're right, I apologize if I came off condescending,” He voiced under his breath. “I didn't realize how deep this went. But if they truly are one in the same, how does any of us hope to fight a System that has been in planning and development since the damned Middle Ages?!”

There was another minute of silence before Doctor Lockwood had her say. “The Hand of Light has been fighting this battle for some time now...We understand that this is a process, nothing happens overnight. And I know you and most of the world have heard some terrible things about us. But they are purported by The System's media; the rumors are simply not true! I wouldn't blame you for doubting anything we've told you and I can't say that what you've heard today doesn't sound crazy.

But I will tell you that I've seen and heard the evidence...from people I love and trust. We are *not* the problem; we are fighting *for* the people, not against them! During the years, we've made plans to slowly infiltrate and destroy relevant vulnerabilities of The System, parts that will directly affect the whole. The attacks that are being carried out; they are designed to hit them where it will cause the most damage. So far, we *are* winning the final war."

Cole sat in contemplation for a while. "And who authorizes all of this; who makes the decisions? Who tells you what to do and how to do it?"

What harm could it be to tell him now? "His name is Quentin Rand. He is the founder and leader of The Hand of Light. He dictates what takes place and formulates the targets. Trust me when I tell you the information we have comes from very reliable sources from around the globe."

So there it is: the man who runs the shop. *How on earth did I end up here*, Cole thought to himself. It felt surreal; as if he had just been dropped into the set of an action thriller, only he didn't know which part he was to play... Things had been simple once and now it was filled with revelations that were both unsettling and disturbing. His life as he knew it had changed drastically in a matter of months, but then again...so had he. The Hand was fighting for a just cause and each member had their own reasons for being there, as did he.

"Where is this Rand; when do I get to meet him?"

"Cole...I can't authorize exposing Rand to an *outsider*..."

She was right. When Cole first arrived at the compound, he'd been shocked to hear that it was The Hand that saved him. Throughout most of his young life, he'd come to believe these people were terrorists, causing havoc against The System to overthrow their rule. But this was not the case, not at all. He had enough regrets from past choices he'd made and that guilt, he always carried with him.

This time, he had a chance to turn things around. Within moments, Cole made up his mind to support their cause; he wanted to be a part of it. His parents had always raised him to fight for his beliefs and ideals, no matter what the cost; these horrors against the people needed to end! Besides, his own curiosity demanded to know more...

"I want to help, Ayla."

"You don't know what you're asking, Cole. We're fighting a real war here; this isn't some game! Besides, you are not even a member of The Hand, I doubt that-"

"Then *make* me a member, Ayla! These people...they murdered my mother! If anyone deserves a chance at payback, it should be *me*, right?!" *What? What the hell am I saying?!* The more logical voice in the back of his head spoke up; at least *it* had some common sense. *Me, a member of the resistance?*

"The boy has a point," Katya observed.

What did I just get myself into? Damn it Lucien, why aren't you here? "I can't just..." Ayla began, "He doesn't have any military training or-"

"Then *train me*," Cole insisted, "Look – you are the one who told me I can learn things faster and better than a normal human being. These Nanites...they're good for something, take advantage of that. Lucien said he needed a weapon; make *me* that weapon!" *What is wrong with you? Shut up before you entangle yourself in something that's way over your head!*

"Again, he *has* a point," Katya stated.

"Oh *shut up,* Katya! You are *not* helping," Ayla pleaded, "Anyway, there is no one here who can take the time to teach you what you need to know, nevermind training you. It's-"

Yelena who had sat silent listening to the argument, finally spoke up. "I'll do it. Lucien was once my instructor and I have mastered most of what he has taught me. Until he can take over, I will be his...mentor."

"*You,* a soldier," Cole blurted out, before reddening in embarrassment. *One of these days, your mouth is going to get you into something deep...*

"Do not be so surprised," Katya cut in, exchanging an amused glance with Yelena. "She *is* my daughter after all. Believe me when I tell you – Yelena has been through her share of trials, she is more than capable of doing this. She will stay here with you and Ayla until I return."

Ayla appeared to be in shock, but could not find the words to argue any further. She didn't look very happy with the outcome of events. If she didn't agree with what had transpired, she also did not fight against it. Putting up her hands in mock surrender, she replied. "Fine, you win...Lucien's not going to like this...neither is Tom."

"You let me worry about Tom, darling."

"Okay...okay."

Katya Prulova was grinning from ear to ear. "Good, then it is settled."

Pushing his empty plate aside, Cole had one more question. "When do we begin?"

AUTHOR BIO:

Do you remember when you were young and carefree? I do. As kids, we used to dream of grand and enchanting adventures, free from the hustle and bustle of responsibilities that came with the burden of becoming an adult. With maturity, we began to lose much of that childhood innocence, and the simple things that used to astonish and inspire us faded with time.

Two years ago, the wonder and imagination hibernating deep within me came back ten-fold. Maybe it was a mid-life crisis or perhaps the better part of me finally caught up with my serious side. Either way, after all these years, my longing for excitement and adventure needed an outlet. So I decided to do the only thing I could think of - write a book.

For those who know me, I have a penchant for truth. I've always believed that we, as a people deserve the right to know what's going on around us. There are too many unanswered questions, things we should be aware of and comprehend, and undiscovered knowledge that is too often buried in lies and hypocrisy. As such, some of my inspiration comes from revealing these ideas and beliefs through my fictional stories.

The story contains elements from a number of genres and falls into several categories: young adult; science fiction; religious; action adventure; horror; suspense, and dystopian thriller. It was not planned this way, but the elements all came together perfectly and if any of these classifications are of interest, there will be a story for you.

You could say that my goal is to explore those possibilities; to make you think; to create discussion; and possibly to open your eyes to a world that may not truly be what it seems...I hope you enjoy it!

ACKNOWLEDGEMENTS:

First and foremost, I would like to thank my Father, Neil Austin Kumaraperu. He was extremely proud of me once I wrote my first ever book and I truly appreciate that – God rest his soul. Thanks also to my wonderful family- my wife Sarah and my kids: Ethan, Cyerra, Cain, Sydney, and Ashlynn – love you guys; Jeff Smolinski who helped me with the main design; Seb Marley [www.AlphaPublishing.org] for an amazing video; my friends on Facebook who supported this venture; and my Mother, Indrani Lewis, my brother, Raji Kumaraperu, and my sister, Amy Kumaraperu; and of course, all the Readers of this Novel in progress.

Look for Book II, soon to be released.

Find out more about The Brand:

Web: www.TheBrandNovel.com
Facebook: https://www.facebook.com/TheBrandNovel
Twitter: https://twitter.com/thebrandnovel
Google+ https://plus.google.com/u/0/111437231917032217589/posts
Pinterest: https://www.pinterest.com/TheBrand_Novel/
Amazon Author Pages: http://www.amazon.com/Nishan-A.-Kumaraperu/e/B002BLP51K?ref_=pe_1724030_132998060

Scan Me with your Smartphone

www.ingramcontent.com/pod-product-compliance
Lightning Source LLC
Chambersburg PA
CBHW070612130626
46556CB00001B/344